HEALER

BOOK THREE OF THE AFFINITY SERIES

J. S. LENORE

Praise for
The Affinity Series

"…a nail-biting mystery novel that did not disappoint and kept me intrigued. The ending is an absolute gem. *Burner* is a very beautiful book for the minds that are open to innovative urban style writing."

Jeyran Main, *Review Tails/Underrated Reads*

"Relate-able characters, great plot, easy to follow world in an urban setting, and a great balance of romance and action."

K. T. Munson, *Creating Worlds with Words*

"The immensely likable female protagonist combined with the theme of the afterlife and deadly spirits and detective work had me thrilled; these attributes combined ensure that no reader will ever be bored."

Aime Ann, *Red Headed Book Lover Blog*

"*Reader* does everything the second book in a series should do and so much more… [it] is an addicting read that fans of the paranormal, mysteries, and crime dramas won't be able to put down"

Danielle Zimmerman, *Hypable.com*

Books in *The Affinity Series*

Burner

Reader

Healer

Speaker (Coming 2020)

HEALER

August 2019

Published by Paranoid Shark Productions, LLC

Indianapolis, Indiana

This is a work of fiction. Names, characters, places, and incidents
are the product of the author's imagination or are used fictitiously.
Any resemblance to actual persons, living or dead, events, or
locales is entirely coincidental.

Copyright © 2019 by J. S. Lenore

Cover art by Natasha Alterici

ISBN-13: 978-0-9987560-7-3

affinityseries.net

To my dad

CONTENTS

PROLOGUE

I knock again, and I hear Taka yell from inside. After another moment, he pulls the door open, smiling broadly at me.

"Kim," he says, gesturing to me to enter. "I'm so sorry. I was showing our guest to the restroom and didn't hear you knock."

He shuts the door behind me, and I bend down to untie my boots. "That's all right," I say, listening to his feet pad off toward the kitchen. I can smell tea, and my cold hands ache for a warm cup. "I've got your books in my car. Don't let me forget to grab them for you before I go."

"You're welcome to hold on to them," he says as he walks back into the room. There's already a cup of tea steaming on the small table in the center of his living room. He passes me the one from his hands, and I take a deep, happy inhale.

"You made my favorite," I say, taking a slow, careful sip. I'm greeted by the familiar tang of green tea and roasted rice.

"Of course," he says as he sits. I join him on the floor, my feet tucked under my legs, cup carefully balanced in my hands before I set it on the table.

"So, where's this guest of ours?" I ask, looking toward the back rooms.

"Andi will be done in a moment."

"Andi?" I ask, frowning at him. "I thought you said this was your friend's daughter?"

"Yes," Taka says before taking a sip of his tea. "She prefers the shortened version of her name."

"What's Andi short for?" I ask, the words passing my lips as I turn to see Taka's guest walk into the main room. Time doesn't precisely slow, but it does take longer for my brain to catch on to what my eyes are telling me than I'd like to admit.

She's not wearing business dress this time, but she still has the same commanding presence she had when I first saw her. Blue-black sweater, gray jeans, and white socks, and topping it all off, a wolfish grin that makes her storm-gray eyes spark with mischief.

"Detective," Banks says quietly, moving toward the table and bending down to pick up the extra cup there. "Pleasure to see you again."

Fuck.

CHAPTER ONE

Taka's living room is so quiet the silence echoes. I don't remember standing, but I'm on my feet, hands clenched by my sides. He looks up at me from the low table that fills the room, confusion evident in his eyes. Banks—calm and collected and so smug it hurts—takes a slow sip of her tea. Her eyes on mine, she takes a seat at the table with practiced ease, like she's been here a hundred times before. I glance from her to Taka and back again, unwilling to accept the implication of her easy movements.

"What is *she* doing here?" I ask Taka angrily and turn to Banks. "What are you doing here?"

And you were doing so well, Priya sighs.

"This is Andi," Taka says carefully, frowning. "I told you she would be here today."

"But you didn't tell me it would be *her*." I gesture again, trying to encompass all of Banks with the motion. As if I can somehow describe her cocky self-assurance and the way she gets under my skin by waving my hands in the air.

It doesn't seem to work.

"Taka is an old friend of my father's," Banks says. "He said he needed my help, so I came."

"And you couldn't have said something sooner? Like yesterday?"

"It didn't seem pertinent," Banks says.

I catch a glint of that familiar predatory light in her eyes and my hackles rise. "It *was* fucking pertinent," I say through gritted teeth. My hands clench at my sides, fingernails biting into my palms.

"Kim," Taka bites back, "watch your tone."

"She's… I mean… It's…" I wave my hands at Andrea again, and she smirks. "What the hell?"

"I've known Andi for five years now. Her father and I became friends after you completed your training. And, as I mentioned before, she is Sighted and an expert in rune work." He turns his eyes to Banks. Andrea. Andi. *Whatever*. "She, however, failed to mention that you knew each other."

"We've encountered each other in a… professional setting. I was helping her with a case," Banks offers. She takes another sip of tea, her eyes dipping to the table in a subtle sign of guilt. A flash of sympathy sneaks through my anger, but it's extinguished when she raises her eyes to mine, looking at me through her eyelashes with a barely repressed self-satisfaction that sets my blood boiling.

"You call extorting information from me help?"

"I was simply finding out what I could about a story I'm working on," Banks says primly.

Taka cocks his head. "The Harris girl?"

"She wasn't helping me," I say blisteringly before turning my attention back to Banks. "And I still don't understand what in the hell you're doing here. What kind of game are you playing at?"

"No games." She sets her cup down and meets my eyes. "Taka told me about the runes you found, and I was intrigued. I'm here to help." Her gaze is stormy and gray, enigmatic yet calculating at the same time. "That's all."

I scoff. "Sure."

"Kim," Taka says sharply, "you are being rude to our guest. Sit. Now."

There's command in his voice, and though it annoys me, ingrained courtesy and years spent following his directions finally force me to move. I tuck my legs under the table, barking my knee against the wooden edge. I fight back a wince, unwilling to show any sign of weakness in front of Andrea. I can already feel a bruise forming as my knee gives a sharp twinge when I settle to the floor.

You're acting like a child, Priya scolds. *Calm down and behave rationally.*

She's not supposed to be here. My hands tense beneath the table.

But she is, and you're stuck with it. We have to figure out what's going on with those grave markers and the energy around them. At least hear her out.

You're assuming she actually knows something.

And you're assuming she doesn't, Priya says. *Let the woman speak before you make an ass out of you* and *me.*

I grab my tea from the table and take a quick swallow. The hot liquid scalds my tongue, and I fight through the sting of pain.

"Kim, show her the pictures," Taka says sternly. "She has taken time out of her day to help you. Do not let this be a waste of her time—or mine."

"Fine." I put my cup down on the table with a crack. Taka glares, and I duck my head, avoiding his eyes as I grab my phone from my pocket.

I quickly pull up the photos from the second grave marker and slide my cell across the table. Andrea stops it with her hand and carefully picks up the phone. She studies the picture for a long time, frowns, and leans closer to the screen, squinting.

"That's interesting." She zooms in, graceful fingers sliding across the glass screen, and tilts her head to the side. "I've never seen this kind of rune work before. It's similar to the American school, but with hints of European and Asian influences here as well. Very unique. Whoever scribed this… I mean, do you see this linkage?" She turns the phone back to me, excitedly pointing to a certain configuration of runes. If there's something worth noting, I don't see it. "This is almost a fusion of all three."

Turning the phone back toward her and cradling it gently, she shakes her head. "This is absolutely fascinating."

"Sure," I say, remembering the pool of dark, corrosive power gathered before each of the grave markers with a shiver. "Fascinating."

"And you said there were *two* like this?" she asks, finally tearing her eyes away from my phone.

I nod, hand outstretched, and she reluctantly passes the phone back.

What'd you say about her not knowing anything? Priya Sends with more than a little smugness.

Shut up.

"Would you be able to show me the grave site?" Andrea asks, leaning forward. "Or at least send me those photos?"

"Not until you tell me what you can gather from those runes."

"Right now?" She shakes her head. "Not much, I'm afraid. It's hard to tell how the marks on the different sides of the obelisk interact with one another without being there in person. The geometry of it all would be critical based on what I saw. It's an unorthodox formation, so the angles between the various runes and sigils will drastically alter the intention and power of the scribing. If I had more time with the pictures, perhaps I could tell you more. But it would be ideal if I could have access to the marker."

"But since you don't have access to the marker, what can you tell me *now*?"

She frowns. "It's some kind of binding, though not like anything I've seen before. I can't tell exactly what it's looking to contain, but many of the runes have to do with restriction, constraint. With more time and access…" She trails off, letting the fading words make her point for her.

"Fine," I snap. "I'll take you. But if you try to pull anything, you can go fuck yourself."

"Kimberly." Taka slams his hand down on the table, the crack of skin against wood startling me into silence. Even Andrea jumps a little. He doesn't glare, just stares at me with barely banked fire in his eyes. I fight the urge to duck into my shoulders, sitting straighter instead. "You are welcome to leave if you can't be civil."

I flinch but refuse to apologize to Taka where Andrea can hear me. Glancing at the time, though, I sigh and stand. "I *can* be civil, but I have to leave." I glance at Andrea's smug expression. No doubt she's taking my words as an excuse to leave. "I've got paperwork waiting on me."

"I'm sure you do." Taka's voice is unbending steel, and I start running through ways I can make up for my behavior later, once she's gone.

"I'll see you on Wednesday?" I hedge.

"Yes," he says, some of the anger fading from his voice. "Of course."

"And you?" I turn back to Andrea, pinning her with a glare. She's finished her tea and is idly playing with the cup, still as calm as when I first arrived. "I'll talk to you later."

"I'm looking forward to it, Detective." She smiles at me with such genuine warmth, I'm taken aback. Still off-kilter, I nod curtly, stuff my feet into my boots, and stomp out of the house.

When you were in kindergarten, Priya says idly as I start the car, *did your first report card home say something about not playing well with others?*

I wouldn't know, I Send back as I drop into Second-Sight, lurching the car into gear and speeding off toward HQ.

I bet it did. You're terrible with people.

I'm terrible with her, I counter.

She counts as people. Priya shakes her head and settles into the passenger seat. *You may not like her, but you need her help, Kim.*

I sigh. *She's a pain in the ass. I could've told you that the symbols were for a binding. No huge wealth of knowledge about rune work necessary.*

Could you tell me the difference between the schools she mentioned?

I frown. *Maybe. When I was in college.*

Don't forget that I was there with you. I know how you did in those classes. She gives me a pointed look. *You need to admit she knows more than you.*

I could relearn it, I insist. *But I'd need more time.*

Which you don't have.

Priya has a point. I have no idea what those grave markers do or why they're here. And as much as I hate to admit it, even to myself, Andrea clearly has a better understanding of scribing runes than I've ever had. If I knew anyone else or had the time to research it myself, I'd tell her to get bent. Instead, it looks like she's my only option, at least for now. It grates on my nerves, though, especially after I thought I'd seen the last of her with the closure of the Harris case. Now, I'm back to square one: needing her help when it's the last thing I want.

You're pouting, Priya Sends with tired exasperation.

Maybe I am. I'm not exactly thrilled here.

I couldn't tell. She's deadpan, her voice flat and sarcastic. She shakes her head and rubs at the bridge of her nose, then chuckles. *I could have sworn that Taka was going to put you in time-out at the end. I mean, he called you* Kimberly. *No one calls you Kimberly.*

That's because it's not my name, I say, taking a right toward the highway. *He only does it when he's pissed.*

He was definitely that, she says with a sigh.

It'll be fine. *Just… stop talking about it.*

Fine, Priya says, sounding slightly satisfied but still disapproving.

The interior of the car grows quiet, the only sounds the low hum of the engine, my wheels on the road, and the other cars that zip by me. I consider turning on the radio but quickly discard the idea. Something about the silence feels welcoming, rather than anxious. Even with Priya's annoyance echoing down our bond, there's love behind it, soothing the rough edges of my lingering anger. The silence wraps itself around me, softening the harsh emotions roiling inside of me and leaving only a sense of calm acceptance, though it's half-amused and half-annoyed.

You didn't bring up training Cross, Priya says, breaking into my thoughts. I curse quietly.

I completely forgot. How did I completely forget? I rub at my temple, pushing a nascent headache back.

You going to call Taka about it? Priya asks.

I'm going to have to. I need to start training Cross sooner rather than later, even if it's only the basics. With how quickly his powers are developing, we're going to have to act quickly before something bad happens.

Can't be worse than Baker possessing him, Priya says sardonically. *But you're right. There are more Turned ghosts showing up, and an untrained Sighted person is asking for trouble.*

I don't know that he's only Sighted. I frown. *I get the sense that there's more going on than we know.*

Priya raises an eyebrow. *What do you mean?*

I mean, I say, *I think he might have the potential to be a Medium. He learned how to fall into Second-Sight pretty quick.*

Cross is a pretty quick guy.

He still should've struggled with it at his age. Most Sighted people start showing signs in childhood when it's easier to learn that stuff. It's harder to learn when you're an adult. You're more stuck in your way of seeing the world. Makes it more difficult to break through to the power.

Priya nods. *Good point. Even more reason to act on this—and fast.*

Agreed.

And speaking of acting on things, Priya says, her mouth curling up into a slow smile that's only a short distance from a leer, *when are you and Cross going to acknowledge what's going on between the two of you?*

Letch.

That's not an answer. She's definitely leering now, and I wish I could jostle her—put my hand to her shoulder and give her a friendly shove. Instead, I wave a hand through her, my skin turning icy within seconds, and watch as Priya wiggles away.

Quit it. You know that feels weird. She shudders.

Don't worry about Cross and me. I'm not doing anything about it and he isn't either. He's my partner and my trainee, and I've got enough trouble in my life right now.

Sure. Priya scoffs. *You're all about avoiding trouble. It definitely doesn't have to do with you being scared of being open with people.*

I'm plenty open with people, I say without meeting her eyes.

Uh-huh. Her eyes flash white for a second and dim back to gray. *If you keep sitting on your hands here, you're going to miss out on the opportunity to grab onto something special.*

Have you been reading romance novels while I sleep again?

She flushes, her skin darkening, but she shakes her head. *You're dodging the question,* Kimberly.

The name startles a laugh out of me, and Priya cracks a smile before settling close enough that we would be shoulder to shoulder if she were alive.

I worry about you being alone all the time, she continues. *And Cross is a sweet guy who clearly has the hots for you. I don't understand why you haven't made any kind of move yet.*

It's not that simple. I shake my head. *For one, he's my partner—*

Potential partner.

I nod, conceding the point. *Potential partner. Second, I'll be his trainer until he finds an actual Mentor who can take him on. That means I'm his teacher and his confidant. Could you imagine if Taka tried hitting on me when I was studying with him?*

I'd rather not, Priya says with a poorly concealed wince, *but Taka is also three decades older than you. Cross is what, three years?*

Five, I think, I say as I turn into HQ's parking lot.

Cross's car is nestled into a spot near the back, and I pull up next to it and park. Priya raises her eyebrow at me, and I lock her in the car. She floats through the door, laughing. *Age isn't the issue here, though. It's about respecting boundaries.*

Right. Boundaries, she Sends. *Whatever helps you sleep at night.*

I'm getting rid of the romance novels, I Send back half-seriously. *They're making you see things that aren't there.*

Kim, I'm a ghost. I know plenty about seeing things that aren't there. This *is not one of them.*

I shrug off her comment, though she's right. I may have been able to avoid it so far, but Cross and I will be spending more time together, whether we're partnered or not. Medium training is intense and deeply personal, and I may not admit it to anyone but myself, but I'm a little scared at how that vulnerability will impact the tension between us.

I roll my shoulders, trying to push back the invasive thoughts. *I've got bigger problems to tackle right now*, I Send. *Like getting off of desk duty, figuring out what those grave markers mean, and finding out why my powers are suddenly changing. Oh,* and *dealing with Banks.*

Priya sighs. *Okay, Kim. But you know you're going to have to face up to it eventually.*

I let her have the final word, pushing my way through the front doors of HQ. *Later*, I think. *But not right now.*

Chapter Two

The bullpen is fairly empty, though there are a few officers who nod curt hellos as I walk past. Cross is tucked into the back of the room, most of his body hidden by a thick support pillar. His face is visible, though, as he's bent over his desk, writing carefully on a stack of papers. Brow furrowed, he bites his lip and flips the top sheet over and back again.

I cough as I approach and grin a little when he jumps. "Good morning, Detective."

"Detective," he says with a grin, brushing his hair from his forehead. He's dressed down today, a worn CPD police academy sweatshirt hugging his shoulders, the sleeves pushed up around his elbows. I nearly stumble, caught off guard by how vulnerable the soft jersey makes him look. I'm used to him in suits. His tattered jeans and worn sweatshirt almost feel like an assault. I shake myself, breaking my momentary trance. Green eyes twinkling with mischief, his grin softens a bit, and my mouth curves in unconscious response.

Yup, nothing going on between the two of you at all, Priya says with a knowing look.

I choose to ignore her.

"Nice outfit," I say as slip my jacket off and pull out my chair, its familiar screech causing a few heads to turn in our direction. "What're you working on?"

"You should be asking me what I've finished." He passes me a neat stack of papers. "I couldn't sleep, so I came in early to get the Harris paperwork together."

"If you have a cup of coffee for me, you might be perfect," I say sarcastically as I thumb through the pages, nodding at his precise notes.

"No coffee, I'm afraid."

"Well, your paperwork is perfect, at least." I hand the pages back to him. "Thanks for doing that."

"From what I hear, you're terrible at it," he says with a wink, "and I didn't want to mess anything up before we talked to Walker."

I look toward the Lieutenant's door. "Is she in today? It is Sunday."

"She's supposed to be." Cross tucks the paperwork into a manila folder and closes it. "Her door's been shut all morning, and I figured I'd wait for you before knocking."

"And what are we telling the Lieutenant?" I ask.

"I figured we would tell her the truth."

"You want to tell her… everything? Even about the Reading?" I ask, thinking back to the sensation of drowning, the weight of water filling my lungs, followed by terror and eventual surrender.

Cross shakes his head. "I don't think we need to go into that. We've got a solid explanation for how we found Jackie, and trying to tell the Lieutenant about your…

situation? I don't see what we gain from it other than Walker trying to get you a psych eval."

"Keeping secrets from the Lieutenant," I say with an arched eyebrow. "I must be a bad influence."

"Probably." He grins. "Maybe I should reconsider this whole partner thing."

"Maybe," I say, with a twinge of guilt.

Cross looks thoughtful for a moment and shakes his head. "Nah, I'd get bored. You, at least, keep things interesting. You can make it up to me by refilling my coffee."

"Only because you did the paperwork."

"Cream, no sugar." He passes me his CPD mug.

"I remember," I say and head to the small kitchen in the back of the bullpen.

The coffee in the pot is still warm. I fill Cross's cup, finishing with a healthy dollop of half-and-half from the nearby fridge. I grab a disposable cup for myself before turning back to our desks. Walking carefully, I try not to splash any coffee from Cross's mug and take a moment to savor the normalcy of it all. No ghosts, no visions, no unexplained powers. Simply the deliberate placement of feet on linoleum as I bring another cop a cup of coffee.

Cross's head is bent over his paperwork again when I set his mug down. He looks up at me with a quick smile, then takes a tentative sip. When the coffee doesn't burn his mouth, he takes a deeper drink. I walk around to my desk and sit down, the chair screeching in protest.

"You ever going to get that fixed?" he asks before

taking another sip of coffee. "It's a bit… loud."

I shift my weight and grin, the chair shrieking again. "I don't know, it's growing on me. It has personality."

"It leaves something to be desired." He eyes the chair. "Like WD-40."

"Don't we have work to do?" I raise an eyebrow and tilt my head toward the Lieutenant's office.

"You have a point." Cross gathers his paperwork together and taps it on the desk to line all the pages up before sliding them into a manila folder. "C'mon, let's get this over with."

Taking another quick sip of coffee, he stands. His green eyes meeting mine, he smiles. "Lead the way."

He follows me as we approach the closed door to Walker's office. The blinds are drawn on the picture window that overlooks the bullpen, and though it's hard to tell, I think there's a light on inside. I hesitate for a moment and knock as Cross takes a step closer.

"Come in!" Walker's voice cuts through the thick wood of the door. I turn the knob and walk inside, Cross right behind me with his carefully organized file tucked under his arm. Walker orders him to shut the door behind him, her head still bent over the swath of papers that cover her desk.

She looks up as the door shuts with a soft click, eyes flashing with hidden humor as she gestures toward the empty chairs before her desk. "How are my two favorite detectives today?"

"Favorite detectives?" I ask as I take a seat. "I wasn't

aware I was your favorite anything, Lieutenant."

She leans back in her chair and gives me a tight smile. "Whenever two of my detectives solve one of the coldest cases in the history of the CPD, they become my favorites."

"Speaking of which"—Cross places his manila folder on top of her desk before taking a seat—"this is the paperwork for the Harris case. Everything's in order."

"I wouldn't expect anything less, Detective Cross." She grabs the folder and quickly skims through the contents. "Are you going to explain to me how you managed to solve this?"

Cross coughs. "Just solid police work, Lieutenant."

"Right." She doesn't sound convinced.

"It had to do with her doll." Cross tenses next to me, but I continue. "It was too far under the bush for it to have fallen there. The placement felt purposeful, like someone had placed it there for a reason."

"And based on other interviews, we knew that Jackie liked to go swimming nearby." Cross continues. "Detective Phillips suggested that Jackie might have left the doll under the bush for safekeeping, then went looking for a place to swim."

"It was unseasonably warm when she went missing," I venture, hoping that Walker believes that I would have looked up the weather for that day.

"And that led you to the lake."

"Yes, ma'am."

She glances down again and idly flips through the first

few pages. "I'm sure the report goes into more detail."

"Yes, ma'am," Cross says. "It's all in there."

She looks to me before closing the folder and moving it to a metal bin labeled with IN in bold letters. "The CPD appreciates the hard work you both put into this investigation, and I'm sure Mrs. Harris does as well. Media Relations wants to get a statement from the two of you for the papers. Make time to get that done this week, and don't make me regret putting you in front of the marketing people, Phillips."

"Yes, ma'am," I say, shifting in my seat as her stern gaze bores into me.

The room falls silent for a moment. I glance at Cross out of the corner of my eye. He's dropped his gaze to his hands, his fingers laced together in his lap. I cough quietly, trying to grab his attention. He looks up, then looks back to the Lieutenant. There's another long pause, and Walker sighs and runs a hand over her face. She looks between Cross and me, then shakes her head.

"I get the feeling that you have something else you'd like to talk about, Detectives."

I look at Cross again and back to Walker. He takes my cue and starts talking.

"Yes, ma'am. We both understand that the Harris case was meant to be a trial run. Based on the results of that investigation, however, both Detective Phillips and I believe that we're more effective investigators working together than separately. Ideally, we'd like you to consider partnering us on a permanent basis."

"Uh-huh."

"Lieutenant," I start, placing my hands on my knees and leaning forward, "I understand why you'd be hesitant to grant our request, considering what happened in November, but Detective Cross and I more than proved that we can work well together, without incident, during this last investigation. I promised you then, and I'll promise you now: I will not put Detective Cross in danger."

Walker looks between us, eyes steely and unreadable. My heart's beating so loud, I swear she must be able to hear it. Cross is stiff next to me, back straight, hands still clasped in his lap. I'm about to speak up again when Walker's impassive expression cracks into a smile, and she laughs.

"You should see your faces, I swear." She shakes her head and chuckles. "Upper brass already asked that I partner you two up, so consider it done. But," she says, pointing first to me, then to Cross, "one toe out of line, and it's over. That goes for both of you. Am I clear?"

I nod, throat tight with relief, while Cross mumbles something in the affirmative.

"Good." She stands, gesturing toward the door. "You've already got your first case. Someone called in a double homicide off Sixty-Fourth and Wolcott. Uniforms were first on scene and are currently securing the area. Forensics is on its way. You'll probably beat them there; the scene is pretty close. There's a patrol car outside. Take that instead of one of your personals. A crowd's gathering, and I want the community to see an official presence."

After she hands Cross a set of car keys from her desk, I

stand, knees a little shaky.

"Thank you, ma'am," Cross says. "We appreciate the opportun—"

"Understood, Detective. Get moving. You've got work to do." Walker waves a hand at us dismissively, then reaches for the Harris case folder, opens it, and starts reading.

I make my way to the door in a daze, Cross close behind. My feet take me to my desk, and I'm grabbing my coat from the back of my chair before I fully realize it.

"Well, that was easy," Cross says, grabbing his jacket. His expression is confused but somehow pleased. "I thought we'd have to fight more."

He cuts an imposing figure in the black wool of his coat, its hem brushing right above his knees. It covers his sweatshirt and most of his jeans, making him look like he's dressed nicer than he actually is. With his hands tucked into his pockets, his expression solemn and professional as he continues to muse over our turn of luck, he looks like the poster boy for the Bureau of Detectives. Then he smiles, excitement lighting his green eyes, and the picture-perfect moment is broken, his boyish charm coming through strong enough to send a low tendril of heat coursing through my stomach. I shake it off, shifting my focus instead to getting my arms into my jacket sleeves.

"Never say that," I say, trying to cover my momentary lapse as I finish settling my jacket on my shoulders. "You're tempting fate when you say that."

"Duly noted," he says with a warm chuckle that teases a grin from me. That wicked curl of heat comes back, teasing and frustrating at the same time. Priya's right. I've got to do something about this.

We head out of HQ, looking around for the Interceptor. The patrol car's number is printed on a fob on the keyring, and Cross and I find it parked along the back edge of the lot where its fenced boundary borders a line of row houses. The car is one of the newer Ford Interceptors, the white and light blue body surprisingly free of dirt from the salt-encrusted streets. The doors unlock almost silently, and I slide into the passenger seat as soon as I have my door open, trying to find shelter from the wind.

Cross starts the car and the police radio crackles to life. I quickly call our status and location into Dispatch, then pull my badge from my pocket and hang it around my neck. Cross does the same, and we pull out of the parking lot.

"So," I say as Cross turns right onto Sixty-Third Street, "while we're alone, we need to talk about your new abilities and getting you trained on how to use them."

He lets out a relieved sigh. "I was hoping we'd get around to that. I'm still getting the hang of Second-Sight, but it's disorienting when it cuts in and out."

"Yeah, I remember that. Always made me a little nauseous."

"Exactly," he says. "What can I do about it?"

"Read, mainly. I've got a couple of books you can borrow. They'll cover the basics, including some meditation exercises that will help your control. After that, you and I will need to schedule time outside of work to do some practical exercises."

He shoots me a look, eyebrows raised, mouth quirked into a half grin. "Practical exercises?"

"Like what we did at the diner," I say, trying to make my voice authoritative instead of exasperated. "There's a lot of useful information available online for Sighted people and Apprentices, but you need guidance from someone who's already been trained or you run the risk of going too far. You remember Jerry Richardson, right?"

Cross's expression becomes more serious. "The guy who nearly drowned you in the lake? Yeah." He nods. "I remember him."

"What happened to him happens to more people than the Medium community would like to admit," I say, turning to look out the window of the car. "Having the Sight is amazing, but it's also dangerous. There's a lot of shit out there that we still don't fully understand, and it's only been in the last century or so that Mediums have been able to work together without fear of Mundane folks burning us at the stake or locking us up in asylums. That means that there are still plenty of Sighted kids who fall through the cracks."

"Gotcha. Practical exercises, then. What're you doing Wednesday?"

"I've got a weekly dinner with my Mentor that night," I say, "and I kind of pissed him off this morning, so I don't think he'd appreciate another guest."

"You, pissing someone off?" Cross scoffs. "I can't believe it."

I laugh, startled. "Okay, smart-ass. What about Thursday?"

"That might work," he says, turning left down Wolcott. "Let me double-check when we get done here and I'll let you know."

Even from a block north, Cross and I can clearly make out the blue flash of police lights and a small crowd of people standing idly across the street. Nervous excitement hums through me. Cross pulls up to the corner of Sixty-Fourth and Wolcott, slotting our Interceptor next to the other police cruisers sitting out front. I unbuckle and let my fingers wander over the weight of my gun and the small notebook I carry in my jacket. Cross goes through the same motions and turns to me.

"You ready?"

Nodding, I reach for the door. "Let's catch a killer."

CHAPTER THREE

T he crime scene is in part of a residential neighborhood that's fallen on harder times. While some of the homes are fixed up, with thick, wrought iron bars on the doors and windows, the building that's cordoned off by yellow police tape is abandoned, the first-floor windows and front door boarded up with plywood. The brick structure was once stately, but the now-crumbling mortar, broken front steps, and sagging roof give it a sad, ramshackle appearance, like a war hero on his deathbed.

"C'mon," I say as I step out of the car and into the dim shadow of the house. It stretches toward a run-down Baptist church that's across the street. Blue lights flash on the church's facade and the faces of the growing crowd that gather at its feet, adding to the forlorn and forgotten atmosphere that lies over the neighborhood like a funeral shroud. There's a uniformed officer standing near the edge of the outer perimeter holding a clipboard. He spots us almost immediately and waves us over.

"You Homicide?" he asks, looking for our stars.

"Detective Phillips"—I hold my badge up for him to see—"and Detective Cross. What's your name, Officer?"

"Taylor, ma'am," he says before waving us past the barrier. He holds out the clipboard and a pen to Cross. "I'll need you to sign in and grab some PPE before going inside. It's a mess in there."

Cross takes the clipboard and signs his name before passing it to me. I sign and pass it back to Officer Taylor.

"What're we dealing with?" I ask.

"Someone called 9-1-1 to report that there were two bodies in this house. The dispatcher wasn't able to get any ID, and whoever called used a pay phone. Dispatch is going to see if they can trace the call, but I haven't heard anything back from them yet. Me and my partner, Hernandez, arrived about four minutes after. She and I found the door to the lower level broken open. We entered and located the victims—two adults, white—in the basement. Neither of them were breathing or had a pulse, and they were both cold to the touch. Based on that and how much blood was on the floor, we didn't try to render aid and instead worked to secure the scene."

"Any sign of weapons?"

Taylor shakes his head. "Not that we've seen, ma'am, but we didn't move the bodies. Figured Forensics and the ME would have our heads if we started messing with their crime scene, you know? Hernandez secured the outer perimeter, and I set up the inner. I blocked off the entrance with red tape. Seems like whatever happened was limited to the basement."

"Did you or your partner move anything?" Cross asks.

"Not that I could tell, sir. It's pretty dark inside, so it was difficult to determine if we may have disturbed something when we first entered. We did our best to avoid the area around the bodies after checking for vitals."

"Forensics will have lighting rigs," I say offhandedly. "Should make it easier to see inside. Is there anything else we need to know about?"

Taylor shakes his head again. "No, ma'am."

"All right, thank you, Officer," Cross says. "We'll take over from here. If there are any extra uniformed officers on scene, see if you can have them start questioning that crowd. Maybe someone who lives nearby heard or saw something."

"Yes, sir," Taylor says and heads back to the staging area.

Cross and I turn to the house and head toward the basement entrance. A double sidewalk leads down the side of the building, running parallel to Sixty-Fourth. It turns into a short set of steps leading into a sunken entrance that's boarded up like the front. Someone either pried off the wood or broke it down, though, because all that's left are some broken pieces around the edges and a discarded sheet of ply leaning against the outside wall. Red barrier tape stretches across the entry, warning us "DANGER– DO NOT CROSS."

"You got a flashlight?" I ask, peering into the inky blackness beyond the doorway. It's slightly overcast today, and what little light is available isn't able to penetrate the darkness inside the abandoned home.

"Yeah," Cross says, pulling a small Maglite from his pocket and clicking it on. The thin beam of light cuts through the darkness, showing a cracked concrete floor covered in dust and a few scuffed shoe prints. I sigh.

"Forensics is going to kill us if we disturb those." I turn back to him. "So, do we break down the front door, or risk it?"

"Depends on who from Forensics shows up," Cross says, biting his lip as he thinks. "The prints could belong to Taylor and Hernandez."

"Maybe. Let me have the light?"

Cross hands the flashlight to me, and I shine it more directly on the shoe prints. They're hard to see, but there's a bit of a wavy pattern to them, not like the geometric tread of the boots most CPD members wear. "Could be from tennis shoes," I hedge while I try to get a closer look, leaning into the doorway but not entering the scene fully. "Uniforms wouldn't be wearing those."

"Let's see if there's a crowbar in the car," Cross says with a sigh.

I turn off the flashlight and hand it to him, and we trudge back up the concrete steps. There's a pair of uniformed officers across the street, starting to interview the milling crowd. Pulling up from the south, lights flashing, is a Forensic Services van.

"Just in time," I say as Cross opens up the trunk of our Interceptor. I hear him dig around inside as I watch the Forensics van park nearby, then turn when he lets out a quiet cry of success.

"Got it." He holds a crowbar up. "You want to take down the front door, or do you want me to handle it?"

"Ladies first." I reach for the crowbar. It's heavy and

cold in my hand when he places it there. "You go get Forensics up to speed."

"Let me know when you get inside." He shuts the trunk.

I nod and head toward the front door, jogging up the low steps to reach the porch as Cross goes to meet Forensics.

The front door is boarded up with two pieces of plywood, one higher than the other, with the bottom overlapping the top of the other piece. I wiggle the crowbar under the edge of the top board until it's firmly seated, then lean my body weight against the metal bar. The wood flexes under the pressure, whatever nails or screws holding it in place fighting to keep the ply attached to the house. With a loud crack and a sudden release of pressure, the wood breaks into two pieces, splitting down the center. It's still hanging from the top of the doorframe, so I grab one half of the board in both hands and jerk it back and forth. It gives way eventually, and I catch the weight of it before turning to the side and letting it fall onto the small porch. The lower board is easier to remove, and it comes away without too much trouble in a single piece. I head back to the cruiser to exchange the crowbar for a couple of pairs of gloves, then head over to Cross, who's still talking to a Forensics tech.

"I've got alternate entry established," I say to the tech as I approach. "You want us to go in now, or wait for your guys to get some lights in there?"

"We're not sure the house has electricity," the tech says. "Still trying to work that out with the power company."

"We'll get started on our own, then," Cross says. "You guys can follow once you get the power situation settled."

"Just don't mess up the evidence, Detective," the tech says, turning back to his van to face another tech sitting with a radio in hand. "Gary, what bullshit is ComEd spewing now?"

Cross and I turn and head back to the house before we can hear Gary's response. Cross passes me a heavy-duty flashlight, an older Maglite that rivals the crowbar for weight.

"Grabbed it from the techs," he explains. "Thought it'd help."

"Yeah, if I need to mug anyone. This thing weighs a ton," I say, turning it on. The beam is wide and bright, casting stark shadows on the porch as we head up the stairs. I point the beam of light through the doorway, and the front hall jumps into sharp focus.

There's a set of stairs to the left leading to the second story and a sitting room off to the right. Straight back from the front door is a centralized hallway, ending in an open room with a broken table lying in the middle of the floor. Dust covers everything in a thin layer that turns the interior a uniform gray. Unlike the cellar, there are no footprints up here.

"No signs of activity," Cross says and follows me through the doorway. He turns his smaller flashlight on and starts scanning the room to the right. "Whoever was in here kept it limited to the basement."

"Seems like," I say, testing the floor under my feet

carefully. Some of the older abandoned homes in Englewood have rotten floors, but this one feels pretty solid. Other than the dust and boarded-up windows, the place isn't in awful shape.

"You see an entrance to the basement anywhere?" Cross asks, walking out of the front room to join me in the center hallway of the house.

"Haven't seen one yet," I say, walking past another room and into what used to be a kitchen. There are obvious gaps in the counters where appliances once were. The doors are missing from most of the lower cabinets, with one of the remaining ones hanging crazily from a single hinge. Faded contact paper covers the shelves, but there's little else in the room. I check a door that turns out to be a pantry, the shelves fallen and empty.

I hear Cross shout "Found it!" from deeper within the house and turn back to the main entrance. Catching a flash of light, I follow it across the main hallway into a back room. After passing a dark hollow of a bathroom, I find Cross in some kind of storage room where a set of wooden stairs trails down into the basement.

"That looks safe," I say, eyeing an obviously broken step cautiously. "What d'you think?"

Cross runs his light over the steps slowly, almost walking the beam down until it reaches the basement floor.

He places a foot lightly on the top step. It lets out a loud groan under his weight but holds. "I think," he says, shifting his weight, "that we should see if there's another entrance into the basement. You and I might be able to get down this way, but I don't know about a whole Forensics crew coming up and down throughout the course of an investigation."

"You think we should look for it from the basement, though?" I say as Cross takes another careful step down.

"Yup," he says, and I slowly follow his lead. The walk down doesn't take long, but my heart is in my throat the whole time, waiting for one of the creaking steps to give way beneath the stress of our weight. Instead, we end up in the basement without issue.

The first thing I notice is how dark it is. If there are any windows in the basement, they've been boarded up like the rest of the house. A few feeble beams of muddy light cut through in dust-filled streams, but otherwise, it's a murky black down here. Even our flashlights seem to struggle to cut through the darkness. Their beams move straight through but don't cast any ambient light. Instead, they flash across the room and bounce off the painted cinder block walls on the far side. Groundwater seeps through cracks in the foundation and runs in rivulets to eventually pool on the floor where the water meanders in slow, snaking lines toward a drain in the center of the basement. And mixed with the water is a darker liquid—blood from the two bodies lying in the center of the room.

They're both facedown, one lying slightly on top of the other. Neither of them is wearing any kind of winter jacket. Instead, the victim on top is wearing a long-sleeved shirt. I can't tell what color it is or if it's been dyed by the blood, but it's something dark. The victim underneath seems to have a sweater on, but it's hard to tell from this distance. Again, the color is obscured by dark, wet stains.

They're both wearing jeans of some kind and sneakers. Blood spreads in an inky pool around them, slowly trailing toward the floor drain in a coagulated stream.

"You see any footprints between us and the bodies?" I ask, and Cross's flashlight dances from the bodies to the foot of the stairs. There's nothing in the expanse of dusty concrete between us and them, and he shakes his head before taking careful steps toward the victims.

I put on a pair of latex gloves and follow after him, trying to keep my footsteps in his. It's so dark, it's hard to see where there may or may not be evidence. We're both stopped short by the blood pool, and Cross and I make a careful circle around the bodies, stopping once we come across the shoe prints we saw from outside. The cruiser lights are easier to see from here, too, and the blue flashes are distracting in the darkness. I shield my eyes, trying in vain to block the light.

"Looks like one male, one female," I say as I crouch down. "It'll be easier to tell once we roll them."

"I think you're right," Cross says. He shines his light on the bottom victim's head, and something glints back at us from the darkness. A large hoop earring, gold and gaudy, catches the light. "I wouldn't put it outside the realm of possibility that I'm wrong, but that looks like a woman's earring to me."

The victim on top, the male, has his face turned away from us. His hair is shaggy and dark, slightly matted either from dirt or blood. This close, I can see that there are older tears in his shirt and jeans, and the sneakers are scuffed with the soles coming away from the body of the shoe.

"Maybe homeless?" I turn and look at Cross. "This guy's stuff looks pretty worn."

"Hers doesn't," Cross says, shifting to the other side of the bodies, where the view of the female victim is clearer. "Her shoes look new, and her nails were done recently."

I join him and see what he's looking at. She's got fake nails on. A few of them are broken, ripped off at the nail bed in a way that makes me wince. But the polish is still bright and glossy, and there are small rhinestones encrusting one of the nails. Not something that would last long after her visit to the salon.

"She fought her attacker," I say, noting the blood coating the tips of her remaining nails. "That'll give us some DNA to match against. You see any weapons?"

Cross shakes his head. "It's like the uniform said. We're going to have to roll them to make sure the murder weapon isn't under the bodies, but the killer may have taken it with him."

"I don't smell gunpowder," I say, taking a deep breath of iron-tinged air. "Just blood."

"Probably a knife, then."

I stand, nodding toward the far side of the basement. "You think there's a door back there?"

Cross gets to his feet and shines his flashlight toward the back wall, trailing it from one corner to the other. The soft reflection from the painted cinder blocks is interrupted by the dull sheen of old wood, and we both share a slightly triumphant glance.

"Would've been faster to tear down *that* door, huh?" Cross says with a grin.

"Shut up," I reply as I walk carefully toward it.

I'm about halfway to the door when the fine hairs on my arms rise in a wave, and then pain, like lightning, arcs through my body. It buries itself in my stomach, and I bend in half, fighting the sudden urge to vomit as the pain ricochets through me.

"Phillips!" Cross shouts, heading toward me at a run.

"I'm fine," I say through gritted teeth, fighting back tears. "Don't damage the crime scene, for fuck's sake."

He stills, and I drop into Second-Sight. Beneath my feet is a sluggish coil of dark red power, a viscous river of supernatural blood that twists and roils on the cement below me. I stagger to the side, stepping out of it into sudden, overwhelming relief. My body wants to sag to the floor. I fight it, slowly standing upright again, though my arm is still wrapped around my middle.

Now that I'm in Second-Sight, I'm surprised it took so long for me to walk into the sickly energy. Thick lines of the stuff weave through the cracks in the foundation and the floor, carving a red path that blends with the blood staining the floor. In Second-Sight, the basement is cast in a dingy, red light that makes something instinctual in me rage. From the corner of my eye, I see ethereal flames of red and blue light covering my body. I clench my hand and watch the power swirl, then concentrate around my fist before it settles, waiting. *Shit.*

Priya, I Send, and she's next to me in a second, eyes white and crackling with her own power.

I see it. She floats through the basement, avoiding the patches of corrosive energy. *This is bad news, Kim.*

Cross finally reaches my side. He takes my elbow in a gentle grasp and helps me move toward the back door. "You all right?" he asks, voice gentle and soothing.

"There's more of that stuff here," I say, throat tight. "That energy from the marker, it's all over this place."

I watch Cross's brow furrow and his eyes go slightly out of focus as he forces himself to fall into Second-Sight. He frowns and turns to me.

"I'm not seeing it." He shakes his head.

I look at the tendrils of energy coiling around the floor and shudder. "You'll get there," I say, taking another step back. "But in the meantime, we need to get out of here."

No shit. The unfamiliar voice cuts through me, and I turn, looking to find where it's coming from. A ghost slowly appears from the darkness behind the stairs, floating around the lines of energy covering the floor. His hair is matted and dark, clothing worn and stained with blood. His eyes, the irises a dark gray, catch mine, and I freeze.

Took you long enough to notice.

CHAPTER FOUR

C ross must feel me tense because he shines his light toward the far wall, trying to find what's spooked me.

"Drop into Second-Sight," I tell him, keeping my eyes on the spirit, "and stay close."

He nods before his eyes lose focus again. A sharp inhalation is the only sign he's seen the victim's ghost.

You're Mediums, the ghost says, floating closer. *But what are you doing here?*

He looks me over carefully but keeps his distance. He also avoids the streams of energy covering the floor in careful, snaking movements that bring him from one side of the basement to the other.

We're homicide detectives, I Send with as soothing a tone as I can manage. *We're here to investigate a murder.*

My *murder*. He looks at the bodies on the floor with a frown. *Well, damn.*

What's your name? I ask, looking for Priya. I can feel her nearby, though she's no longer manifesting.

Steve. He floats closer to his body. *I do not make an attractive corpse, do I?*

I pause. *You don't seem that upset*, I say, taking a careful step back toward the door. Cross follows my lead, his flashlight hanging by his side and lighting up the floor by our feet.

Steve watches us move away. *I think I'm just a little numb.* He looks back to his body. *I didn't think this was how it would end. I thought it would be, I dunno, more glamorous.*

It's never glamorous. I give Cross a slight push toward the door.

"Get it open," I say quietly. "I don't know what to expect here."

"On it," he replies, already trying the knob. It rattles quietly, and Steve's head kicks up, eyes wide.

Are you scared? He pauses, glancing between us and the door. *Of me?*

We need to get Forensics in here, I say, dodging the question. *This is safer than the stairs.*

Steve looks up, then back to his body. *Yeah, I guess that makes sense. Jesus.* He crouches down again and tries to touch his hair. His hand passes through his body's head instead, and he visibly shudders, eyes flashing white, then black.

Not a good sign.

"It's locked," Cross whispers. "Feels like there's a padlock on the outside."

Priya, I Send, reaching out for her. There's a quiet acknowledgment down our bond, but she still doesn't appear. *A little help, please.*

I feel a pull of energy—Priya using our bond to fill her

power reserves—and hear something metal click outside, then rattle against the door. Steve's eyes lift from his body and he tilts his head to the side, listening.

What's that?

Just the door, I Send. *Like I said, we need to bring a forensics team down here.*

No, he says slowly. *There's something else there.*

Little faster, I Send to Priya, not liking the expression crossing Steve's face. There's a hunger to it, one I haven't seen before but immediately don't trust.

I feel Priya pull on our bond again, and I push as much of the flaming power that coats my body down it, hoping to give her enough strength to force the lock. My vision starts to gray at the edges, and Steve stands, eyes flickering black again.

I shove as much power as I can down the bond, grabbing at Cross's arm as my knees weaken. He quickly bolsters me, pulling my body close to his so I don't fall. Steve starts to move closer. My heart's racing and I reach out desperately for Priya. Then, there's a quiet clunk from outside. Cross tries the door again, twisting the knob with his free hand. This time, it creaks open.

Thank you, I Send to Priya. All I get is a soft answering pulse down our bond and nothing more.

Steve, his interest shifting back to his body, runs a translucent hand over his face. *This sucks*, he says, voice sounding distant and vague. *I had so much left to do.*

It's all right, I Send as Cross pulls me through the now-open door. *We're here to help.*

Steve's eyes meet mine again as I back out of the basement. He crouches over his body, staring at me until my heels knock into a set of concrete steps, and then he's hidden by the doorframe as Cross and I hurry up the stairs and tumble into the backyard.

Though it's January and the grass is gray and crackling, it's still tall and overgrown. So, when I fall to my knees, breath heaving from my lungs in huge gasps as nausea and nerves crash into me, it scratches against the sleeves of my jacket and digs into my palms. Cross crouches next to me, his hand on my back rubbing gentle circles as I slowly regain my composure.

"Hey," he says, tone reassuring but serious, "you need to get yourself together right now. I know that was unexpected, and it's real bad news that there's more of that shit here, but we're at a homicide, we're the detectives in charge, and we've got a job to do."

I nod and get back to my feet. "Yeah." I sigh. "Yeah, you're right. Sorry, it's just…" I run a hand through my hair and shake my head. "That's not normal."

"From what you've told me and from what I saw at that cemetery, no, it's not."

"No, not only that," I say, shaking my head again. "That ghost. He's not acting right. There's something… off about the guy. I can't put my finger on it, but we need to be careful around him. Ghosts are never stoic when they see their bodies, especially when they've been killed violently. He should be raging or weeping or *something*. He's just… cold."

Cross looks back down the steps. "Do we need to be

worried?"

"I don't know," I say, looking around for Priya. "Priya's hiding, too, and I don't understand why."

She pops into existence next to me, eyes whirling with bright white energy. *He's not right,* she Sends, flitting toward the steps leading into the basement, her hair flaring around her face as she stops suddenly. She whips around and moves closer to Cross and me. I can feel her pulsing with nervous energy as she throws a small shield around us, then dissolves it almost immediately. *There's something very wrong with that ghost.*

Are you okay? I reach through our bond and feel her grasp at it tightly. It buzzes with anxiety and fear, and I push a low thread of calm down it, trying to help ease her tension. Her eyes meet mine, and the white light fades slightly. With a shiver, she lets go of the bond and nods.

I'll be fine, she Sends as her eyes fade back to their normal pale gray, *but you need to Burn him right now. We can't leave him here. It's too dangerous.*

I shake my head. *You know I can't do that.*

Cross must come to the same realization I have. "If we've got a victim's ghost down there, we're going to have to get his testimony."

I don't want you interviewing him, Priya says hurriedly, eyes flashing again. *He's not right, Kim.*

"I'm going to have to figure out how to do that with all the energy around," I say to Cross. "You'll need to take lead on this scene until I figure out how to get rid of it. It doesn't seem to affect you the way it does me."

Priya puffs up and flies between me and Cross.

Are you listening to me? she Sends. *You can't do it, Kim.*

There's no one else who can, I snap back. *I'm the only Burner on the force.*

"Okay, I can do that," Cross says with a nod as Priya flares with anger. "I'll let Forensics know we found a better entrance into the scene. Take a moment, get yourself in order, and we'll figure out how to move forward."

I nod. "Thanks."

There are other Burners in Chicago. Bring one of them in. Priya's nearly yelling, and I shut my eyes, trying to bolster myself against the power she throws into her Sending. My stomach lurches, the darkness behind my eyelids making my disorientation worse. I swallow down the nausea and start walking away from the house.

The building overshadows us, the windows boarded up but still watchful. Cross walks from the unfenced backyard to the front, and I slowly make my way to a pitted one-lane road behind the house. It must serve as an alleyway for the block as there are one-car garages stretching down it and trash cans sitting on the curb. The distance from the house and the dark energy that fills its basement helps, and I take a deep breath of cold, January air. It burns in my lungs, but it's clean and leaves me feeling purified.

I turn to look back at the house and trace the lines of power that radiate toward it. A huge tree towers over the backyard, its trunk and bare lower branches choked with ivy. The higher branches reach like skeletal fingers toward the gray-clouded sky. And threaded through the limbs like pulsing arteries are more lines of deep red power.

Kim, Priya says, her forceful tone pulling my attention back to her. *We've got to talk about this ghost.*

Yeah, I say as I walk into the back alley.

He has to be Burnt. Now. By you or by someone else.

And you know I can't do that yet, I say, frustrated and still slightly nauseous. *There's protocol that I have to follow first.*

She opens her mouth to speak, and I hold up a hand, stopping her. *Look, I get it. There's something seriously fucked up about this, but being a Burner isn't my only job. I'm also a detective, Priya, and that means I have to interview witnesses, especially victims. I'm* sorry. *I'll put up wards. I'll get a binding circle scribed. I'll make sure every tool I have at my disposal is ready to go in case this guy Turns, but I* have *to talk to him first. I'm not going to bring someone else into this and put them at risk. We don't know what that energy is or how it'll affect other Mediums. For now, I have to be the person to deal with this. Okay?*

Her shoulders sag as she turns her face away, but she nods slowly. *Okay. But I don't trust him. Even if it's just whatever that energy is interfering with things or making him act weird, there's something wrong here that I can't explain. I just* feel *it, and it's not good.*

I know, I say. *I can feel it, too. Even if he isn't Turned, there's something off about him, and the energy down there isn't helping anything.* I look at the lines again, watch as they slowly meander toward the basement as if drawn to it. *It's not quite the same as in the cemeteries.*

She pauses, then traces the lines of power with her eyes, following them up the branches of the tree. *No, this doesn't seem as directed or contained in any way. It's more…*

Random, I finish before letting out a low groan. *I really don't want to have to bring Banks over here. Fuck.*

Priya's eyebrows rise. *You think there's a marker nearby?*

Or a broken one. We've only seen trails of energy like this around them. Could be there was one nearby that got damaged or corrupted, and now we're seeing the aftereffects of it. If I take her to one of the other markers, then back here, she might be able to tell us something about it.

I'm sure your Lieutenant will love that, you bringing a reporter to a double homicide.

I snap my latex gloves off and rub my temples. *You have a special knack for giving me headaches.*

A low thread of healing energy courses through our bond, and the ache in my head eases. Priya gives a small shrug when I turn and smile at her.

Thanks.

You need to be careful, she Sends. She hovers closer to me, wrapping her transparent arms around my shoulders like a cold shawl. The hairs on the back of my neck stand up from the icy touch, but I let it calm me as it centers her. After a moment, she lets out a breath and drops her arms.

What do we do next?

I'm going to let Cross take the lead for now, I say, turning back toward Wolcott. *I can't go down there until I talk to Andrea and find out what I can about the bindings on the markers. Maybe it'll tell us more about what that energy is and how to get rid of it.*

You need to make sure Cross is protected, Priya cautions.

I curse softly. *I think I've got some liquid chalk in my desk or my car. We'll get him warded before he heads down there again.*

Priya smiles a little, trying to break the tension. *You're not going to enjoy that at all, are you?*

I glare at her quickly, then start heading toward the flashing lights of the cruisers and the Forensics van. *Now's not the time for jokes.*

Someone's got to lighten the mood around you. You'd be all doom and gloom otherwise.

My mouth tilts up into a reluctant smile. She has a point.

I pull my shoulders back to hide any lingering effects the basement had on me and head toward Cross. He's standing next to the Forensics van as the techs unload large rigs of lights.

"They got the power situation figured out?" I ask.

He nods. "Yeah, ComEd turned it back on for us. They should have the whole area lit up in an hour or so."

"Okay. I'm guessing we're holding back while they do that?"

"Yeah," Cross says, turning away from the van to head toward our cruiser. I follow after him, and once we're away from the other officers, he adds, "I thought it would give us some time to get things figured out. With the ghost, I mean."

"I need to make sure it's safe for the two of us to be down there," I say as I dig through my coat pockets. "Long-term, that means figuring out where that power is flowing from and what's drawing it in. Until I figure that out—and how to get rid of it—I shouldn't go down there.

And, in the short term, we have to get you warded."

"That sounds concerning." Cross takes a step closer and frowns at me, watching my hands as they dip in and out of my pockets. "Should I be concerned?"

"Probably." I shrug. "You're newly Sighted, which means you're prime meat for ghosts. Most people become Sighted when they're kids, and it's less likely they'll run into anything nasty. We put some low-key protections on their clothing, or they stick by a fully trained Medium, and that's often more than enough to keep them safe."

"So, I'll stick with you," he says. "You're a fully trained Medium. You can keep me safe."

"Your faith is reassuring," I say with a slight smile, "but I can't go into the basement without the risk of getting hurt, and, in case you forgot, we've got a crime scene to investigate. That means you need more protection than what I can offer. I'm going to have to break out the big guns."

"Okay, now I *am* concerned."

I hold my hand up, a piece of chalk held between my fingertips. "It's only some chalk sigils and runes, Cross. Nothing to worry about. And," I add, pressing the tip of the chalk into his chest to leave a small, white speck on his dark coat, "you have to listen to me while we're anywhere near that basement. If I tell you to get out, you get out. No questions."

"You think I'll need to run?" He looks back at the house.

"That room is full of blood and power," I say, and my throat is suddenly tight with fear for him, myself, and any of the other investigators who will be working inside. "It's a dangerous combination, especially with a ghost inhabiting the space. Chances are he'll stick with his body—most ghosts do—but he might linger in the place instead. If he does that, there's no telling if he'll Turn or not. And since I still don't fully understand what that power is or what it's doing, I can't rule out other... things making themselves known."

"Like whatever came out of Baker's knife in the storage room," he says with a nod.

"I doubt that, actually," I say, and the tension in his shoulders eases. "I think that was Baker manifesting in some form, rather than a random spirit. It's a one-way street into the afterlife. We only need to worry about the ghosts in our world." I roll the chalk between my fingers, staring past Cross to look at the brick home. "Problem is, I don't know if Steve's the only ghost in the area. That power may draw them, and with how many homicides, suicides, and natural deaths have happened in this neighborhood in the last thirty years? There's no telling how many others may join in the party."

Cross swallows and looks at the chalk. "Okay. Let's get these wards in place, then."

My cheeks heat. "Yeah, we can't do that here."

"Why not?"

"If you were a kid or Mundane, I'd put the warding into your clothes and power it myself. Since you're Sighted, we need something more powerful, and that means chalk and blood," I say. There's a full blush on my face now.

"You have to bleed on me?" Cross asks, looking vaguely disgusted.

"Not *my* blood," I say. "Yours. Wards work better when they're powered by the person they're protecting. I'll have to scribe them on your skin in order to tap into your powers."

Understanding rushes over Cross's face, and his eyes meet mine. "Oh," he says on a soft exhalation, and tension flares to life between us. He shifts his body weight, leaning toward me in what has to be a subconscious movement. There's a long moment where we're both frozen. I can't decide if I want to move away from or toward him. Our breaths frost in the air between us, tangling in a misty cloud that's blown away by a sharp wind. Cross finally ends the uncertainty of the moment as he pulls his eyes from mine, breaking the tension enough that I can breathe again.

"Where are you going to do it, then?"

"HQ, I think," I say, and my voice comes out gravelly and rough. I want to cough to clear my throat, but I swallow instead.

"We'll need to sign out of the scene, let Forensics take control." He takes a slow step back and motions toward the perimeter. "I see Taylor. I'll take care of the handover."

"No," I say quickly. "I don't want you getting too close to the house until you're warded. Like I said, you're vulnerable right now. I don't want to put you at risk."

"What about you?" he asks, eyeing the chalk in my hand. "Are you warded?"

"I'm a Burner," I say. "Of course I'm warded."

"You know that power messes with you. You don't know what it can do."

"I know more than you do, and I'm at least able to see it." Cross scowls at me, and I instantly regret the words. "Sorry. We'll start working on your Second-Sight today, but until you can see where it is, I don't want you near that stuff."

"Fine." The word is curt.

"I'm watching your back."

"I know," he says. With a long exhale, he looks at me. "I'll wait in the car. Sign me out of the scene?"

"Yeah, of course."

He brushes past me to head to the cruiser. I swear I can feel the heat of his body through his coat and mine, but it's gone in a second as a brisk January wind whips past. I shiver and head back to the perimeter. Taylor is standing near the staging area, clipboard still in hand.

"Hey," I say, waving at him to meet me by the perimeter tape. "Detective Cross and I need to sign out of the scene. Forensics is going to take lead."

Taylor hands me the clipboard. "Anything we need to know about?"

"Yes," I say, head bent as I fill in the form with Cross's and my information. "One of the victim's ghosts is still down there."

Taylor's eyebrows go up, his expression disbelieving. I sigh.

"I'm a Burner," I add.

"You're *that* Phillips," he says with sudden recognition and a bit of awe. "I was wondering if you were, but I wasn't sure."

I'm not exactly happy that I apparently have a reputation in the district, but I move on.

"Like I was saying, there's a ghost down there. He seems fine right now, but anyone entering the inner perimeter needs to be made aware of the potential danger. I've got to get some Medium stuff from HQ to handle him. We won't be gone long, but while we are, try to keep people entering the inner perimeter to a minimum. Other than that, let Forensics do their job."

"Understood," he says, taking back the clipboard as I hold it out to him. "Thank you, Detective."

I tip my head and head back to the car. Exhaust puffs from the cruiser as the engine idles. Cross is in the driver's seat. His head is tilted back against the headrest, one of his arms resting on the door with his fingers touching the steering wheel. He raises his hand to rub the space between his eyes, and a small cloud of breath fogs the air in front of his face. Something aches in my chest at the picture he makes, and I rub at it idly as I come around the back of the car to open the passenger side door. He watches me as I slide in, and I have to turn away, looking at the seatbelt to escape his too-green eyes.

"Let's go," I say as I keep my eyes focused on the run-down neighborhood outside my window.

He doesn't say anything but puts the car in gear and pulls away from the scene, blue lights flashing.

CHAPTER FIVE

R un-down houses pass as we head north. Our cruiser jolts as it hits a pothole, but Cross doesn't seem to notice. He's still silent when we reach the stop sign at Sixty-Third Street, and I find myself unable to sit in the uncomfortable silence any longer.

"I wasn't trying to imply that you couldn't handle yourself," I say, turning to look at him. "You don't put yourself in risky situations, and when you do find yourself in them, you know how to stay out of trouble. Hell, you've saved my ass at least once, and we've only worked three cases together, including this one. But you were knocked unconscious by a Turned ghost, what, *three* days ago? Maybe I'm a little gun-shy, but the whole thing makes me nervous."

I turn and look out the window again, sinking a little deeper into my seat. The only sound in the car is the quiet click of the turn signal and the crackle of radio chatter. After Cross makes his turn, he sighs.

"Look," he says, and I turn to face him again. "I get it, I do. But I don't like being this… vulnerable, I guess. I don't know this supernatural stuff like you do, and that makes me defensive. And the way that energy affects you, it…" He takes a deep breath. "You're not the only one who wants to keep their partner safe, all right?"

I smile a little. "Thank you. Priya's got the overprotective thing handled, though."

"She's clearly reasonable and intelligent, and I'm sure she'd appreciate the help keeping an eye on you."

Priya laughs. *I really like him.*

Hard not to, I admit begrudgingly. *He's a good guy.*

He's a great guy, Priya Sends, hovering behind Cross in the cruiser. She bats her eyes at him, and I laugh. He glances in my direction and brings his eyes back to the road.

"She's talking about me, isn't she?"

"I promise, it's all very flattering."

He grins. "Like I said, she's intelligent."

"I'm glad you two don't talk to each other." I shake my head. "You'd be unbearable."

"Is that something I *can* do?" he asks.

"Send to Priya?" I shrug. "Probably. It depends on how Sighted you are. We know you can see ghosts, and you can tell when Priya and I are Sending, even if you haven't heard anything so far. We'll work on it as part of your training."

"How do I do it?" he asks as we pull up to a red light. He turns to look at me fully, his arm resting over the top of the steering wheel as he twists in his seat, excitement gleaming in his eyes.

"Sending works like Second-Sight," I start. "The same way you have to look without looking to See, you have to listen without hearing."

"That doesn't make any sense." He frowns.

I continue. "It's communication outside of the physical world. You're not using your body to listen or speak. Instead, you're tapping into your connection to the afterlife to do it for you. Relax into that feeling as you do for Second-Sight, and it should click."

"What? Just *think* at her?"

"That's one way of framing it," I say. "We've got a few more blocks till HQ. You're welcome to try now if you don't think you'll get too distracted."

I watch as his brow furrows, then eases as the light turns green. Priya leans forward in the back seat. We drive to the next intersection, the radio crackling with police chatter as boarded up business fronts pass by, and she laughs. I see her mouth move but don't hear what she's saying. Cross's eyes gleam, and he turns to look at me, his expression a little smug.

How'd he do? I ask Priya, who's still grinning in the back seat.

He sent me the alphabet song, she says with a laugh. *It was a bit in and out, but he made it all the way to L-M-N-O-P before I couldn't hear anything else.*

And what'd you tell him that's got him looking so smug?

Nothing, Priya says a beat too fast.

Nothing.

She dips her head into a quick nod as she fights a smile, her face flushing slightly.

There's no way I'm believing that.

She tries to give me a look of pure innocence and fails.

I'll get it out of you eventually, I say before turning my attention to Cross.

"The alphabet song is a good approach," I say. "Starting with something you know by heart is a great way to focus on the process instead of what you're trying to Send."

"Can you Send to other Mediums?" Cross asks, glancing at me as we wait to turn into the HQ parking lot.

"*I* can't," I answer. "But Speakers can. There's something special about their Affinity that allows them to Send with other Mediums, but they're the only ones who can communicate that way."

Traffic breaks and Cross makes the left into the parking lot. "How do Mediums talk over distances, then?"

"Cell phones?" I offer with a grin. "Or our ghost partners relay messages. Most of the time, it's not an issue. We tend to work alone."

Cross parks the car and shuts off the engine before turning to me, eyes serious. "I'll keep working on that and Second-Sight. And you're right. I can't see this stuff, it's dangerous, and I need to be prepared to keep myself out of trouble."

"The wards will do a lot to keep you safe." *I hope,* I think to myself, uncertain any wards will stop that energy from doing *something* to Cross. With his sudden shift from Mundane to Sighted, he's his own set of unanswered questions.

"Speaking of which," Cross says, shifting

uncomfortably in the driver's seat, "what, exactly, is that going to entail?"

"These are personal protections," I say with a shake of my head. "Scribing them on your skin in chalk allows the natural power you have as a Sighted person to keep the runes working. It's one of the more basic protections, but it's basic because it works, even on people who aren't full Mediums. If it looks like you need more than that, you'll need to scribe them yourself in blood."

He blanches a little, and I hold up a calming hand.

"Don't worry. We'll start with the basics first, then go from there. If it turns out that you need the beefed-up version, I'll walk you through everything." I give him a thoughtful glance. "For a homicide detective, you sure don't like the idea of blood."

"I don't like the idea of *my* blood," he says. "Other people's blood doesn't bother me." My eyebrow raises, and he sighs before opening his door. "Way to make it weird, Phillips."

I smile and climb out of the cruiser. "You know, if your powers keep growing, you could train to be a full Medium."

He spins to face me, eyes wide. "You really think so?"

"If it's something you want to do, sure. We'll need to figure out how strong your powers are, but I haven't seen anything that would tell me it's out of the question."

He looks stunned.

I walk to stand next to him and place my hand on his shoulder. "And Cross?"

He looks down at my hand, then meets my eyes.

"You use a *hell* of a lot of your own blood when you're a full Medium."

I give his shoulder a commiserating squeeze and head toward my car, leaving him to stand, dumbstruck, in the middle of the parking lot.

I open my trunk and start rummaging through its contents, searching for the backpack of Medium supplies I usually keep inside. There's a first aid kit, some discarded fast-food bags, a few pieces of mail from last month that I need to toss, and other random bits of trash floating around in the trunk. Eventually, I find the beat-up, black backpack that has my extra supplies buried under a threadbare blanket I keep in case of emergencies. I pull the bag out, shut the trunk, and toss it over my shoulder.

Cross is waiting by the front door and holds it open for me as I walk inside. Walker is out of her office talking to a pair of uniformed officers and catches sight of us coming inside.

"What're you doing back here already?" she asks and checks her watch for the time. "You've barely been gone an hour."

"There's a ghost at the scene," I say. "I needed to stock up."

She groans. "You'd better get your paperwork in order, Phillips, or so help me. You *know* defense attorneys love to go after supernatural evidence."

"Understood." I point to Cross. "I'll make him do it."

"*Perfect*," Walker says with more enthusiasm than I feel

is strictly necessary. "Get your shit and get back to the scene." She turns her attention back to the uniforms, dismissing us with a wave. I head toward our desks, the backpack bouncing against my body with each step.

As he walks next to me, Cross looks at me and squints. "How bad, exactly, *is* your paperwork?"

"I plead the Fifth," I say before tossing my backpack down on my desk, followed quickly by my jacket.

I unzip the bag and shift its contents around until I find a large bottle of liquid chalk. Giving it a quick shake, I grin when I hear sloshing inside. The bottle's definitely cold, but it's unfrozen. Cross eyes it warily.

"It'll be fine," I say as I hold the bottle tight in my hand, hoping to warm it up some. "It'll be a bit cold."

"I don't like the sound of that," he says reluctantly.

I roll my eyes. "I'll run it under hot water or something. C'mon, let's get you warded."

He sighs and tilts his head in the direction of the locker rooms at the back of the building. "Ladies first."

As I head down a small hallway, I'm flanked on both sides by interview and conference rooms. Most of the doors are closed, though muffled voices stream from a few of the rooms. At the end of the hallway are two doors labeled with bathroom signs, one for women, one for men. I push my way through the women's door, and Cross hesitates for a brief moment before following me inside.

The room we walk into is lined with floor-to-ceiling metal lockers. Small pieces of tape with Sharpie-written names label each officer's space, mine included. Most of the lockers don't have names on them, though, and the room is, as usual, empty. There's a slight jog to the left that leads into an open shower space, but to the right are a series of gray metal stalls for changing clothes. Rubber mats cover the floor, a few of them still wet from where officers have changed after showering earlier in the day. There's a slightly musty smell to the place, a mix of old sweat and mildew that seems to fill every locker room in existence. I ignore it and head to the largest stall.

It's tucked into the back corner of the room, and I push its creaking door open and gesture for him to walk in. He ducks past me, and I follow him inside, shutting and locking the door behind me.

"I'll try to get this warmed up a bit," I say as I roll the bottle between my hands, my eyes watching it move back and forth, "while you get ready. Take off your shirt whenever you're comfortable."

I turn to face Cross, who's already pulling his CPD sweatshirt over this head. He's got a worn white T-shirt on underneath. The hem of it is dragged up slightly by the sweatshirt, showing a thin strip of muscled skin with a narrow line of dark hair that disappears into the waistband of his jeans. I draw my eyes up quickly, then get caught on the way the slightly worn collar of his shirt reveals the hollow of his throat. His neck flexes as he swallows, and his arms drop, the sweatshirt tangled in them, as he meets my eyes.

"Can you put this on the hook?" he asks as he holds the sweatshirt out to me. I nod and take the still-warm garment from him. I turn away, hanging it by the hood on the small hook attached to the stall door. With a deep breath, I frantically try to calm my suddenly racing pulse. *Professionalism*, I remind myself. *You're here to do a job, an important one. You're keeping him safe. That's it.*

With a swallow, I shift back to face him. He's already got his shirt off and folded carefully on a small, plastic bench in the stall. His back is a spread of lightly tanned skin over muscle and bone, all of it dusted with a hint of freckles. My mouth goes dry and my hands tighten on the bottle of chalk as the sight of him washes over my senses. As he flexes his hands, his corded arms jump and lead to taut shoulders. He rolls them, sending the planes of his back into a gentle shift that has my breath catching. When he turns, I watch the motion cascade down his body, his abs tensing and relaxing as he finishes the careful stretch. I force myself to meet his eyes, distracted for a moment by the scarred symbol in the center of his chest. They're tilted up with a hint of masculine pride, and his mouth curves into a matching grin as he gestures toward himself.

"You going to do this or what?" he asks, his voice filled with more than a hint of challenge and bravado.

I nod, unscrew the top of the bottle, and move closer until we're toe to toe.

"I promise I'll be gentle," I say, trying not to let the implied dare in his voice throw me. Thankfully, my words come out glib and confident, and I find myself relieved that my nervousness isn't as obvious as it feels.

I slide my finger into the bottle of chalk and tilt the container until cold liquid meets my skin. It's like ice; my feeble attempts at warming it have made no noticeable difference in the temperature. I don't warn Cross before I press the pad of my finger against the heated skin of his chest. For a brief moment, I'm overwhelmed by the warmth of him, the solid feel of muscle beneath my hand, and then he gasps and flinches back with a curse.

"Fuck, I thought you were going to warm it up," he says quietly. After a beat, he purposefully shifts his weight forward to bring my finger back in contact with his chest. I watch as goose bumps appear on his skin, spreading from where I'm touching him.

"My bad," I murmur and turn my attention back to his chest and scribing.

My finger drags the liquid chalk across his skin, leaving a thin, white smear. I dip my finger into the bottle again and bring it back up, lingering as I finish the first rune. As I reapply the chalk, finger retracing the already-scribed symbol, Cross speaks.

"What do they mean?" he asks. I look up to find him staring at the mark I've left on his skin, his eyes hooded, brow furrowed.

"Self," I say and start drawing the next rune. "Body."

I recite the meanings of the runes as I write them, distracting myself from the muted friction of his skin and the slowly warming chalk.

"Spirit." I drag my finger down the soft ripple of muscles along his side. "Mind." I graze the slope of his neck. "Enemy." My finger moves along his chest. "Power." I paint from the top of his arm to the dip of his inner elbow. "Protection." I move my finger over the back of his hand and down each of his long, graceful fingers.

His breath catches with each touch even as the chalk warms. Goose bumps still cover his body, the small hairs on his arms lifting to meet my hand as I scribe over his skin. His chest rises and falls, deforming the runes as I go, forcing me to redraw them again and again until their shapes no longer crack with his every shivering inhale.

As I finish the last rune, I take a step back, surprised at how unsteady my legs feel. I take a deep breath and consider what I've written, fighting for impartiality in the face of the heavy weight of blood in my veins and the reckless pounding of my heart.

"It's not perfect." My voice comes out on a raspy whisper. I swallow and try again, and my voice steadies. "The scar complicates things."

Cross traces his hand over the raised mark in the center of his chest, following the outer circle and ending on the longer line that extends past it. The white lines of chalk covering the back of his fingers draw my attention to the careful motion, and I find myself losing track of whatever composure I found with distance.

"Is it going to be a problem?" he asks, his voice deep and muted, a feeling more than a sound, before he meets my eyes. His are a darker shade of green than I've seen before, his pupils blown wide as he waits for my answer.

"I don't think so."

"That's it?" he asks.

I swallow and shake my head. "No. I need to tie them together now. It won't be much longer, I promise. I'm nearly done."

He nods, and the muscles of his chest tighten as I step

forward again, chalk-covered finger raised and dripping with fresh paint.

The sigils flow easily, binding the various runes together. And though I'm still distracted by the feel of Cross's body beneath my hand, the gentle rasp of skin and hair as I finalize the wards, I find myself falling into the pattern of the sigils. Some instinct takes over and my hand moves faster, symbols flowing like water from my mind, through my hand, and onto his body. They swirl and twist across the canvas of his chest, moving ever closer to the scarred symbol in the center of it. As if it's a lodestone and my hand is some kind of compass, I'm drawn to the raised mark until my finger touches the edge of the symbol, and my mind is torn from the normal world into Second-Sight.

The stall is outlined in twisting red and blue-white light, and in the center of it all is Cross, a pillar of blinding, golden energy in the shape of a man. The runes and sigils on his skin shift and pulse with that same power, sending it in crackling paths across his body. I lift my hand, marveling at the twined red and blue light that outlines my fingers. As I bring it closer to Cross, energy leaps between us, a shock of power that arcs into a curl of rainbow light. When my finger touches his skin, drawn to the intersection of the lines in the center of his scar, a pinpoint of jade green light appears. There's a sensation like falling, and then everything in the room—from the beat of my pulse to the unsteady inhalation of breath—*stops*.

Something builds within my body, a power that refuses to be restrained. It flows out of me in a slow, agonizing wave, traveling down my arm in a bolt of blue-white light that fills the symbol in the center of Cross's chest. The lines of the scar start to beat in time with his heart, with mine, and the power changes in color from blue-white to red to green, and finally to the golden glow that coats his body.

With a gasp, I press my palm to his chest and watch as the chalk smears and leaves my palm print glowing on his skin. My ears pop, and a silent explosion radiates out from where my hand is pressed against his skin.

The shockwave moves across the room, wiping out the bright light of Second-Sight in a wash of pure darkness. I cry out involuntarily, lost, my fear animalistic. I can't see anything, and for a moment, I'm enveloped by a sense of utter desolation and emptiness. All I can find in the darkness is more of the overwhelming sense of loss that threatens to overwhelm me completely. Heat crashes over me, dragging me out of whatever void I fell into and bringing me back to the world. Light slowly grows, golden and warm, and I gather it around me like a child with a favorite blanket. That bright energy flows into my body in a rush, and as I fall out of whatever dark world I stumbled into, I find myself pressed up against Cross. His arms are tight around my body, my forehead resting in the center of his chest. And my palm pressed against his scarred Burner symbol is the first thing I see when I open my eyes.

CHAPTER SIX

K im! Priya's voice is so loud, it leaves me reeling. My hands dig into Cross's chest as I flinch and let out a pained gasp.

What happened? she asks again, this time softer. *What was that?*

I don't know, I Send. It makes my head ache, and I close my eyes against the pain.

"Was that normal?" Cross's voice shakes.

"No." I try to pull away, but he stops me, his arms tightening around me. Fingers flexing against his skin, I pull my head away from his chest and look up. He looks the way I feel, as if all the energy in my system was sucked away into that endless dark place.

I try to pull away again, and this time, he lets me go, though his touch seems to linger before he releases me. His arms fall limply to his sides and he stumbles back and collapses to the small bench. I lock my knees to stay standing, then laugh weakly.

"You're warded." I point to his now-clean skin. "The chalk's gone."

"You, too," he says, grabbing my outstretched hand to

steady it. "Your pointer finger."

He's right. The chalk that had been coating my finger and hand is nowhere to be seen. With a groan, I fall into Second-Sight. It hurts to do, but it's worth it for the brief glimpse of Cross's heavily warded body, the runes and sigils glowing like gold in sunlight as they dance over his skin. My pointer finger glints up at me, covered in a similar metallic sheen.

"It's like it's stained," I say as I flex my finger to watch the light glimmer across my skin. I sound drunk, but I keep speaking even as I drop out of Second-Sight with a grimace. "Like I dipped it in gold."

Are you two okay? Priya asks slowly, looking between me and Cross and our hands. *I don't think I should have left you two alone.*

I look at her, then back at Cross's hand holding mine. Pulling away with more strength than I need, I fall back a step before awkwardly leaning my weight against the stall. *No, you shouldn't have.* At some point, I must have dropped the bottle of liquid chalk because it slowly rolls on the floor to settle against my boot. I slide down the stall and pick it up, forcing myself to stand again. I give the bottle of chalk a shake, then hold it up to my eye. The contents are gone, taken in the wash of power.

"What the hell was that?" Cross asks, drawing my attention from the bottle. "What just happened?"

"I have no idea," I say, tossing him the bottle. He catches it clumsily and looks inside for a beat before setting it on the bench.

"You're the expert here. You've got to have some

idea."

"I was warding you, and then…" My voice trails off as I struggle to find an explanation.

"And then…?" he prompts, leaning forward.

"And then it all went hazy. I don't know what to tell you." I sense my strength returning, and I lift my back from the cold metal of the stall to stand. My knees only wobble a little, and I'm almost smug when I keep my feet.

I'll be better in a bit, I Send to Priya who looks both worried and aggravated. *Whatever happened, it seems temporary.*

I nearly got blasted out of the building, she says, turning to Cross. Her mouth starts moving, but I don't hear anything as she tries to Send to him.

Angling his head toward her, he frowns. There's a pause. Priya's lips still for moment and she starts speaking again.

Hey, over here, I Send, interrupting whatever exchange they're having. Priya turns to me with a concerned glare. *We're fine.*

I hate that word. And that's not what he says, she says, waving her arm toward Cross. *He says something seriously weird just happened. Considering whatever that was nearly threw me out, I'd say he's right.*

He's not wrong, I Send as Cross reaches for his shirt and slides it back on. He stands up carefully and holds his hand out.

"Sweatshirt," he says. I grab it from the hook with stiff fingers and toss it at him. He catches it and stuffs his arms into his sleeves before giving me a long, considering look.

"You need to start talking. Now."

"What do you want me to say?" Frustration makes my voice rise. "I don't understand anything that's happening with you. You're too old to be developing powers, especially when you've been Mundane up to this point. Maybe if you'd had a bit of the Sight as a kid, this might make sense…" He shakes his head, and I exhale sharply. "I didn't think so. Whatever is going on started after Baker possessed you, and I did whatever I did"—I wave toward his chest, hoping he understands that I mean the scarred symbol—"to get him to leave. And now? I honestly don't know what's happening. You're… *changing*, and I don't know why."

He stares at me, expression unreadable, and pulls his sweatshirt over his head. When his head pops back into view, his hair is ruffled. Tugging the sweatshirt down around his waist, he walks into my space and I take an unconscious step back.

"We have a problem," he says quietly, looking down at me, "a big one, and we're going to have to figure it out."

I lift my chin, meeting his eyes with my own, powering through my racing heart and tight throat with sheer stubbornness. "No shit."

My pulse races as I continue to hold his gaze. I tighten my hands into fists to keep myself from putting them to his chest. In the moment, I don't know if I'd push him away or pull him closer. Something sparks in his gaze. His eyes darken, and his mouth parts on a harsh exhale.

"I swear," he says, voice dark with emotion, "there are days I could…" He spins around and runs a hand through his hair, his back turned to me. I shiver, suddenly cold.

"You're warded," I say with force, my voice trembling. "Aside from whatever happened here, you won't have to worry about the guy in the basement."

"How can you be sure?" he asks as he faces me. "You keep… doing things to me that you don't understand. First, there's the scar. Now, whatever the hell that warding was. Excuse me if I don't have a lot of confidence that you know what you're doing right now."

Anger flares.

Priya, I bite out, his words stinging. *Show him.*

Kim, she says with hesitancy. *Are you sure that's a good idea? I know you're both feeling a little vul—*

Just do it, I snap, unlocking the stall door and storming out. After a moment, I hear Cross's heavy footsteps coming after me; then they stop.

I can't help it. I swing around and watch as Priya hovers, fully manifested, in front of Cross, her hands held in front of her. I think it's the first time he's seen her, maybe the first time he's ever seen a ghost, because he's staring at her with brows raised, his mouth hanging open. A ball of energy forms in her hands, and his eyes dart to it, widening.

Sorry, she Sends, her mouth twisted into a sheepish expression.

"What's she doing?" he asks, looking at me with disbelief and confusion. "What'd you tell her to do?"

Then Priya throws the ball. It races toward Cross, white light that sparks as it moves through the air like lightning.

With a crackling flash and the sudden overpowering smell of ozone, it splashes against his body, spreading out in a wave of light that slowly fades.

All that's left is a golden glow that emanates from his body. Even through the fabric of his shirt and sweatshirt, the light from the symbols covering his body can be seen. He bathes the small room with it, the runes and sigils of his wards briefly covering the walls around him in ghostly marks. The glyphs on his neck are the brightest, the lines of power unobstructed by thick fabric, and the golden light leaves his eyes shadowed and dark. As the wards finally fade to nothingness, he looks up from his chest and meets my eyes.

I try not to let my own surprise show, but it's hard. I've never seen anything like it, and I cross my arms to stop my hands from shaking. Slowly, I lift my chin, meeting his eyes with a confidence I don't entirely feel.

"You're warded," I say again before I turn and leave the changing room. The conference rooms are a blur as I walk down the hallway, my mind reeling.

What was that? Priya asks as she flies after me, her voice high-pitched with confusion. *What did you do to him?*

I don't know, I Send, grabbing the bag of supplies on my desk like a lifeline. My hands fist around the black fabric of the straps, and I stare at them, wondering and terrified. *I don't know.*

He lit up like a goddamn Christmas tree. That's not... I mean... What's...

Something happened while I was warding him.

That's exactly *why I left you guys alone!* She throws her hands up. *I thought you'd kiss or* something, *not whatever* that *was.*

I ignore her. *It was like something else took over. An instinct or… I don't know. I don't think I've seen half of the sigils that I used, Priya. They just… appeared.*

She stills, then settles on the desk by the backpack. *What do you mean?*

I mean, my hands were moving, and I could see and feel them, but I wasn't the one in control, not really.

Do you think you could scribe the wards again? she asks softly.

Yes, I say. I can feel the shape of the warding under my fingers, held within chalk and skin.

I think you need to call Andrea.

I drop my head back, eyes closed, and sigh. *I think you're right.*

I know you don't like—Wait, what?

I'm in over my head. I need help.

Cross's footsteps draw my attention, and I slowly face him. Any sign of emotion is gone from his face, replaced instead with a professional calm and stoicism that make my stomach twist uncomfortably.

"We need to get back to the crime scene," he says, voice flat as he takes the backpack from my hands. "I'll meet you outside."

He's mad, Priya says softly.

He's in over his head, too, and scared. I need to be better at this.

You're trying, she offers. *That's something.*

It's not enough. I grab my jacket and rush after him,

nearly jogging out of the building. He's a few yards ahead of me, and I struggle to pull my jacket on.

"Cross!" I yell, but he doesn't slow. "Riley!"

His given name makes him stop. Shoulders tense, he stands in the middle of the parking lot, waiting without looking at me. I slow as I approach his side, my steps echoing around us.

"You had Priya *attack* me," he says through gritted teeth.

I'm suddenly ashamed. "You wouldn't have been hurt."

"You had Priya. Attack me." He starts walking again. "We are *partners*, Phillips. Fuck, I thought we were at *least* friends."

He reaches the squad car and wrenches the door open, throwing my backpack into the passenger seat. "What is wrong with you? Do you get off on making stupid decisions? Is pushing people away your kink or something? Because I can't think of another reason why you keep insisting on doing this shit."

Stunned, I gape at him.

"I get that you don't know what's happening with me. *I* don't know what's happening with me. And as for whatever that fireworks show was back there"—he waves a hand over his body, indicating the now-invisible wards— "whatever you were trying to do seems to have worked. This supernatural shit, we'll get it figured out, but there are better ways to prove your damn point than having your tamed ghost *assault me*."

Hey now, Priya says, affronted.

"No offense," he says, acknowledging Priya before bringing his focus back to me. "You, on the other hand, are a different story."

I wince. "I got carried away."

"No shit. What if the wards hadn't worked? What then?"

I go to answer, and he cuts me off.

"You don't *think* sometimes and it's infuriating," he says and climbs into the Interceptor. I stand, stunned, near the car as he starts it up. He rolls down his window, then turns to look at me. "Are you getting in or what?"

I walk around the back of the car and open the passenger door gently. I move the backpack to the floor and fall into the seat. I don't put on my belt, and Cross sighs, resting his head on the steering wheel, eyes closed.

"You need to get this shit under control before someone gets hurt." His hands tighten on the steering wheel before he sits up and meets my eyes. "You got me?"

"I got you," I reply, throat tight.

I wouldn't have hurt you, Priya Sends gently, broadcasting it loud enough that I can hear. *It would've felt like static, nothing more. Kim's an idiot, but it did make sense to test the wards.*

"You're right about the idiot part," Cross says. "And I'm sorry I yelled. You caught me off guard."

I understand, she says, smiling gently. *Those wards are pretty good, though. Nothing's getting through them anytime soon.*

I look at Cross, then back to Priya. Slowly, understanding dawns.

"That's some comfort, I guess." He reaches for his

seatbelt and shakes his head. "I would've appreciated a warning or something, though."

"Cross," I say carefully, looking between him and Priya again. "What are you doing?"

He opens his mouth to respond but stops.

Priya, I Send. *Say something else.*

Huh? She furrows her brow. *What's going on?*

Just say something. Anything.

Priya rolls her eyes and speaks. *Rutabaga. Congressional decree. Go Bears.*

Cross's eyes widen. "Is she Sending to me?"

I nod my head.

"I can hear her." Then he frowns. "She's a Bears fan?"

"Not important." I shift in my seat. "Are you doing anything differently than before?"

He shakes his head. "No, nothing. Why can I hear her so easily?"

Maybe he's a quick learner? Priya suggests, and Cross snorts out a laugh.

"I think," I say, reaching a hand toward the center of my chest, then stopping the motion, "it has to do with your scar."

He looks down at his chest and rubs at the center of it idly. "My scar? What're you talking about?"

"You became Sighted after you got it. And the first time you used Second-Sight," I say, thinking back to the darkened parking lot of the diner from a few days ago, "it lit up then. It wasn't as bright as today, but I could still see it."

He frowns. "I didn't see anything."

I didn't see anything then, either, Priya Sends to both of us. *There was some light, but nothing like today.*

"I think I might be attuned to it." I cringe a little. "Since I put it there."

"You got Baker out," Cross says with more kindness than I think I deserve. "You didn't mean to leave a mark on me."

"But it does act up whenever I'm around, and when I was warding you, I felt drawn to it somehow," I stress. "That's the symbol that was on my grandmother's diary. I'm pretty sure it *means* Burner. That's part of why I scribed it in November. Something about it… called to me."

Like the warding today.

I nod. "Exactly."

"So, what's next?" he asks, looking between me and where Priya hovers in the back seat of the cruiser.

"I think," I say with resignation, "you're coming to Wednesday night dinner."

You'd better call Taka, Priya Sends.

I'd better call Taka, I agree before putting my seatbelt on. "And we've got a crime scene to get back to."

"You're sure it'll be okay?" Cross asks.

"About eighty-five percent, yes," I offer with a wry smile.

"That'll have to do for now." He sighs before reversing and heading back to the crime scene.

"If Priya says it's strong, I trust her. But there is

another thing." I bite my lip and continue. "I have to call Banks."

His eyebrows shoot up, expression confused. "Andrea Banks? The reporter?"

"Yes," I say with a wince. "She's going to help me look into that energy and the grave markers I found."

"Andrea Banks, the *Chicago Tribune* lifestyle reporter, is going to help you with the nasty supernatural energy."

"Yes."

"And the creepy-ass ghost lady."

"Yes." I force the word out through gritted teeth.

"Why would she do that?"

"She's an expert in rune work," I say, frowning at Cross as he fights, unsuccessfully, to suppress a grin. "Apparently."

"All right," he says with a quiet laugh. "I forgive you for being an ass. Karma's already gunning for you."

"I am sorry," I say quietly. "I shouldn't have lashed out. It's only… I've always been so *sure* about my powers, but lately, they've been all over the place. Having you call me on my shit, I guess it pushed a button. And while Priya's right that we should've tested your wards, there are better ways to do it than that."

Cross sighs. "And I shouldn't have said those things about you pushing people away. It was out of line."

"No." I look down at my hands and out the window. "No, you're right. I *do* make rash decisions, and I *do* keep people at a distance."

"Doesn't matter if I was right. I shouldn't have said it

that way. It was out of line."

"Maybe." I let out a slow breath and keep going. "Look… this kind of stuff wasn't a problem with my last partner. We worked well together, but he didn't push. You're different. You want to be friends for some reason."

"You're an interesting person, Phillips."

I scoff. "I'm a pain in the ass."

"That, too. But you're also a good cop and a good person, and dammit if I don't like you even when it's against my better judgment." I flinch slightly, and he must catch the slight movement from the corner of his eye. "That was a joke. I'm joking."

"Well, I'm still sorry."

"Me, too."

The car falls quiet, the air between us still somehow uneasy. I reach for my backpack, desperate for distraction, while Cross's fingers drum idly on the steering wheel.

You're both idiots, Priya says with exasperation. *Now, what are we doing about Steve?*

CHAPTER SEVEN

The Forensics techs are nearly finished arranging the lighting rigs when we arrive. The entrance into the basement from the side of the house is brightly lit and already being processed as Cross parks the cruiser. We climb out of the car, and I swing my backpack of supplies over my shoulder.

"First things first," I tell Cross as we approach the perimeter, "I'm going to put some wards on the house itself. They should keep Steve contained to the basement for the time being. If it looks like he's going to stick with his body, rather than the crime scene, I'll drop them so he can leave when they transport his body to the ME's office."

"And if he Turns?"

"Then everyone gets out of the basement ASAP. The wards should hold him."

He nods. "What about the energy?"

"So far, its effects seem to be limited to me and the ghosts who've come into contact with it. We'll get you more comfortable with Second-Sight so you can identify where it is and keep people away from it. Assuming your sudden ability to Send translates to Second-Sight, it shouldn't be too much work." I run a hand through my hair. "We'll start on that after I get the wards in place."

"I'll get working with Forensics to get the scene cataloged," Cross adds. "Supernatural stuff aside, we've got a double to work and we're losing time."

"Agreed."

Taylor signs us in, eyeing the backpack slung over my shoulder, though he refrains from saying anything. As Cross and I approach the back of the house, one of the techs—Gary, I think—stops us.

"Detectives Cross and Phillips?" he asks.

"That would be us," Cross says, holding up his badge. "Are you in charge of the scene?"

"For now," he says. "It's a mess in there."

"Has there been any activity since you started setting up the lights?" Cross asks.

"No, nothing. Your ghost seems to be keeping to himself."

"That's great," I say. "I'm going to put some basic protections up as a precaution. I'll keep them to a minimum."

"It's going to contaminate the scene," he grumbles.

"I'll place them outside of the inner perimeter. That'll keep the interior uncontaminated while still offering the people on scene some protection."

"And," Cross adds, "a little contamination is better than someone getting hurt."

Gary rolls his eyes. "All right, Detective. Just stay out of the way while you're doing it. There are other people here trying to get real work done."

Cross frowns and goes to say something, but I place a restraining hand on his arm and smile tightly. "Understood. Detective Cross will be working the scene with your guys while I work outside."

Gary gives Cross a cursory glance and points toward the Forensics van pulled up in the alley behind the house. "Go get gloves and booties, Detective. I'll walk you through what we've found so far."

Cross gives me a long look before heading to the van while I move into the yard, away from the entrance to the basement.

So, wards, Priya says, eyeing the overgrown backyard carefully. *What are you thinking?*

The yard isn't big, but it's thick with grass and weeds. No stone that I can see, other than the concrete steps leading into the basement at the back, which means that I'll have to put the wards down pretty close to both basement entrances. I move around the back corner of the house and consider the doorway where our offender likely entered the building. There's a lip of concrete peeking above the ground, edging the stairs as they drop down.

What're the chances that this guy put his hands all over that wall? I ask, pointing toward the brick exterior of the house near the underground entrance.

He would've had to pull the plywood off, either with his hands or a tool, Priya says. *So, when he finished, I'd think he would've at least touched the brick, maybe the retention wall, too.*

I sigh. *That's what I was thinking, too. I'll have to put the wards farther back, maybe all the way along the edge of the sidewalk to the street.*

And the entirety of the front door, Priya adds, *and the windows.*

I groan. *This is going to take forever.*

You could amp them up, see if they'll extend farther up the house?

On concrete? I ask, incredulous. *Maybe if it were solid rock. Concrete's a pretty shitty conductor.*

Your powers are stronger than they have been, Priya offers. *Ever since you started Reading, I mean. Look at what happened with Cross. It could be that all of your wards have increased in power, too.*

I consider it, feeling the pool of energy that lives in my gut. It *is* different: deeper and more chaotic. I remember the spinning orb of energy, the bright flashes of unpredictable fire that leaped from its surface, and I reach for it, feeling the warm tendrils of power—now calmer, less riotous—tangle with my fingers and settle in my hands.

It can't hurt, I say as I let the energy sink back into that inner well of power. *Let's get started.*

Since most of the activity is centered around the secondary entrance that Cross and I opened up earlier, I begin with warding the likely point of entry for our offender. Moving out to the sidewalk in front of the house, I start scribing. The chalk scrapes across the concrete with a quiet rasp, leaving white runes and sigils in its wake. It's slow going as the broken surface requires me to be creative with some of the symbols and their placements. Forensics techs are careful to avoid me, and I catch more than one person giving me doubtful looks.

Twenty minutes later, I have a somewhat neat line of wards circling from the front porch to the street and to the entrance at the side of the house.

I pull my knife from the sheath at my ankle, draw power into my hands with a slow, steady breath, and cut the tip of my finger. Blood beads on the tip, and after a moment, I press it gently to the last sigil in the line stretching from the house to the street.

Power flows into the chalk and moves down the line of symbols, erasing them as it weaves through the symbols to leave glowing marks in its wake. As the mark farthest from me bursts into blue-white light, the whole line shivers, then springs up into a swirling mix of blue, red, and green light that rises high above the street in a wall of twisting, multicolored power.

Priya's brows raise as she follows the light to where it fades near the second story of the house. *Well...* she says, *I think that answers* that *question.*

No kidding. I'm a little stunned by the strength of the wards. Tentatively, I reach my hand out, feeling the edge of the protections. They spark against my hand before settling, recognizing the Medium that put them there. *I don't think he'll be able to get past these anytime soon.*

I don't think I'm *going to be able to get past them,* Priya quips, pressing her own hand against the wall of light. Her fingers meet resistance, then stop before the light slowly engulfs her hand in a gentle glow. After a moment, it fades and her hand passes through. *These are pretty complex, Kim. When'd you pick up this level of warding?*

Probably the same place I learned how to turn Cross into a human light bulb. I take a moment to consider the wards, feeling uneasy, before grabbing my bag and heading toward the front door. *C'mon, we've got more places to ward before we can call this done.*

The wards on the front door go down easy, chalk, power, and blood melding into a glowing shield over the entryway. Priya is able to get through them, though they force her to stop for a long moment before entering, as if considering whether to allow her to pass. There's some kind of intelligence to the wards, something I've never seen—much less implemented—before. I don't know if I should be worried or impressed and decide to deal with it later. For now, the wards are strong and steady, and there's still plenty of house left to ward.

The back entrance that Forensics is using as their primary entrance to the scene is more complicated. The backyard is filled with snaking lines of energy, twining with the roots of the old tree and weaving their way across the yard toward the steps into the basement. One thin tendril of power breaks through the concrete retaining wall to ooze down the steps and meander into the basement itself. Though techs walk straight through it, I can't see any hints of the supernatural energy impacting them. In my case, though, I can feel it licking at the edge of my senses, sending goose bumps up and down my arms as I draw closer.

I have to wait for a break in the foot traffic to start scribing. I do it quickly. Between the few people entering and leaving the inner perimeter, I get progressively more nauseous the longer I stay near the red energy. I have to pause momentarily to get a new piece of chalk from my bag, gritting my teeth the whole time, but within ten minutes, I have a line of wards across the entry. I press my blood to the marks, watch as they fill with light, then immediately fizzle as soon as my power crosses the dark energy flowing through the wall. The few symbols that had sparked to life slowly fade, leaving nothing—no chalk and no ward—behind.

I try again, but this time, I create shorter lengths of warding, small barriers that I do my best to interconnect. They flare to life in broken walls of power, but each time they cross one of the lines of darker energy, they sputter, fade, and disappear.

That's a problem, Priya says quietly.

I let a tech walk past me as I consider things. There are a few successful barriers still stretching into the sky, twisting with the same power and protection as those in the front of the house. But the dark energy leaves gaping holes in the wards, like pieces of a wall that's fallen in on itself. Perfect doorways for Steve—or any other nearby spirits—to pass through.

How did the markers do it? I wonder, staring at the breaks in my wards. *The barriers around them worked. Why won't mine?*

I sigh, head to the Forensics van for gloves and booties, and walk briskly into the basement. Cross has a notepad out as he crouches next to the bodies and talks to a Forensics tech. He raises his head when I enter and excuses himself. Slowly, he walks toward me, avoiding the small yellow plastic markers that identify various pieces of evidence spread around the basement.

"You all set?" he asks as he approaches, nodding up the steps. "That didn't take too long."

"No, not yet. There's something about that energy that's preventing my wards from sticking." I shiver and take a step toward the exit. Down here, the pricking sensation of the energy is amplified, turning what had been an annoyance into pain. "Let's talk about it outside."

Cross eyes me. "This stuff really messes with you, doesn't it?"

I'm not standing directly in any of the energy, but it's tugging at me. My instincts are screaming at me to do something about it, a visceral reaction that I have to fight every second I'm near the red, caustic power. A metallic taste coats the back of my throat, and the energy coiled in my gut pulls at me like a dog on a leash, desperate to attack. And through it all, there's a feeling of fire on my skin, of ethereal power searing my skin and bones, demanding I do *something* about the wrongness of the energy seeping into the world around me.

"Yes."

I head back up the steps to the backyard. The feeling follows, but in the open air, the pain lessens, and I can at least breathe. Cross follows after me, shedding his gloves and booties once we leave the inner perimeter. I do the same, then walk to the side yard.

"What've you found?" I ask before he can speak.

"Interviews of the crowd out front were a bust. No one knows anything about the house, who owns it, how long it's been abandoned, or when someone might have broken into the basement. Apparently, this is a neighborhood where people like to keep out of each other's business."

"What about in the basement?"

"There's a lot of blood evidence," he starts. "Spatter on the ceiling, walls, and floor. The tech says there's what he thinks is arterial spray in the back corner, but he's going to have to bring Scene Reconstruction in to piece it all together. He's pretty optimistic that they will give us more to work with in terms of identifying our offender."

"And the murder weapon?"

"Based on the blood patterns and what wounds we can see on the vics, it looks like a knife. We're pretty sure it's under the bodies," he says, "or stuck in one of them. The other option is that the offender took it with him after committing the murders. The ME's office will be here soon to pick up the bodies. We'll know for sure."

"And the footprint we saw?"

"Got it marked and cataloged. There are actually a few more down there. I don't think we would've seen them with our flashlights, but once the lighting rigs were in place, they were pretty obvious. We're looking at five to six different tread patterns, most from what appear to be athletic shoes. Taylor and Hernandez are both wearing boots, which should make it easy to identify which prints are theirs, and you and I know where we walked when we entered from inside. I already pointed those out to the tech, and he's got them marked. There is one set, though, that has a completely different tread pattern from the rest. They don't look to match either of our victim's shoes, either."

"That's promising."

"Yeah. Forensics snapped pictures and added them to the scene map. As for what kind of shoes they're from, we'll find out more once they've been analyzed. Now," he says, tone serious, "quit stalling and tell me what's going on with your wards."

"I wasn't stalling."

He doesn't say anything but leans back a little and crosses his arms.

"That energy? It's stopping the wards from working." I tip my head in the direction of the side entrance to the basement. "Drop into Second-Sight and look at those."

Cross's eyes go distant, then move slowly over the concrete. "Those look pretty impressive to me," he says as he shifts his focus back to me. "Or, at least *I* think they're impressive. Are wards not supposed to look like that?"

"That's what they're supposed to look like," I agree. "But the ones on the back entrance? They aren't working right. The wards won't take if that energy is anywhere near them. I'm not going to be able to get any further with warding the house until I find out how to contain it. That means going back to one of the grave markers that I found to see how they work. If I can figure out how those bindings were able to contain and work around the energy, then I might be able to get a full ward on the house."

"Which means you have to call Banks."

I sigh. "Yes, and sooner than I wanted to. I'm also going to need the keys to the cruiser."

"Where do you need to go? I thought you just needed to talk to her."

"I'm going to have to bribe her a bit," I say. "She wants to see one of the markers, so I'll take her to one. Are you comfortable working the scene on your own?"

He reaches into his pocket and tosses me the key. "Yeah, I've got it. I'm waiting on the ME while Forensics finishes processing the scene. I'll grab a ride from one of the uniforms if I need to leave."

"Until I complete those wards," I say, getting serious, "Steve can leave that basement at any time. You're going to be the only person here who can see what he's up to, so be on guard and stay in Second-Sight as much as you can. You're the only warning system for the people here if he Turns. You see his eyes go black, you get everyone out."

"Understood. Staying in Second-Sight is going to make cataloging evidence a little difficult, though," he says. "I can't see anything in the real world while I'm in it."

"I know." I wince. "You'll have to switch back and forth between the two while you work. It'll give you a headache, but power through it."

"Is that safe?"

"Kind of?"

It's not, Priya interrupts. *You can burn yourself out when you're new to this, and flipping back and forth between normal vision and Second-Sight's a good way to do it. You could try to get your vision somewhere in between the two, but that's more advanced. Right now, there's not a better option while Kim's away from the scene.*

Cross nods.

"Speaking of our resident ghost," I say, looking toward the basement, "how's he been?"

"Still absent," he says. "I didn't see or hear anything from him while I was down there."

"That's either a good sign or a really bad one. What about seeing the energy? Is it getting any clearer?"

He shakes his head. "No, unfortunately. I believe you when you say it's there, but I must be doing something wrong. I don't see it at all—only glowing yellow lines."

"Okay," I say. "I'll get it mapped out for you for now. It won't be perfect, but it'll be better than nothing."

"You'll call me when you're on your way back from seeing Banks?" he asks as he starts to head toward the primary entrance. I follow after him, digging into my backpack for a notepad as we walk.

"Of course. You'll let me know if the ME finds the murder weapon?"

He smirks. "No, I thought I'd keep that to myself. Figured it would make the investigation a bit more interesting."

"I don't think we need more interesting right now," I say, flipping to a blank page in the notebook. "Let me get this sketched out for you. I don't want to leave the house unwarded longer than I have to."

"Sounds good, partner." He smiles a little at the word, and my mouth curves in an answering grin. "You need me, I'll be walking the outer perimeter. I want to see if I can figure out which direction our offender may have gone when he left the scene."

"I'll find you when I'm done." I head down the steps leading into the basement, hugging the wall to avoid the snaking lines of energy that trickle down the stairs. From the safety of the small landing at the base of the steps, I drop in and out of Second-Sight to draw the lines of power that snake through the basement. After making sure I have them all drawn in, I head back up the stairs and, using the extra light from one of the lighting rigs set up in the backyard, I copy the map to another page. I find Cross in the back alley talking to a man wearing a CSI jacket. I rip one of the two maps out of my notebook and hold it out to him. He pauses in his conversation to take the page and wave me off. With a quick, sarcastic salute, I head to the cruiser.

As the car warms, I pull out my phone and Banks's business card, then dial her cell number. It rings a few times, and I'm half-hopeful that it'll go to voice mail and I won't have to talk to the woman when she answers the phone.

"Detective Phillips," she says. "To what do I owe the pleasure?"

"You know that marker?" I ask. "How would you like to see it today?"

CHAPTER EIGHT

Forty minutes later, I'm parked in a small circular courtyard at the Bohemian National Cemetery. I step out of my car and lean against it, watching the entrance gate for Banks. She pulls up next to me in her black two-door coupe after a couple of cold minutes.

Banks climbs out and gives my cruiser a pointed once-over.

"Are you here on official police business, Detective?" she asks, closing her door and approaching.

"Not your concern, Banks." I walk toward the first marker I found. I hear her hurry to catch up, her shoes crunching on the gravel drive. At first, I consider slowing but pick up my pace instead until I'm in front of the marker.

"I'd argue the point, but I find I don't particularly care at the moment. What am I looking at?" she asks as I crouch down to the base of the marker.

"This"—I look back up at her—"is the marker."

She studies the obelisk for a long moment, walking around it in a slow circle before coming to stand next to me.

"While this is as interesting as the photos you showed me this morning," she says with a shake of her head, "this is not the same binding."

She's sharp, Priya says with more than a little admiration.

"This is the *first* binding." I brush my fingers over the base of the obelisk. "The pictures I showed you were from the second."

"The second." Banks joins me on the ground. "Do you think there could be more than these two?"

"That's what I'm assuming," I say.

"How many?"

"At least two."

She glares at me.

"Stay focused, Banks. What can you tell me about this one?"

She moves closer to the stone marker, and I shift to make more room for her. She fishes in her pocket and pulls out a small pair of glasses. The thin silver frames glint as she places them on her nose and leans closer to the stone. Her eyes go unfocused as she drops into Second-Sight, and the corner of her mouth twitches up into a soft smile.

"I have to admit," she says, ignoring my question as she traces her hand over the barely visible marks etched into the stone, "you do have a way of showing a girl a good time."

"I'm not trying to sho—"

"Hush," she says. "I'm working."

Eyebrows raised, I stand. "Well, then. If you're done

with me, I've got a homicide to get back to."

She laughs and looks up at me. "I never said I was done with you." Her eyes glint with excitement. "How'd you even find this thing?"

I drop into Second-Sight and let out a soft groan. The great, pulsing lines of power that had previously crawled their way through the cemetery to pool at the base of the marker are almost entirely gone. What few remain have lessened to rivulets, rather than streams, the energy naturally dissipating into the ground like rainwater.

"How good is your Second-Sight?" I ask, watching the thin lines of energy as they meander their way to, then through, the marker.

"Pretty good. Why?"

"Do you see that?" I point to the line of energy and wait. She squints a little, then nods. "That's what led me here."

"It seems pretty innocuous," Banks says. "I'm surprised you even noticed it."

"It was bigger before. A *lot* bigger."

"That kind of makes sense." She leans closer to the obelisk, her dark, graceful fingers trailing against the stone. "This isn't the same binding you showed me this morning, but it is similar. Look at this series of runes. Just like the photo, they indicate entrapment and containment, but they're also harnessing something. There are a lot of symbols here I don't recognize. I'll need to look them up to figure out what the sigils are targeting, but it could be a focus for the natural energy here."

"But why? The energy from death is dangerous, and stockpiling it is asking for trouble."

"Whoever it is could be using it like a battery," Banks says. "If the Medium who did this wasn't able to store enough power on their own, they could dip into this source instead."

"And damn the risks?" I ask.

Andrea shrugs. "The binding suggests that's what it was used for. I'll have to do more research to be certain."

I think back to the ghosts at both markers, Turned but not Turned, unpredictable and dangerous, maybe even deadly. "Besides the energy, there were ghosts bound to these markers. They were… Odd is probably not the best word for it, but they weren't what I'm used to. Do you see anything that would explain them?"

"Maybe," Banks hums quietly, then stands. "I can't be certain, though."

"How long is it going to take you to figure this out?" I ask.

She raises an eyebrow at my tone. "What aren't you telling me, Detective?"

I stare at the obelisk and the Burner symbol etched over and over again into the stone. Tightening my hand, feeling the soft ache of the nearly healed cut in the center of my palm, I wonder if I can tell her about my blood and how it reacted to this ghost, how my powers have been changing ever since I first found the symbol—a circle, quartered by a cross with one arm longer than the rest.

"Judging by that pause, I think it's safe to assume it's

quite a bit." Banks crosses her arms and shifts her weight to one leg, giving me a long, thoughtful look. "Are you going to fill me in here?"

"That symbol," I say, pointing to one of them on the marker. "I've seen it before, but I haven't been able to find out much about its meaning or how it's used. Have you seen it before or read anything about a symbol like it?"

"Okay, you're going to ignore me, then," she says with a sigh before reaching into her sports coat to pull out a notepad and small pencil. "I'm not sure that I've seen it before, no. It doesn't look familiar, but most of this binding is new to me, at least in terms of how it's executed. I'll take a few pictures so I can study it at home. I have some reference books that might explain the configuration, and it's too cold to come out here with them. I'll make a note to look into that symbol in particular."

"Great," I say a little grimly. "You didn't answer my question about how long it's going to take you to figure this out."

Banks's eyebrow raises. "Maybe tomorrow at the earliest, but it could be longer. This is my lunch break, and I won't be able to go home until tonight. I'm already pushing my luck as it is with work. Unless you'd like to give a statement for the *Trib*?"

I glower at her and she laughs.

"I can tell you this." She tucks her notebook into her jacket and pulls her phone out to snap photos of the grave marker. "Whatever it *was* doing, it's broken now."

"Broken?"

"Yes." She walks around to the back of the obelisk, leans down, and snaps another photo. "No energy being channeled or collected. No ghosts, Turned or otherwise, being held by it. Even if you were to put more power into it, I don't think it would function. Whatever you did when you found this thing, you've destroyed some integral piece of the binding in the process."

Do you think, Priya asks slowly, *that it was the ghost? The one you…*

The one I Burnt, I say, finishing her thought. I frown, confused. *Is that something you can even do? Blood powers bindings. Ghosts don't bleed.*

No, we don't. Priya moves closer to the obelisk, mirroring Banks as she finishes circling it with her phone.

"Would you be able to find out what the missing piece is?" I ask her.

"I'd certainly like to. This is one of the most interesting pieces of rune work I've seen." She flashes me a conspiratorial grin, her sky-gray eyes flashing. "And if there's another marker like this, I'm willing to bet there's a whole bunch more. Whoever put this here, they knew what they were doing, which leads me to think that it's not the first or the last of these markers. You finding a second one confirms that. I'm sure you're less than happy to hear it, but you and I will be spending a *lot* of time together in the near future."

"If you can tell me how this thing worked, I'll put up with it."

She laughs, and the sound makes her seem younger, less dangerous than I've come to think of her. "Careful,

Detective. I might think you're starting to like me."

"Can you at least tell me how the binding was able to direct the energy?"

"I can make a guess," she says. "Come take a look."

I move back to the obelisk and let my eyes settle on the configuration of runes and sigils that Banks is pointing to.

"This grouping seems to be the center of the binding. These runes describe the location and intent"—she points at various symbols as she speaks—"and these sigils tie them all together into something that should contain and control. If I had to guess, this would be the heart of the binding, with the rest of the rune work describing the more subtle aspects of it. And"—she holds up a hand, stopping me from responding—"before you ask, I'm going to have to do more research to figure out what those are."

I pull my phone out and take a quick picture. "Call me when you get something."

"When do I get to see the second marker?"

"Later," I say as I head toward my cruiser.

"Later?" She runs to catch up to me, caught off guard. "What's that supposed to mean?"

"It means focus on this one first, then I'll take you to the second."

"And the others?"

I sigh and wait for her to catch up. "We don't know that there are others."

"Oh no," she says slightly out of breath. "*I* know there are more of these things out there, and I think you do, too."

"If I find any, I'll call you."

"*Before* you break them."

I glare at her. "I'm not breaking them."

"Before you do anything, then."

"Fine. Just call me when you get this one figured out."

She smiles. "I know you've got a case to get back to and all, but do you want to grab a cup of coffee first?"

Taken aback, I stumble a little, then turn to gape at her. "What?"

"Coffee," she says slowly, drawing the word out. "It's a hot drink with caffeine and, if you make it right, lots of cream and sugar. Would you like to get some with me?"

I struggle to answer, and Priya laughs.

She's great, she Sends with a wide grin.

"No," I finally say, "thank you."

"Maybe next time, Detective." She winks at me and gets into her car. I watch as she turns it on, puts on her seatbelt, and drives off. As soon as her taillights pass through the limestone gate of the cemetery, I open the door to my cruiser and climb inside.

"Coffee," I mutter as I start the engine. "Right."

Were you able to get what you needed from that? Priya asks.

Does a headache count?

She was perfectly pleasant, and you know it.

I sigh and start driving. *I may be able to use some of it, yes. Trying is better than leaving that house unwarded.*

I'm very proud of you, Priya Sends with a grin. *You didn't even cuss at her. I'd call that progress.* And *she does seem to know her stuff.*

I nod begrudgingly.

Maybe she'll be able to find out something about that symbol, Priya continues.

I pull my phone out and call Cross. He answers halfway through the first ring.

"Phillips," he says breathlessly. "You need to get back here now."

"What happened?" I ask, suddenly afraid. "Did the ghost Turn? Is everyone okay?"

"No, that's not it. The ME came and rolled the bodies. We found the murder weapon."

"That's great." Relief washes over me. "Was it a knife?"

"Yes," Cross says. "I think it's a Medium's."

"What?"

"Just get your ass back to the scene, okay? I need you to confirm."

"Okay. I'm already on my way."

"Fantastic." He starts talking to someone on the other end of the line, his voice muffled enough that I can't make out the words. After a moment, he comes back on the line. "Hey, I've got to go, but find me as soon as you get here."

"Consider it done."

The line goes dead, and I set my phone down in one of the cup holders.

That sounded exciting, Priya says.

Cross says the murder weapon is a Medium's knife.

That's not good. Priya looks shocked. *Is he sure?*

He wants me to confirm. We need to get back.

Yeah, no kidding. Priya sits quietly for a long moment, then starts speaking again. *Did you consider that if Banks is able to find out where that symbol came from or what it means, she might be able to explain some of the things happening with Riley?*

Riley? Since when are you on a first-name basis with Cross?

Since he told me to use his first name, she says primly. *You're missing the point, though.*

I've considered it, but I didn't want to put the cart before the horse. I give her a suspicious look. *How much have the two of you been Sending?*

A fair bit, actually. Her mouth dips down into a small frown. *It's like his powers were jump-started after you warded him.*

The car falls silent, both of us lost in memories of this morning. I wonder again at how those wards reacted to him, the light literally pouring off of him as Priya's attack struck.

It's got to have something to do with that symbol, I Send.

You don't think it has something to do with him being possessed by a Turned ghost from the 1970s?

I stare at her, and she throws her hands up. *Just a suggestion.*

Maybe Banks will figure it out, I say, frustrated. *I just don't want Cross in any further danger because of me.*

Right now, I think the only danger he's facing is from unresolved sexual tension.

Nope, not going there, I say as I merge onto the highway.

You're going to have to talk about it eventually.

I don't respond, and Priya stares at me, impassive, for a

long minute. I turn the radio on.

She frowns. *Are you being difficult on purpose, or is it a natural talent?*

Both. I fight a grin. *It's not that big of a deal.*

Uh-huh. She doesn't sound convinced.

We'll talk about it later.

And would that be after you finally rip each other's clothes off or before?

There will be no clothes-ripping, I say, shaking my head. *We're adults. There's no reason we have to act on... whatever this is.*

And you're sure that's what you want? she asks, giving me a long look.

I want to figure out what's causing Cross to develop powers. I want to get to the bottom of the markers and the dangerous energy they contain. I want to solve this double homicide, Burn Steve, and move on to the next case. It doesn't matter if, mixed up in all of that, there's a desire for something else. Compared to the rest of it, it's unimportant.

I sigh and nod. *Yes.*

Priya sighs. *Remind me to play poker with you more often.*

You can't hold the cards or spend the money.

She glares at me. *You get my point.*

I scoff, and she shakes her head again, exasperated.

You know it's not one-sided, Kim. You Read his memory. You know he has feelings for you.

I know no such thing.

She scowls at me, then slumps onto the passenger seat,

arms crossed. *Fine, if that's the hill you want to die on, be my guest. But when the sexual frustration makes your brain leak out of your ears, don't come crying to me.*

You were a doctor, I say, exasperated. *You know that's not going to happen.*

It might, she Sends primly. Then a sudden grin tinged with mischief splits her face. *Since* you *aren't going to talk to me about it, maybe I'll talk to* him *instead.*

I stare at her, mouth open. *You wouldn't dare.*

Try me.

Shocked laughter bursts out of my chest. *You're evil.*

She grins. *Maybe a bit.*

Promise me you won't. Please.

The grin stays on her face for a moment longer, then falls into a pout. After a moment, she nods. *I won't—not until the two of you finally talk about it. I understand what you're doing, but I also think you're stupid to keep ignoring it. The situation is only going to get more complicated the longer you stay quiet, and then what?*

I shrug. *Then nothing, I guess. It's all moot since there's no reason to talk about it.*

Priya rolls her eyes. *All right, Cleopatra.*

Cleopatra?

Queen of Denial.

I glare at her.

Fine. I'll let it go. For now.

Thank you, I Send. *We're almost to the scene, anyway, and we need to prep to finish the warding, and I need to look at this knife.*

When did you figure out how to get around the energy?

I'm not sure I've got it figured out yet, but I'm going to try something.

Didn't you and Riley just *have a fight about you being reckless?*

I'm not being reckless, I Send.

Nothing good ever happens when you just "try something," Kim, Priya groans. *Can you at least tell me what you're planning?*

I'll explain it when we get there, I say, enjoying her annoyance when I don't go into detail. Turnabout is fair play, as far as I'm concerned. If she wants to hound me about Cross, I can leave her in the dark about my plans for ten minutes. *But make sure you're powered up, just in case.*

In case of what? Priya asks, leaning forward in her seat. *Kim, in case of what?*

I start humming along with the radio, turning the volume up louder.

I hate you, she Sends loudly as I start to sing along with the song, my voice raspy and slightly out of tune. *I hate you so much.*

CHAPTER NINE

I t's getting dark when I arrive back at the scene. January means that night falls early, and my headlights cut through the settling gloom as I approach the scene. I park and make my way to the perimeter. Taylor is nowhere to be seen, but a different uniformed officer signs me into the scene with perfunctory motions. I ask him where Cross is, and he points me toward the basement of the house. As soon as I walk through the back entrance, Cross hurries toward me.

"Hey, come here," he says as I slide on a pair of gloves and booties. "You've got to see this."

The bodies are absent from the middle of the scene. In their place is a dark bloodstain and more of the yellow evidence markers. In the dead center of it all is a knife, the silver handle and blade covered in dark red. The bottom of my stomach drops out from under me.

So much for a normal murder.

"It looks like a Medium's knife to me," Cross says as I take a hesitant step forward, and he moves closer, avoiding the blood that surrounds it. "What do you think?"

I inch closer, but I'm hampered by the blood pool. "We're going to have to move it," I say with a shake of my head. "I can't tell what I'm looking at from here."

Cross waves a Forensics tech over. "Hey, we need you to bag and tag the knife. You guys are finished with the photographs, right?"

The tech nods. "Yes, Detective. It'll only take me a minute to process it."

"Have it ready for her"—Cross points at me—"as soon as you're done."

He stands, gesturing for me to follow him to the base of the interior stairs, away from the scene markers and the tech.

"Another thing," he says quietly, his voice lowered so that it doesn't carry. "Steve showed up when we moved the bodies. He didn't do anything, though. Just watched as the ME took them away."

"Great," I say, dropping into Second-Sight to confirm that the ghost is still in the basement. I catch a flash of blue-white light, and then it disappears. "That means he's tied to the location, rather than his body. He's still here but not manifesting."

"Is that normal?"

"Sometimes, yes. Inherently, ghosts are people who didn't handle the end of their lives well, whether that end is violent or natural. It makes them… temperamental."

"You think he's moping," Cross says, raising a brow. "Because he's dead."

"Or he's getting pissed off," I suggest quietly. "Be respectful. We don't want to give him any reason to move from temperamental to furious, okay? With all of the blood and power that's down here, I don't want to take any unnecessary risks."

He flushes but nods. "Gotcha. What did you find out from Banks?"

"Let's go outside," I say. "I don't want an audience."

Cross catches my drift and heads for the exit. I reach out with my supernatural senses, questing for Steve's presence. Something brushes against my mind from the back corner of the basement, and I drop into Second-Sight to find him silently watching me, his eyes too shadowed to tell their color. I fight to suppress a shiver, an instinctive reaction to an uncertain threat, and leave, feeling his eyes on my back the entire time.

It's fully dark when we step outside. Night and a thick cover of clouds have rolled in while we were inside, and wind whips its way through my jacket. I shiver again, pull the latex gloves from my hands, and stuff my fingers deep into my pockets, searching for warmth.

"So, what'd you learn?" Cross asks as he snaps his own gloves off.

"Not much more than what I already knew," I grouse. "She's going to research the rune work and get back to me. There was one configuration that I'm going to try to use here. I'm not sure if it'll work or not, but it can't be worse than leaving this place unwarded, especially since Steve's decided to stay."

Cross frowns. "I'm not looking to piss you off or anything, but are you sure that's a good idea?"

"Of course, I'm sure. What's the worst that could happen?"

I've told her not to say that, Priya Sends, appearing next to Cross with her arms crossed, *but I think she likes to tempt fate. If I could knock on wood...*

"I'll do it for you," he says. "What're you going to do when everything goes sideways?"

"It's not going to go sideways." Annoyance is heavy in my voice. "Just... keep the stairs clear for me, all right?"

I brush past him, and he grabs my arm. I nearly shake his grip loose, but stop, meeting his concerned gaze.

"Be safe," he says quietly, green eyes dark and serious. "I've got your back if you need it."

"I'll be *fine*," I say, gently pulling my arm free. "Don't worry."

Priya groans. *There she goes again.*

You're not helping.

"Just shout if you need anything," Cross reiterates. "I'll be right here."

Oh, trust me, Priya says pragmatically, *if this goes bad, she won't need to yell.*

I turn my back on both of them and stop at the top of the stairs. Pulling a piece of chalk and my phone from my pocket, I crouch down and start copying the central motif from the binding on the marker onto the concrete by my feet. I have to zoom in on the picture more than once, and the cold air numbs my fingers quickly. It makes for clumsy scribing, but I take my time, blowing on my stiff fingers to help warm them back up. Still, after only a few minutes, I have a copy of the rune work spread out before me.

I take a long time reviewing the symbols, making slight

adjustments where I see weaknesses in the marks. Finally, I pull my knife, nick my thumb, and hesitate a moment before pressing it to the chalk. As power flows from my blood into the chalk, I flip my knife around to rest at my wrist.

Just in case.

The symbols start to pulse, rising high above the ground. Slowly, their glow spreads, reaching toward the other wards encircling the entrance into the basement. There's a flash of light, bright enough that I have to close my eyes against it. When I open them, blinking away the afterimage, I'm met by an aurora of red-blue-green shifting light. I grin and fight the urge to laugh at the successful, completed wards. I reach out to test them and feel their reassuring strength echo down my arm. Just like the wards at the front of the house, these are solid and strong.

I stand up, brushing gravel from my knees, and head back to Cross who's so tense, I can sense it coming off him in waves. I flash him a shit-eating grin and watch as he sags in relief.

"Told you it'd work," I say smugly, turning back to appreciate my wards. "Our resident ghost won't be going anywhere soon."

Well, damn, Priya says. *I've gotten so used to everything blowing up around you, I don't know what to do right now.* She looks to Cross. *Is it weird that I'm slightly disappointed?*

"Other than the knife, is there anything else we need to do here tonight?" I ask him, ignoring her.

"Forensics is nearly done processing the scene. The ME should get back to us tomorrow with the autopsy results, though Dr. Abramo said cause of death is probably hypovolemic shock from all the stab wounds. After we look at the knife, we can head out."

"Still no luck with witnesses?" I ask.

Cross shakes his head. "No. Uniforms are going to keep canvassing tomorrow, but it's not looking good."

"Let's find that tech, then," I say, heading toward the Forensics van. She's in the back, copying a number from a paper evidence bag onto a clipboard. I knock on the side of the vehicle, and she jumps.

"We all set?" I ask, holding my hand out for the bag.

The tech frowns and passes me a box of latex gloves instead. She doesn't hand me the evidence bag until I finish putting on a fresh pair.

"Here you go, Detective," she says, keeping a close eye on the bag. "I'll need that back as soon as you're done"

"I know how chain of custody works," I say before opening the bag. The knife, dulled by blood, still glints in the lights from the van. Cautiously, I reach inside and pull it out.

The knife is solid metal and heavy in my hand. I turn it over as I examine the runes etched into the blade and handle. I'm not enough of an expert to say what *kind* of Medium it belonged to, but it's definitely a Medium's knife. Remembering Casey's knife, I hope that we can solve this quickly, get the blood cleaned off the thing, and put it somewhere safe before anything is drawn to the heady combination of blood and the power in the knife. I place it back in the bag and hand it back to the tech.

"If you haven't already, identify that as a Medium's knife," I say, pulling the gloves off.

"I knew it," Cross says, looking both triumphant and nauseous. "Can you tell what Affinity it's associated with?"

"If it were a Burner's knife, maybe," I say, "but I don't know enough about how the other Affinities mark their blades to tell you the difference. There are people out there who can, though."

"We'll find a resource in the morning," he says and pulls a small notebook out of his coat pocket to make a note. After putting it back in his pocket and pulling his coat closed, he looks at me. "You ready to go?"

I nod.

We're silent on the drive back to HQ. The car's still warm, and as Cross reviews his notes, I find myself thinking of the knife and the two bodies in the basement, and the dark, caustic energy that winds through all of it. I turn into the lot and park the Interceptor near our personal vehicles. When Cross moves to get out of the car, I stop him.

"One more thing," I say. "I know it's a lot to ask, but I think between what happened this morning and finding a Medium's knife at the crime scene tonight, it can't wait. I've got some resources in my car, and I want you to start working on controlling your powers as soon as you can. You need to get to a point with Second-Sight where you can be both in and out of it at the same time, and you need to do it as quickly as possible. It'll look a bit like an overlay when you get it right, but it'll allow you to keep an eye on Steve and the scene at the same time. If you can do that, you'll have plenty of warning if something goes wrong."

"And that knife makes you think that something is going to go wrong," he says.

"I don't like what it implies about those murders," I say quietly. "Blood is power, and if a Medium is behind those deaths…"

"I understand." He tips his head back, looking out the windshield to the dark clouds above before exhaling slowly. "What do you have for me?"

I turn the car off and climb out of the car, Cross following. "It's mainly books."

I walk to my car, quickly unlock it, and open the back door. Taka's books are scattered across the back seat, and I lean in, piling them up before grabbing the stack and working my way out of the car.

"Looks like I've got a lot of reading to do," he says, eyeing the slightly leaning pile.

"I'll see if I have anything else at home that'd be useful." I pass the books to him, and he jostles the heap of books as he struggles to grab them all. My hand shoots out, catching a book before it can fall to the ground. I set it carefully on top and take a step back. "Start with Second-Sight. There are some basic meditation exercises in the books that'll help you find that middle ground I mentioned."

"You want me to work on Sending, too?"

"That's a little more difficult. Priya can't go with you. She's tied to me, and it's unlikely you've got a ghost in your building. No recently deceased neighbors you can practice with, right?"

He gives me a blank look from over the stack of books in his arms.

"I'll take that as a no, then. I'll talk to Priya tonight, and we'll figure out a way for you to practice. In the meantime, read the books." I shrug. "They're a little dull, but they'll help. And if you have any questions, you've got my number."

"Sounds good." He doesn't move, and I can hear the engine of the Interceptor ticking quietly as I wait for him to do something. It's awkward, both of us staring at the other, waiting for something to happen. Finally, Cross coughs out a laugh.

"I can't get my keys," he says, glancing from the books that fill his arms back to me. "A little help?"

Warmth creeps its way into my cheeks. "Shit, yeah. Hold on a second. Where are they?"

It's his turn to flush. "Front pocket," he says. "In my jeans."

Jesus fucking Christ, I think. *Like this morning wasn't bad enough.*

"Got it." I move closer as he angles the books away from me. Doing my absolute best to not touch him more than absolutely necessary, I slide my fingers into his jeans pocket and start fishing for the keys. His pockets are deep, and I pray to any higher power that's listening that I'll find the damn things quickly. After a long, awkward moment, I find the key ring, loop my finger around it, and pull the softly jangling mess out. I back up from Cross like I've been burned, then jostle the keys in my hand.

"I'll get the door for you."

I flip through the ring and hit the unlock button on his key fob. His headlights flash, and the door lock clicks. I open the door, and he leans in, setting the books in a neat pile on the passenger seat. I turn my eyes to the front entrance of HQ, absolutely *not* looking at Cross's ass as he crawls over the driver's seat. He backs out slowly and I pass him the keys.

"All set," I say.

"I'll let you know if I have any questions. See you tomorrow, partner."

My mouth kicks up at the corner. "Partner."

He climbs into his car, and I head to mine as he shuts the door. He's pulling out of the lot as I'm turning my car on, and I watch his taillights as he disappears down Sixty-Third Street.

CHAPTER TEN

Thirty minutes later, I place my keys, knife, and gun on the small table by the door as I look around my apartment for something to take my mind off of Cross. My fridge calls to me, and, as soon as I lock the door, I make a beeline for it. On the bottom shelf, next to old takeout containers and a bag of lettuce that's seen better days, are three brown bottles. I grab one and pop the cap off against the end of the kitchen counter. Priya lets out an aggrieved sigh as I take a long drink.

You're never going to get your deposit back on this place, she Sends, eyeing the counter.

It was my grandmother's deposit, I say as I head back to the front room, *and no, I'm not.*

The bookshelves in the front room grab my attention as I pass them, and I let my fingers run over the spines of my old Medium Studies textbooks before I pull a couple of volumes out. They're a little more advanced than the stuff I sent Cross home with, but I figure he'll enjoy the more in-depth analysis. Considering I majored in the subject, I never really cared to get into the nitty-gritty of being a Medium. If it didn't help me with Burning, I'd learn enough of it to pass the test, then promptly forget it.

Knowing how intense Cross is about his research, though, he'll probably like having more materials to cross-reference. I set the books on the coffee table and wonder whether he'll have a binder for all of this shit by the time he's done. A small smile crosses my face before I can stop it.

I set my beer on the table and fall gracelessly onto the couch, kicking my feet up onto the coffee table. My foot bumps into Comfort Bell's diary. It's facedown from when I'd left it on the table before hurrying out the door this morning. Looking at it now, I'm unsettled. The Reading from the night before replays in my mind. Joseph Baker's defiance in the face of Caroline Moore's anger, my grandmother stepping between the two with something like tenderness in her expression as she looked at Baker. And something about *tears* and ghosts Turning…

There's something in the memory that's important. Hopefully, finding the matching entry in Bell's diary will explain some of what I've seen. I toe off my boots and lean forward, swiping the diary from the coffee table, figuring the normalcy of Bell's day-to-day life will, at least, get my mind off of Cross. The leather cover is somehow warm when I pick it up, the feeling of it familiar under my fingers though I've only had the book for a little more than a day. I chalk it up to the Reading the night before and Comfort Bell's memories still echoing in my mind. Tracing the faded gilt along the edges, I open the book, looking for where I left off before being swept up in the Reading last night. I find the last entry I remember reading: a summer day in 1941 that's mainly a complaint about humidity and mosquitoes.

I skim through the diary from that point forward, looking for anything that grabs my attention. Nothing jumps out at me, but there are hints of something happening in Bell's life. References to Caroline Moore increase as I near the beginning of 1942, though the details are sparse. It seems like Bell met Moore during some kind of Medium rally in Chicago that spring, their relationship cemented through a shared belief that Mediums deserved more recognition in the Mundane world.

She is a strong woman, Bell writes. *Outspoken, though eloquent. Beautiful, but restrained. You can't help but watch her. To listen when she speaks. I do not believe she accepts defeat, no matter the contest, and I have yet to see anyone bring her close to it. She is not a woman who loses. She, instead, conquers. I am in awe of her, though that is sometimes tinged with fear.*

I shiver, remembering the harsh woman who'd quelled a room of Mediums with only her voice and power, but it doesn't bring me any closer to an explanation of what Baker had been talking about before Moore cut him off, or of the tears that my grandmother mentioned in the last memory I Read from Bell's diary. I'm cradling it in my hands, half-considering Reading it again and taking my chances when Priya appears.

Anything interesting? she asks, settling next to me on the couch and peering over my shoulder at the diary.

I sigh. *No, I haven't found anything like the Reading. Bell hasn't even mentioned my grandmother yet. Same goes for Baker. I think I could skip ahead a couple of years and get closer to when the memory happened, but at the same time, I don't want to miss any of the background. She's just met Caroline, and I feel like that's where all of this starts.*

What if there's no matching passage in the diary? Priya asks.

Then I'll try Reading it again, I Send with a shrug. *The vision I had yesterday was spontaneous, uncontrolled. If I go into it with an idea of what I'm looking for, I may be able to guide the Reading. And if that doesn't work, we can always go back to where I finally Burnt Baker. I can always try Reading something at the Mental Health Center.*

I don't like that idea, Priya says, looking nervous. *I don't know what Reading the memories of a Turned ghost would do to you. And we still don't understand how Baker's possession impacted Cross. There was way more going on with him than we saw—I'm sure of it. Reading something of his certainly doesn't* feel *safe.*

I don't disagree, but if that's the only option left…

You could talk to Andrea about it. Her father was a Reader. She may be able to offer insight into the process.

She's only Sighted, I Send, *not a full Medium. I'm sure there's another Reader in Chicago I can talk to instead.* I frown. *I'm already going to be spending enough time with the woman. I don't want to look for more reasons to. I know you like her—I have no idea why—but I don't.*

She puts your hackles up, Priya says matter-of-factly, *which is always fun to watch. But honestly? I get the feeling that she's not as bad as you think she is. She's intelligent and driven. On top of that, Taka trusts her, and while she's been a bit overzealous at times, she's never been cruel.*

That's because you're not on the receiving end of that overzealousness. The woman is a pit bull.

And you're not? Priya shakes her head. *I think you don't like her because you're too much alike.*

Well, whatever we are or aren't, I'm keeping my interactions with her limited to those grave markers, and that's it. If I need a Reader to help with this—I hold the diary up and shake it a little—*then I'll find one. In the meantime, I'll stick with normal reading.*

Priya rolls her eyes but lets it go. *If you find anything useful, let me know.*

Of course. I open the diary to the last entry I read, and settle into the couch, pulling my grandmother's quilt around my legs. Most of the entries are dull, just quick peeks into Bell's day-to-day. It's not until the winter of 1943 that things start to get interesting.

Caroline called me earlier today to set up a meeting, but about what, she wouldn't say. She warned me there would be others attending, other Mediums, but that I should not be afraid. I had not felt any trepidation about the meeting until that moment, but something about her tone has set my heart racing. I cannot help but wonder what, exactly, she has planned. Jeremiah worries as well and has spent the morning gathering energy in preparation for a battle we do not know will come. It is hard to break old habits.

The entry ends there. I sit up a little, unconsciously bringing the diary closer as if that will shed any light on what Bell means. Hurriedly, I turn the page, hoping for a further explanation in the next entry. Instead, there's a four-day gap and the next thing she writes about is her Healing work at a small local hospital. I skim through the next couple of entries and find nothing. No Caroline, no mention of their meeting, *bupkis*. Frustrated, I set the book down on the couch and let it fall open, the pages spreading out in a white fan.

Bell's entries are usually detailed, leaving little of her day-to-day routine to the imagination. She also rarely missed a day, taking the time to write at least a short note about the weather every day. To have four days missing would have been suspicious in any context. In this one, it's a bright red flag.

"There's a meeting with Caroline," I say quietly to myself, rubbing at the space between my eyes and trying to work it through. "One that Comfort was worried about, one with other Mediums. Nothing in the diary for four days after that, and then it's back to normal, like the meeting never happened. So, why doesn't she write anything about it down if she was worried?" I shake my head. "It feels off. Why would you *not* write about something when you've written about everything else before?" I pause, considering.

Maybe she removed the pages? Priya asks from the corner of the room, watching me as I stare at the book.

"No, there are no missing pages. It simply jumps in time." I look at the book, letting my eyes fall into Second-Sight as I think. "Why would you do that?"

The room falls silent. I watch the lines of energy that make up the world in Second-Sight move around the room in slow, undulating waves of blue-white and red. They flare and flicker around the room, thin tendrils of power that center me as I think. I breathe slowly, letting my mind still. Then, I start speaking again.

"You don't write something down," I say slowly, "when you don't want others to find out about it. Which means there was something about that meeting she wanted to keep secret."

Falling out of Second-Sight, I slam the book shut and get up from the couch to start pacing next to the coffee table.

"In the visions I've had so far, there was always a group of people. With Baker's Binding, six. And with the Reading from Bell's diary, four who I recognized—Caroline, Baker, my grandmother, and Bell—but more people around the room who I couldn't see. And of the people I *could* see, they were all involved in Binding Baker."

How many more were there? I ask myself, trying to remember how many shadowed figures had been on the edges of the memory. I look back at the diary, my steps slowing. Could that meeting have been where it all started? Where the Mediums who eventually Bound Baker met?

"But she hasn't mentioned any of the other Binders besides Caroline and my grandmother up to this point." I run my fingers through my hair, frustrated at the puzzles that keep appearing. I grab the diary and flip through it again, my eyes rapidly skimming the pages in search of any familiar names. "She *has* to have written something about it."

When I get to the end of the diary, I flip back through the pages again. But if one of the other Binders is mentioned, it's not by a name I recognize. "Damnit. There's nothing. No names, no explanations. *Nothing.* What was it about that meeting that had her so spooked?"

You're not going to try to Read it, are you? Priya asks, startling me from my thoughts

I don't think I have a choice. I set the diary down and head toward the table by the door to pick up my knife. The tip slides through my skin like a breath, and I watch as blood wells on the pad of my thumb. *I'll let you know if I learn anything.*

Still standing, I grab the diary from the table. My blood beads against the leather cover. I wait for it to sink in, but instead, it sits on the surface, stubbornly refusing to disperse. I try rubbing it in, but the blood only leaves a trail of small droplets behind, bright red against stained and faded brown.

I don't think it's going to work, I Send to Priya.

I'm not so sure about that, she replies, her voice hesitant, almost frightened.

Confused, I drop into Second-Sight. The light nearly blinds me. Power so bright it washes everything out is concentrated in my hands. The diary is ablaze, ethereal energy licking over its edges like crimson flames tipped with blue light. My blood burns brightest, a white-hot streak of energy crossing the back cover. Amazed, I reach for the pooled energy, trying to dive into the memories clearly contained within the book. But as I try to Read the diary, to fall into it, something stops me. I push, brow furrowed as I force myself deeper into Second-Sight and into the diary. But whatever other power is in play, it's stalwart, refusing to move aside.

I stop trying to force it, and energy flows out of me in a knee-shaking rush. I stumble a little and slowly make my way to the floor. Priya is next to me in the space of a heartbeat, cool hands running over my shoulders and face.

Like a soft breeze, she brushes my hair back from my face, her eyes blazing white with the energy it takes to manifest physically. After a moment, she settles back, floating above the ground, legs tucked under her as she studies me carefully.

You okay?

I nod, still drained. *There's some kind of protection on the book. I can't get a Reading.*

You were able to Read it last night.

I think it wanted *me to Read it.* I shake my head. *It doesn't want that now.*

Can I look? Priya floats closer, eyeing the diary with apprehension. I nod and slide it closer to her on the floor.

She reaches forward until her fingers almost touch the diary and she closes her eyes. Slowly, she spreads her fingers wide, holding her hand over the cover of the book. Power dances through her fingers, bright light sparking over and around her outstretched hand. Then the energy slows, stills, stops. It coats her skin, a glove made of pure power, and she presses her hand onto the diary. There's a loud, ringing snap, like a steel band breaking, and Priya's eyes fly open in surprise.

She pulls her hand back and shakes it as if burned, the power drifting from it in misty tendrils of smoke that fade almost immediately. *There are some serious protections on this diary, Kim.*

Do you think you can break them?

She shakes her head. *Whatever they are, I'm not familiar enough with the warding to remove it.*

I try to think of how I interacted with the diary last night, if there was something I did differently, but exhaustion clouds my mind. It's been a long day. Warding Cross and the crime scene already took a lot of effort and keeping my still-changing powers in check around the dark energy filling the basement was a struggle, too. Pushing against the wards on the diary has drained the last of my reserves.

Groaning, I lean forward to rest my head in my hands. *I don't think I did anything different from usual when I was looking through the thing last night. I was on the couch and started falling asleep. Then the Reading took me. I didn't* do *anything. It was all the diary.*

Maybe that's it, Priya suggests. *Falling asleep isn't that far from a deep meditative state, and we both know you're terrible at reaching that state on your own.*

Go to sleep and try again? I'm tired enough from the day that I'm tempted.

Or meditate, Priya says with an exasperated grin. *Though it* is *getting late.*

I grab my phone and check the time. Priya's right; it's nearly past eleven. I must have spent more time studying the diary than I thought. *What do you think? Risk it, or call it a night?*

If it were up to me, she Sends hesitantly, *I'd call it a night. Trying to Read through those protections clearly drained you, and it's already been an intense day. But knowing you, you're going to want to try again.*

Today's a day for trying new things, I say as I set the diary on the table and push my way back to my feet. *The diary will still be here in the morning. I'll see if I can Read it before we leave or after we get home from work.*

I head to the bathroom to quickly brush my hair and teeth. I'm careful with my hands. With all of the scribing today, I've had to make more than a few cuts on my fingers, and the palm of my left hand is still tender from where I cut it when Burning the ghost at the first grave marker. I fish through my medicine cabinet until I find a half-empty box of Band-Aids. Pulling out a few smaller ones, I go to bandage my fingers, then pause. Where I nicked my thumbs and forefinger earlier today, there's only a thin, raised line, almost like a shallow paper cut. Even the slice I took out of my thumb a little earlier is already the lighter pink of partially healed skin.

On the list of weird things that have happened today, this is pretty far down. Figuring I must not have cut as deep as I thought I did, I shrug it off and head into the bedroom. I strip down for the night, my clothes landing haphazardly around the room before I fall onto my unmade bed, the comforter bunched awkwardly underneath me. I roll to the side and free the blanket, then drag it over top of me and tight under my chin. With a yawn, I flick off the bedside lamp. Darkness covers the room. Still half in Second-Sight, the room is suddenly, vibrantly outlined in flickering multicolored light. But as I drift to sleep, even that dims, leaving only the black of night and my fading thoughts.

CHAPTER ELEVEN

I roll out of bed the next morning feeling surprisingly well-rested, my stamina level higher than I'd expect after how much power I expended yesterday. I chalk it up to a good night's sleep and make my way to the bathroom for a shower. The too-hot water pounds away the last of the sleep that clings to me, and I nearly bounce into the kitchen, buzzing with unexpected energy.

Sweet dreams? Priya asks.

I start the coffee brewing and shrug. *No idea. I just feel… awake this morning.*

You're never awake in the mornings. Priya settles on the kitchen counter, frowning at me as I wait for my coffee to finish. *Are you sure you're okay?*

I laugh, then dig through the cabinet for a mug as the coffee maker sputters. *Worry about me when I'm bleeding or near death or something. I feel fine.*

I worry about you when you're not feeling normal, Priya says, stressing the final word. *This is not normal.*

Priya, I promise you, there's nothing to worry about. I take a sip of my coffee, the French roast rich and dark against my tongue. Closing my eyes, I enjoy the flavor and inhale the scent deep into my lungs. Pure caffeinated bliss. *But if it'll make you feel better, you're more than welcome to give me a once-over.*

Muted anxiety dances across my bond with Priya, her worry echoing through. *I think I will.*

Let me get comfortable, then. Taking another sip, I head toward the front room to settle on the couch. My mug placed on the table, legs stretched across the sofa, I lie down and lean my head against the armrest. My arms are limp at my sides, and I tilt my head back, staring at the ceiling before I close my eyes. *Do your worst.*

Ha-ha. Just… stay still.

Her hands feel like a cool breeze against my skin. She skims them over my shoulders and neck. Energy flows into me, searching through my body with curious fingers. It's an odd sensation, like an arm or leg as it starts to come awake, but there's no discomfort, only a tingling sensation that makes me want to fidget. I can feel it in my blood, zipping through my veins and arteries in time with my pulse. Priya hums quietly as she works, her hands trailing over my arms and hands as I struggle to stay still.

That cut on your thumb is nearly healed, she Sends quietly, *and I can't sense any other significant injuries, not even from when you Burnt that woman's ghost in the cemetery.*

I frown. *That seems a little fast. The cut on my head should still be healing, same with my palm.*

They are *still healing,* Priya says, *but they're both nearly finished. Your oldest injury—the cut on your head—is from five days ago, but it looks like it's been healing for over a week. As for the cuts on your hands, those look like they're four or five days old, rather than from yesterday. Outside of the physical, they're almost nonexistent. And there's no sense of the injury in your psychic presence. But other than the accelerated rate of healing—which is distinctly* not *normal—I can't find anything out of the ordinary with you. Vitals are all good. Heart rate is normal, oxygen levels are where they should be.* There's a pulse of amusement down our bond. *No signs of significant head trauma.*

I crack open an eye and catch her grinning. *You going to let me enjoy the rest of my coffee now?*

She pulls away, nodding, but she bites her lip. *You should see a physician about the healing. It's probably nothing to be worried about, but it's still out of the norm for you. As for your mood…* She frowns, concern radiating from her. *You don't do perky. It's unsettling.*

I'm not perky, I say with annoyance. *I'm just awake. Can you please let me enjoy it?*

Okay. Priya rolls her eyes but moves out of the way as I grab my coffee and take a too-large sip, burning my tongue slightly. *But I'm only dropping it because that's the first time you've sounded like yourself since you woke up.* She pauses and looks at me thoughtfully. *Since you're so "awake"*—I glare as she uses air quotes—*what's the plan with Bell's diary?*

It's still sitting on the coffee table, brown cover staring up at me as I look over the rim of my mug and take another, more careful, sip. I set the mug down and pick up the book, turning it over in my hand. The now-dried smear of blood is hard to see against the cover, and though it's still bright when I fall into Second-Sight, I wonder if the power contained within it will be enough to break through the protections on the diary or if I'll need to cut one of my fingers again.

I'll try to Read it again, I guess. I set the book on my lap, running a finger around the edge of the cover. *How much time do we have?*

Priya looks at the clock. *About another hour before you have to head in. More than enough time for you to try.*

Okay. I grab my coffee cup and take a final drink, draining it. The rich taste sitting heavy on my tongue, I fall fully into Second-Sight and start meditating. I kneel on the floor, my back straight, and breathe deeply as I settle into a traditional seated posture.

Taka would be proud.

A lot of things have changed over the last four months, but my inability to meditate without a struggle hasn't. This morning—especially with the extra energy zipping through me—is no exception. It takes a long time to get settled. There's a lingering sense of discomfort from Priya's examination, small ricochets of energy that leave me wanting to shake out my arms and legs. I have to move a few times when it gets overwhelming, rolling my shoulders back to shake the sensation from them. As I fail to escape the feeling entirely, I shift from *seiza*, moving my legs to the side so that they're resting next to me, rather than underneath. I can feel pins and needles as my feet start to wake up. With an aggrieved sigh, I lie down on the floor, knees bent, one arm thrown over my eyes, the other stretched out toward the door.

You all right there? Priya asks.

I'm fine. Just… give me a minute, okay?

I take another deep breath, and finally, I start to calm down. Something settles, and as I breathe slowly in and out, eyes shut tight beneath my arm, I let my other arm drag across the floor slowly until it touches the diary. My hand rests gently on the cover, and I run my thumb idly up and down the edge as I continue to drift. My breaths become more even and steady. The flames of Second-Sight flicker around me, brightening and dimming in time with my slowing heartbeat. Around me, the light flares, shifting from red to green to blue, then back to red again. The shock of the shifting kaleidoscope of colors nearly pulls me from my trance, but then there's a familiar tug deep in my gut, and I'm falling into the Reading, the world awash in red flames.

———

Your face is familiar in the mirror: dark skin lined with nearly invisible wrinkles, tightly curled hair pulled back and just starting to gray at the temples, and eyes such a dark shade of brown, they're almost black. Tentatively, you reach forward, trailing your fingers over the reflection, wondering at the marks that time has left on your body. With a sigh, you drop your hand to your diary, the leather warm and comforting. Then you start speaking.

"I don't know who you are or when you're Reading this, but I have no other way to transfer this knowledge without risk. I believe the protections I've scribed into the diary will be enough to stop those who should not access these memories, but I have no way to be assured of the fact. Because of that, I'm afraid I will only give you as much information as I can. You will have to find the rest of it on your own. Decades of history have taught my family that other Mediums are not always to be trusted, so

I will do what I can to guide you on your way, but no more than that. There's too much at risk to be careless.

"First, you must understand that whatever the outcome of the upcoming events, I am only trying to help. I do not fully understand what is happening, but without the proper preparations, I do not know how we'll be able to stop it. There are others working to prevent these circumstances, but I fear that their current plan will only lead to future problems."

You look down from the mirror, unable to meet your own eyes, knowing that someone else will be looking out from them as they relive this moment. Shivering, you force yourself to look up again, your eyes alien in the silvered glass. You don't know when it will happen, but someone else will be staring back at your reflection, reliving your innermost thoughts and feelings. The implied invasion nearly makes you gag.

"Elijah has Seen… terrible, dark things. We must prevent those visions from becoming truth. As for how to do tha—"

There's a knock on the bathroom door that has you jumping, the diary sliding from your grasp to fall loudly onto the floor. You bend down quickly, picking it up and tucking it into your skirts, heart racing.

"Who are you talking to, Comfort?"

It's Caroline, her voice high and piercing through the wooden door. You dart your eyes back to the glass, your dark skin suddenly pale.

"No one," you respond. "Just myself."

Later, you think. *I will continue to explain. But for now, you must go.*

You close your eyes, and *push*, hoping that Emmett's instructions on how to do this were enough. It's hard to tell, though, as you continue to press outward, hoping that you'll somehow—

———

There's a shove, and then I'm hurtling back out of the memory and into the present day. My body jerks, one of my legs gives a sharp kick, and I bang my heel on the floor as I recover. The bright lance of pain brings me fully out of the Reading, and the diary tumbles from my grip onto the floor, landing with a heavy thud.

"Shit," I say, wincing as I sit up and rub at my aching foot. As the sting fades, I pull my knees up and rest my head against them, breathing hard. My hands tremble as I run them through my hair, tangling my fingers together to cup my neck. "Shit."

What happened? Are you okay?

The extra energy is gone now, leaving my hands shaking where they rest against the nape of my neck. I take another breath and hold it as I try to calm my still-racing heart. Too tired to Send, I speak instead. "I Read the diary, but… it wasn't a memory, it was a message. For me, or rather, for someone. I don't think she really knew who she was talking to, other than another Medium."

What? Confused, Priya settles next to me, sending Healing energy down our bond. It helps steady me, but I motion for her to stop. I'm tired, sure, but not to the point where I need Priya to refill my reserves.

"She was in a bathroom, in front of a mirror, talking to herself. Or rather, she was talking to someone *else*." I run my fingers through my hair one more time before finally lifting my head. "Christ, I don't know how to explain it. She was leaving a specific memory in the diary, one that she hoped would be Read in the future. There was this sense of *invasion*, like she knew how the person Reading it would experience the memory, and it made her uncomfortable. But she still did it because her message was more important than her discomfort. There's something coming, something evil. Or at least, that's what she wanted the Reader to know."

That doesn't sound good. Do you think she could've been talking about Baker?

"No, I don't think so. In the last Reading, the one from two days ago? She wasn't afraid of Baker, not like she was afraid of this. Honestly, Baker didn't even come up. She was more worried about Caroline—who was there with her, by the way—but I don't think she was trying to warn me about her, either."

So, if it wasn't Baker or Caroline, what was she warning you about?

"I don't know." I stand and head toward the bedroom, frustrated. "Caroline interrupted Bell before she could say anything specific. She *did* say that she would tell me more later, though how in the hell I'm going to find *that* specific memory is beyond me."

Priya sighs. *So, you'll have to Read it again.*

"I'll have to Read it again," I say in agreement. "I think

it's the only way I'm going to figure out what's going on. I'm going to have to do some research into how to target the Readings, but I think that diary is going to have a lot of the answers we're looking for. And I think this explains why there's a gap in the entries. If I had to guess, she didn't write anything potentially incriminating or dangerous down in that diary because it wasn't secure enough. She left a record of memories instead."

It's clever but feels like overkill. Why not ward the diary and call it a day?

"Paranoia, I think. She seemed terrified, Priya. Whatever she was facing, it had her spooked."

This whole thing has me spooked, Priya says with a shiver. *Those markers, Riley suddenly becoming Sighted, you getting a new Affinity… None of this is remotely close to normal.*

I swallow, my throat suddenly dry. "No, it's not."

She glances up at me, and her expression softens. *Kim,* she says gently before coming close enough that I shiver from the cold air that cocoons her. *Whatever this is, we'll figure it out. You've already learned how to control your new Affinity, and Riley is learning how to use his powers, too. Andrea is going to get the bindings on the gravestones figured out, which will tell us why someone is harnessing that power and also give us an idea of what that symbol means. Sure, it's a lot, but we'll figure out the diary with the rest.*

"That's putting a lot of faith in Banks."

Priya nods. *I know you may not like her, but she's smart. It certainly can't be any worse than where we are now. At least it's a step in the right direction.*

"I hate it when you have a point," I grumble. "I'll call

her later today to follow up. Hopefully, she'll have something."

Oh my God, are you being sensible about this?

"New leaf," I say with a shrug. "Now, c'mon. I'm gonna be late."

Chapter Twelve

I walk to the bedroom, my stamina still low but recovering, and get dressed for the day. I put on dark dress pants and a white blouse with my shoulder holster thrown over top, all covered with a matching suit jacket. Strapping on my ankle sheath, I slide my Medium's knife into it. My Chukka boots go on next, a step up from the combat ones I usually wear. Working a case means I have to dress in uniform. I shrug into a heavy black wool jacket as I head out the door, locking it behind me.

The traffic is lighter than usual on the way to work, so when I walk through the front doors of HQ, I'm only five minutes late instead of fifteen. Shrugging out of my jacket, I toss it over the back of my chair before falling gracelessly into it. Cross looks up at the metallic shriek of the chair, his eyebrows raised. His expression quickly shifts from surprise to concern.

"You look like shit," he says. "You feeling okay?"

"Yeah, I'm fine," I say with a sigh. "Coffee?"

"If you're headed that way…" he says. "You're sure you're all right?"

When I nod, he passes me his mug, brow still furrowed.

I head to the kitchen and the promise of coffee within. The coffee pot is nearly empty, but there's enough left in the carafe to fill the bottom of my disposable cup. I take a quick, lukewarm chug, thoroughly unsatisfied by the experience, and start gathering the stuff to make another pot.

I spill some grounds as I measure out enough to brew a full pot. With a sigh, I start the coffee maker and sweep the grounds into my hand. When I turn to toss them into the small trash can by the door, I nearly run into Cross who is walking through the door, a folder in hand, his head bent.

"Watch where you're going," I say with more fervor than I intend.

"Sorry," he says, clearly caught off guard by my response, before looking back at his folder. "I got some updates on the case to share with you and figured we could cover it while waiting. That work for you, or do you want me to let you stew over whatever's gotten you fired up this morning?"

I give him a blank stare, and he coughs before looking back at his file. "Okay then, work it is. First things first, a couple uniformed officers were able to find someone who knows the owner of the house." He looks up at me, face screwed up in a wince. "Or, rather, *knew* the owner of the house. Apparently, the property's been abandoned for a few years."

"Fantastic," I say. I turn back to the coffee maker, silently urging it to brew faster.

"It gets better," he continues. "The Baptist church

across the street? Well, the pastor there says they've had issues with the homeless population in the area. I was on the phone with him right before you got in, and from what he was telling me, they've been staying in some of the abandoned homes in the area. And according to the city, there are a *lot* of abandoned buildings in this neighborhood—you probably already know that from working the district. With the weather as cold as it's been lately, there's been an increase in homeless folks breaking into these buildings for shelter. That's also why our crime scene was boarded up. The church has a volunteer group that works with the city, and they go around the area to board up abandoned places."

"So, there's a chance that we've had a fuckton of people through our scene, is that what you're saying?"

He frowns. "It's a possibility, yes. I don't know that the evidence backs it up, though. The first floor didn't look like anyone had been in there recently."

"But we don't know." I lean forward against the counter and close my eyes. "Any other good news?"

Cross doesn't say anything, so I turn around to face him. "Well?" I ask, pushing him to respond.

His expression is a mix of confusion and amusement. "You okay?" he asks before closing his folder and taking a small step closer. "I was trying to make a joke of it earlier, but you seem on edge. You're not the cuddliest person I know, but this doesn't feel like your usual brand of standoffishness."

"I'm fine." I go to turn back around, but he grabs my hand. I freeze, more shaken by the gentle touch than I want to admit.

"You can talk to me," he says, his fingers warm against the delicate skin of my palm. He gives my hand a quick squeeze before he lets it drop. I fight the urge to curl my fingers into the lingering heat of his touch and fail, my nails biting into my skin.

"I know," I finally say. "That I can talk to you. I just… It's nothing. What else did you learn from the canvas?"

"Nice deflection," he says. "Very subtle."

He waits for me to respond, but when I don't say anything, he flips the folder back open with a sigh and picks up where he left off.

"Scene reconstruction is going to be working on-site today, while Forensics finishes up on-site. We should know more about the shoe treads in a few days, same with the blood evidence. We'll need to call the ME's office to find out when the autopsies are scheduled. I haven't had a chance to do that yet."

"I'll call Abramo," I say. "With all the work you've already done this morning, I'm surprised you haven't solved the case."

"It was the butler," he says, deadpan. "In the basement, with the knife."

When I don't laugh, he frowns. "You're in a hell of a mood this morning. What's going on?"

"It's nothing," I repeat.

"You know I'm a trained detective, right?"

"It's nothing to do with *you*," I restate. "There's a lot going on right now that I don't want to get into."

"When you say there's a lot going on, do you mean the whole new powers thing, or do you mean the way you turned me into a light bulb yesterday? Or is it the crazy ghost lady we saw, or, wait, maybe the scar I'm gonna be explaining to every date I have for the rest of my life?"

When I fail to respond, he sighs.

"No shit there's a lot going on right now." He sets the folder down on the counter and leans his hip against it, effectively boxing me in. "But I thought we were going to work on it together. Or did I stay up half the night reading for nothing?"

He crosses his arms, and I stop myself from mimicking the movement. Instead, I reach for his coffee mug and fill it from the now nearly overflowing carafe. I slide it across the counter and the mug comes to rest next to his folder. After I finish pouring my own cup, I hold a container of nondairy creamer out to him like a peace offering. Cross takes it from me, the motion somehow goading in its slow precision. He pours a heap of creamer into his cup and hands the container back, the small mountain of white powder dissolving gradually as silence saturates the kitchen.

"Well?" Cross stares at me, and I can feel myself cave the moment before I do.

"It's this diary," I say, collapsing against the counter, my coffee stinging hot in my hands. "And some shit with Baker."

"Baker?" Cross asks. "Do I need to be worried? I thought you Burnt him."

"I *did*," I say, waving his worry away with a reassuring

hand. "He's gone. Don't worry about that. I'm trying to figure out something that I saw right after. A… vision or something, I don't know."

"And this diary has to do with it?"

"It belonged to one of his victims, the genealogist. His ancestor wrote it."

"That's great, but why does it matter?" Cross asks.

"Because she helped Bind him, and I still don't know *why*."

He frowns and rubs idly at his chest. "What question will that answer for you? You have more than enough evidence that he was evil. Binding him was the right choice."

"But how can we be sure?"

Cross looks surprised by the question.

I turn away from him and bite my lip, remembering Baker's expression as he was Bound, the fervor he spoke with when confronting Moore.

"Phillips," Cross says, dragging my attention back to him as he forces me to look him in the eye. "The man killed five people. Hell, he tried to kill you and used my body to do it. Binding him was the right thing. Burning him was, too. Finding an answer to *why* he was Bound isn't going to change either of those facts."

I nod, though my mind is still clouded with doubt. Something about the way my grandmother looked at Baker in that first memory from Bell's diary leaves me unsettled. *How could she love someone that twisted?* I push the thought aside—unwilling to examine it here and now—and stop leaning against the counter.

"You're right," I say, grabbing my cup of coffee and heading toward the door. "I'll call the ME's office."

I try to push past him, but he grabs my wrist, stopping me.

"He's gone," he says softly. "You said so yourself. It's time to move past it."

"How am I supposed to do that?" I ask. My voice is pitched low, so it doesn't carry, but the words are still fierce. "How do I move past it when everything's different now, and it's all because of him?"

"You don't let it define you." He squeezes my wrist gently, his words strong and calming. "Things may be different, but you control how those differences affect you. Baker can't decide how you live your life. He's gone. You're not."

"Is that how you do it?" I ask, my eyes darting to his chest, then back to his face. "Is that how you've moved on?"

"It's one way." His voice is calm, steady. "I'm not saying I've got it all figured out, but I don't let my fear of the unknown make my choices for me. Am I afraid of what's happening to me? You bet your ass I am. But I won't let it control me." He smiles a little, eyes shining with amusement. "I've never known you to let someone else tell you what to do or how to behave. Don't let that asshole be the first."

Cross rubs his thumb across the thin skin of my wrist. He wants to help. I can read it in every line of his body, in the tone of his voice and the way his mouth curls into a teasing, encouraging smile. It's an offering of support, of understanding, and I cling to it like a life raft.

He's right, of course. I shouldn't let my fear define me. But so much of my life has been spent in fear. Fear of the unknown, fear of abandonment, fear of myself. It's made me unwilling to trust, to open up to people. I have few friends and even fewer confidants. Looking at Cross, his eyes full of understanding, I feel that distrust shift a little, and I slowly nod.

"You're right," I say quietly, his hand still wrapped around my wrist. His grip shifts until he's cradling my hand in his, his thumb now stroking over the back of my hand. My eyes fall to the gentle movement, watching as his finger glides over the delicate skin across my knuckles.

I know that the motion is platonic, just Cross trying to calm me down, to help me through this moment. It's a kindness, offered from a place of friendship and nothing more. But something twists in my gut, a reaction that's physical and base and unstoppable. I try to fight it, to repress the shiver that's growing beneath my skin as his thumb continues its inexorable path. Instead, goose bumps spread across my skin, and I shiver as his thumb slows and his hand tightens around my now-sweating palm.

I'm filled with a mix of embarrassment and excitement as his eyes meet mine, unable to hide the flare of response his touch brings. The heat between us flashes, and the gentle half smile on his lips stills, then turns to something more serious, an expression that I can't read but speaks of an answering awareness. He takes a step closer as he starts running his thumb over my knuckles again, though this time his touch is slower, more purposeful.

"Is there anything else you want to talk about?"

He's close enough that I can smell his aftershave. The sharp, musky aroma fills my head as I take a shuddering breath. His lips part as if he's about to say something, and I have to pull away. My feet land heavily as I take a stumbling step back. His touch lingers on the back of my hand. Staring at the linoleum tile of the kitchen, the far wall, the counter, anywhere but him, I take another breath, fighting for balance.

"Kim?" His voice is quiet, but there's a subdued wildness in the way he says my name.

"It's nothing," I say, taking another step back and finally meeting his eyes. Emotion lies heavy in his gaze, matching the feelings roiling within me. "It's nothing."

"Nothing to do with me," he says, challenging me to respond.

I swallow, throat tight. My heart is racing, but this time, all I can feel is uncertainty. My mind races for a response, and the only thing I can think is that Priya's right, that she's been right all along. I can't keep dancing around how I feel about Cross. He won't let me bury it or pretend there's not something here.

Terror lances through me at the thought. This moment matters. Whatever words come out of my mouth next could change everything between us, for better or for worse, and the sensation of standing at the edge of some gaping precipice, deciding whether to step back onto firm ground or fall over the edge, is *awful*. I can't breathe, can't think, but I find myself meeting his gaze, my mouth opening to respond.

And then there's a loud cough from the doorway that makes me jump, and I turn, scalding hot coffee sloshing over the edge of my cup and over my hand. I curse and quickly set the cup down on the counter before shaking the still-steaming liquid off of my now-red fingers.

"Detectives," Lieutenant Walker says, watching me cautiously as I hurry to the sink to turn on the cold water and run it over my burned skin. "I wanted to talk to you about your ghost."

CHAPTER THIRTEEN

"My office, five minutes," Walker says and heads back into the bullpen. I can sense Cross's eyes heavy on my back as I keep the water running, my hand tucked under the faucet. I stare at it, watching as the water breaks into miniature rapids against the ridges of my fingers, hiding my red skin.

"Are you okay?" he asks. "The coffee, I mean."

"I'll be fine." I turn off the water and grab a paper towel from a wall dispenser near the sink. Pressing it to my hand, I flinch a little at the feel of rough paper against the burn. "What do you think Walker wants to know?"

Cross is silent, and I finally force myself to look at him again. He's expressionless, his eyes on my hands. The openness that had been there is shuttered, hidden away. My fingers clench, and I wince as they press too hard into my stinging skin.

"I guess we'll find out," he finally says, grabbing his folder and coffee mug from the counter, not meeting my eyes.

I feel guilty and don't know why. Making sure not to overfill it this time, I pour myself another cup of coffee and even put a lid on the damn thing to be safe before I head back to my desk. I haven't been at district HQ long enough this morning to have anything to grab, but I pull a small notebook and pen from my desk to give my hands something to do. I stand awkwardly as I wait for Cross to finish whatever he's working on.

He keeps typing, eyes firmly on his computer screen. He has to see me waiting, and part of me feels embarrassed while another part starts to get pissed. With a loud punch of the enter key, he pushes back from his desk, grabs his file, and stands. He doesn't say anything but heads toward Walker's office. I follow after him like a puppy on a leash. It irritates me, and as soon as he slows to knock on Walker's door, I push past him and into her office.

She looks up at us and nods. "Sit down. Phillips, I need your input. What has this guy told you so far?"

"His name is Steve." I pull out a chair and sit. "But other than that, he hasn't said much of anything."

"And you don't have any other sense of the guy? Who he is, why he was in that house, who might've killed him? Nothing?"

"No, ma'am," I say. "The only other thing worth noting is that he makes my partner nervous."

She looks to Cross. "I didn't think you could see ghosts."

"No," I say, glancing to where Priya is tucked into the corner of the room. "Not Detective Cross. My *other* partner."

Understanding brightens Walker's gaze. "She tell you why?"

"No," I say quickly as Cross opens his mouth to speak. I turn to fully face Priya. "She hasn't explained her response to Steve other than to say that something is wrong with him. And, I have to admit, I agree."

Cross and Walker both look at me in confusion, though Cross is the first to speak.

"You don't like the guy?"

"I don't know yet," I say with a shake of my head. "There's something... *off* about him, but I can't put my finger on it. Between his response to his own death and the way that he isn't interacting with us, his behavior is odd."

When Walker frowns in confusion, I continue. "Most murder victims want to talk to me. I'm a cop and a Medium, so I'm obviously there to help them in one capacity or another. Once they figure that out, they either tell me about their death or they give me a Sending of it. Steve hasn't made any move to do either of those things. He's just... I don't want to sound flippant about it, but he's just kind of hanging out."

"Hanging out." Walker leans forward slightly in her chair. "Can you explain that further?"

"Ghosts fail to pass on to the other side because of unfinished business or because they're caught off guard by their death and miss the chance. You learn to tell which kind you're dealing with pretty quickly. The ones with a purpose, they let you know what that is and how to accomplish it almost immediately. If they missed the bus"—I shrug—"they need a bit of a push. Even though they know their only choices are to pass on or to Turn, they still need some help taking that first step. Dying is hard no matter how it comes about."

"But then they go," Cross says.

"But then they go," I agree. "But Steve's not acting quite right. He's not telling us his purpose, and he's not hedging around moving on. Instead, he's just… waiting."

Walker leans back in her seat and crosses her arms.

"Detective Cross," she says, "anything about the scene strike you as odd?"

"Actually," he says slowly, "there are a few things, yes."

"Like what?" she asks.

"There was a lot of blood around both of the bodies," he continues. "And while there are signs of an attack around the scene—blood trails, spatter, footprints—for the most part, the blood evidence is centralized around the bodies. That's two full-grown adults who've effectively bled out in a contained location. That means, what, four to six liters of blood? For each of our vics? That's a lot of blood."

He turns to look at me, then back to Walker. "But the pool wasn't disturbed. No transfers, no prints, nothing. Just a giant pool of blood. So, how'd our guy get in there, kill two people with a knife—an up-close-and-personal kind of murder, one that's pretty damn messy—and exit the scene without leaving some kind of blood trail?"

Walker grins. "You're earning your keep today, Detective. That's the exact same question that Scene Reconstruction was asking this morning. There are voids at the scene, so we know there was someone there who blocked some of the blood spatter, but there aren't any transfer stains, or at least nothing that would indicate an offender leaving the scene."

I turn to look at Walker. "None?"

"None that Forensics have found, and they've been looking."

"What else aren't you telling us?" Cross asks.

"I also got a call from the ME's office this morning," she says. "And while our Jane Doe has defensive wounds, our John Doe is missing them. What he *does* have are injuries consistent with a knife slipping and cutting his hand while he was holding it."

"Wait a second," Cross says, his eyes widening. "Are you implying that our John Doe—Steve—is the attacker? How does that explain his wounds?"

"Abramo thinks at least some of them are defensive. It could be that our female victim got the knife away from him and did enough real damage to take him out. Whatever the case, you"—she trains her gaze to me— "need to get back to that scene and get this guy talking. And fast."

"Understood," Cross says, standing almost immediately. "We'll head out right away, Lieutenant."

"Be careful, Detectives," Walker says as I stand. "And Phillips? If you have to Burn him, do it."

"Yes, ma'am," I say, hurrying after Cross as he exits her office. He's already grabbed his coat and is heading toward the front door by the time I get to our desks. I try to block his path, but he brushes past me.

"I'll see you in the cruiser," he says, not making eye contact.

"Okay." I watch as he hurries out of the building and toward the parking lot.

You are terrific at making a mess of things, Priya Sends with a shake of her head. *Grab your coat and go apologize to that man.*

For what? I ask as I grab my jacket and hurry after Cross. *I didn't do anything.*

Kim, Priya groans, *you're doing it again.*

Doing what?

Deflecting, she sighs, and I burst out the front doors. Cross has the Interceptor pulled up to the curb and pointed toward Sixty-Third Street, engine idling. I slow as I approach the car and circle around the back to get to the passenger side door. Hesitantly, I reach for the handle and climb in.

Though the heat is on full, the inside of the car is icy. Cross's shoulders are stiff, his back straight, his eyes glued to the windshield and the road ahead. He glances my way for a moment when I get in, then snaps his eyes forward and shifts into drive, pulls out of the parking lot, and heads toward the scene. It's achingly quiet. The silence coats the inside of the car, filling the spaces in brittle folds that feel like they could shatter at the slightest sound. My emotions are a mix of annoyance at Cross's cold shoulder, embarrassment at my own behavior in the kitchen, and trepidation about facing Steve, knowing that he may have been the killer rather than the victim. It's not the healthiest mix of emotions, and I can sense Priya reaching out, trying to calm the rioting mess inside of me.

You need to say something, Kim, Priya cautions. *If you leave it like this, it's only going to get worse.*

And what do I say? I ask. *Sorry, I don't know how to open up to people, and you make me nervous because I want to?*

Maybe not that. She sighs. *But you can't not say anything.*

You're right, I Send with a groan. *This is going to be so awkward.*

You can do it, sport.

Sport?

I'm trying to be supportive.

Not helping, Priya.

"Look"—

"Phillips, I'm—"

Our words tumble out over top of the other, and I clamp my mouth shut, biting my lip as Cross takes a deep breath.

"In the kitchen," he says, and I'm struck by the hesitation in his voice, "I shouldn't have... I don't know, I'm just... I'm sorry."

"What?" I'm struck dumb, trying to figure out what in the hell *he* has to apologize for.

"I pushed," he says with a scowl. "I shouldn't have."

"I don't... What are you talking about? Do you mean about Baker?"

"No." He sighs. "No, not about Baker. About... After that."

"It's not..." I pause, struggling for the right words.

"You didn't do anything."

"That's kind of you," he says, corner of his mouth kicking up into a smirk, "but you and I both know that I was out of line. Just… If you can, forget about it. It won't happen again."

It's the out I've been looking for. My opportunity to let this thing between us finally die, to bury it and move on. But there's a sudden tightness in my chest, a small ball of grief that's surprising in its strength as I think about letting this thing between us go.

I don't want this, I think, watching Cross's expression slowly turn to stone as I stay quiet.

Kim, Priya says, her voice frantic.

"You didn't push," I say. "You were being a friend, and I'm not going to forget about it." My voice is quiet but firm. "I don't want to forget about it."

He glances at me, then back at the road.

"And it's not nothing," I continue. "But it can't be more than what it is, at least for right now. I'm not… You're… It's complicated."

"That's certainly the word for it." He huffs out a pained laugh.

"I don't know if it's fair of me to ask this," I say, looking down at my hands as I tangle my fingers together, "but if you can wait until things calm down a bit, we'll talk about it. *Really* talk about it."

"And there *is* something to talk about?" he asks. "It's not only me?"

I swallow and clench my hands tighter together. The

car is quiet except for road noise and the crackle of the police radio. Fear holds my throat closed, but I swallow again, not letting it win out this time.

"No."

It's one syllable, but the weight of it leaving my mouth makes me feel lighter. I look up at him and our eyes meet for a brief, heat-filled moment before he looks back at the road. He laughs a little, shaking his head.

"Well, shit." He laughs again, and the sound is filled with warmth. "I don't know if this is better or worse," he says, "but okay. As long as you promise me we'll talk about this… thing. Between us."

I nod, heart racing. Emotion—exhilaration, relief, uncertainty—whips through me, leaving me a little light-headed and giddy. I fight down a grin.

I could kiss you right now, Priya Sends as she swoops from the back seat of the cruiser to the front, her cold body sending shivers through me. *I am so proud.*

I didn't do anything, I Send back to her, a smile sneaking its way out at her response.

Oh, can you shut up and let me gloat? Priya asks with a grin. I laugh, and Cross flashes me a smile that's a mix of relief and excitement.

"Let's get focused," I say, turning away from his smile to hide my own. "We've got a possible murder suspect to talk to. How do you want to handle this?"

"You're the expert here," he says as he turns onto Wolcott. "You tell me."

I frown, considering. "I don't know how that energy is

going to affect things," I start, "but between the wards around the house and on you, you'll be safe to enter the scene when I confront the guy. We'll want to get everyone else out of there to be safe."

"Scene Reconstruction is going to love that," Cross says dryly. "What do we do if he Turns?"

"You run like hell," I say as he pulls to a stop outside the crime scene. "I'll deal with the rest."

"Sounds safe." He turns off the car, then twists in his seat to face me. "Be careful. You owe me a conversation."

I nod, throat tight. "You're not the only one who wants to have it."

"Noted," Cross says, his eyes flashing before he turns away from me. "All right, let's get this done with."

"Agreed." I clamber out of the car and slam the door shut. There are a few other CPD vehicles around the scene. A tired-looking uniformed officer is posted in the staging area, and Cross and I head his way, badges already out.

"Detectives Cross and Phillips," Cross says, reaching for the sign-in sheet. "We're going to need the area cleared while Detective Phillips handles the ghost on scene."

The uniformed officer's shoulders sag in relief. "Thank God you're here," he says, taking the clipboard back quickly and waving us through. "We've been having issues with the damn thing on and off all night. Reconstruction had to leave early. Whatever's down there, it's not letting anyone stay for long."

A thread of disquiet eases its way through me, and I

look at Cross to see the same emotion reflected on his face.

"Start clearing people out," I say before dropping into Second-Sight to check the wards I placed the day before. They're still strong, soaring into the sky in a rainbow of power. Some of my tension eases, but as we walk from the front of the house to the back, any sense of comfort brought by the powerful wards lessens, then fades to nothing.

The thin lines of red energy from the night before have easily tripled in number. Where before there were only five or six streams of energy cutting through the backyard, now there are more than two dozen, and that's only counting the larger streams. Smaller ones, like veins, turn the yard into a tracery of deep red.

It's nearly impossible to avoid them, and I gasp as I trip through one. Cross quickly steadies me, grabbing me by the arm so I don't fall. My power flames and flares over my skin, licking at Cross's hand where its wrapped around my arm. As we near another line of energy, my power spikes, lashing out at the bloodred river in a painful burst of flame. It sings through my blood, leaving me shaking and on edge, ready to attack.

That's not good, Priya says, floating around the energy as much as she can. *What happened?*

I don't know, I Send. It's hard to concentrate, and I struggle to not give into the primal sense of wrongness that arcs its way through me as we draw closer to the basement entrance. Oozing down the stairs in a slow, dark trail, the power pools and settles, a deep, fathomless void of bloody, twisted energy that seeps through the doorway and into the brightly lit basement beyond.

"Cross," I say slowly, taking a hesitant step away from the basement entrance. "Can you see this?"

His eyes go unfocused for a moment, and his eyebrows shoot up. "Is this what you wanted me to see yesterday?"

"Yes, but it wasn't like this. This is worse."

"Do you think he's doing it?"

"I don't know," I say as a twinge of doubt twists its way through me. "But we definitely need to get people out of here. Now."

"I'll get started on that," he says. "Don't go down there until I'm done."

"No way in hell am I letting you go down there by yourself. You clear the scene up here. I need to make a call."

He eyes me for a moment, then nods and heads off to the few CPD members still on scene. I pull my cell out, fingers numb as I pull up Banks's number and dial. She answers almost immediately.

"Detective Phillips," she says, her tone bright and cheerful. "To what do I owe the pleasure?"

"Those runes," I say, walking away from the house, needing distance from the rancid feel of the power boiling up from the basement, "I need you to tell me everything you learned about them. Now."

"That's going to be rather hard right now," she says. I can make out muffled conversation from her end of the line, and I curse. "Why? What's the problem?"

I stare at the pulsing lines of power as they weave their way through the yard toward the basement and trickle down the steps. A sour taste floods my mouth, and I fight against the urge to vomit.

"Detective?" Banks's voice draws my attention back. "What is it?"

"The runes, especially that central motif you showed me yesterday? I need you to figure them out as soon as possible. Call me when you do."

I hang up and curse softly under my breath.

What're you thinking? Priya asks as she continues to avoid the power snaking across the yard.

I'm thinking maybe I shouldn't have tried something.

Her eyes widen. *You think you did this?*

I think, I Send, flinching, *that I tied the wards together with a series of marks we found on one of those gravestones, and now we've got a bunch of energy pooling inside those same wards.*

I don't want to say I told you so…

So don't. I run a hand through my hair, considering. *Instead, what do we do about it?*

Cross joins me a moment later, eyeing my phone as I slide it back into my pocket.

"Scene's clear," he says, "and there hasn't been anyone inside for the last hour. Steve wouldn't let them stay. So, you ready to go down there?"

"No," I say, turning back to the house. "But I don't think we've got a choice."

I bend down and pull my knife from my boot, then throw a shield up around Cross and myself just in case.

Priya, I Send, and she appears next to me, eyes white and crackling with power. *Watch his back.*

What about you? she asks.

I take a hesitant step forward, moving into the thick stream of energy. My gut clenches immediately, twisting with revulsion and nausea. I taste metal in the back of my throat; my mouth floods with saliva, but somehow I keep the vomit down.

I'll be fine, I Send, taking another step. *Let's go.*

CHAPTER FOURTEEN

The feeling of wrongness grows worse as we move down the stairs. Cross trails behind me, his hand on his gun, though we both know it won't help here. It's bright inside the basement, the lighting rigs still up and on. Blood stains the floor and walls. The dark energy twines in and out of the blood trails, scarlet blooms of energy that seem to follow the stains across the floor. A small, dark pool of it gathers in the discolored center of the room, pulsing slowly with a deep, red light.

I don't enter the basement yet, but I do my best to stay out of the caustic stuff, hugging the retaining wall as it offers me a small island of clear ground. Cross stands next to me but a little bit behind. If the energy bothers him, there's no sign. A thread of relief winds its way through me at the confirmation that his wards are working.

Steve? I Send cautiously.

From the back of the basement, the ghost gradually manifests. His hair is shaggier, the holes in his clothes bigger than they were the day before. The knife wounds that cover his body gape open beneath his clothes, and torn muscle shifts as he moves closer. Ghostly blood oozes from his wounds and into his clothing, dripping on the floor to leave a trail behind him that fades as he comes closer.

Detectives, he says, his eyes hidden by his hair so I can't see the color.

Is he Turned? I ask Priya who's almost pressed against me to avoid the energy on the ground.

I can't tell, she whispers. *But he's gotten worse.*

Steve finally brushes the hair away from his face, and I can see that Priya is right. His eyes swirl with a mix of white, black, and gray, a marbled effect that I've never seen before. His expression, combined with the strange color of his eyes, puts a shiver up my back, and my hand tightens around my knife reflexively.

I think I'm getting used to it, Steve Sends again. *Being dead I mean.*

That's good, I say, moving a little closer to the doorframe though a frisson of disquiet courses its way up my spine. *Would you be able to answer a few questions for me?*

I guess that depends on the questions. He circles the small pool of energy in the center of the room. *Maybe you'd answer some questions for me, too, Detective?*

I can do that as long as you answer mine, I respond, unsettled.

He grins, his teeth stained with blood, and nods. *Absolutely. We can make a game of it.*

"This isn't normal, right?" Cross asks from behind me, tone suspicious.

I shake my head. "No, this is not normal."

"Do we need to be worried?"

I eye Steve as he stares distractedly at his reflection in the pool of energy, his eyes swirling. Before he brings his gaze back to me, I nod quickly. "Yes."

What's your first question, Detective? he asks, moving away from the pool and toward the doorway where Cross and I stand.

What's your name?

Steve, he says with a blood-tinged grin.

Your full name, I restate, but he shakes his head instead of answering.

No, that's a different question. That means it's my turn now. He taps a finger to his chin, affecting a thoughtful expression before meeting my eyes with his immutable ones. *How old were you when you saw your first ghost?*

Eight, I Send. *Now, your full name.*

I want to know more than that, he murmurs.

Tell me your name, and I'll tell you more.

Stephen White.

Your full *name,* I say again, my temper flaring, *or my partner and I turn around and walk out of this place. And with the wards I placed? You're not.*

Stephen Christopher White, he snarls. His eyes go black, but they somehow still blaze with light. *Tell me.*

I was walking to the bus. Someone had been struck by a car and killed on my block. Their ghost was still there.

I bet that was terrifying, he says, voice thick with satisfaction. *What did they look like? I imagine all of that metal would do some very unpleasant things to the human body.*

I don't think about it.

I'm sure you don't. You've probably seen worse by now. You work homicide, after all. Were you always drawn to death, Detective, or did that come with age?

Why were you here? I ask, ignoring his question.

Probably for the same reasons as you. Something brought me here.

"What's that supposed to mean?" Cross asks, frowning.

You were drawn here?

Steve smirks. *That's one way of thinking of it, yes. And that's two questions, Detective. You still haven't answered mine. Were you always drawn to death?*

I was Sighted from an early age, I say. *Death's always been a part of my life. What drew you here?*

Power. Does it excite you, your connection to the afterlife?

I don't respond. His face goes stony, eyes flashing with that odd, black light again.

What Affinity?

Burner.

How helpful with your current line of work. Do you take pleasure in it, in Burning ghosts? Does it feel good to destroy them, to watch them fade and know that your hands were the ones to bring about their end?

It's not destruction, I say, tensing. His tone of voice, the way he revels in the words, has my stomach in knots. *It's release.*

Yes, release. He smiles contentedly, eyes lidded. *That's it exactly. What a wonderful way to look at it.*

I pause, considering my next question, when Steve stills like a wild creature scenting danger, then vanishes.

We'll talk again, Burner, he Sends. I feel his words like a gentle caress in my mind. I fight down nausea at the touch, and both the feeling and the lingering sense of the ghost are gone.

"What the hell is going on?" Cross asks as he looks around the basement, eyes scanning for Steve.

"He's starting to Turn." I take a cautious step inside and slowly work my way around the scene. "It should take decades for a ghost to physically degrade to this level. Steve's been gone for a day. I think this energy is messing with him."

"Then we need to get rid of the energy, right?" Cross says.

"I have no idea. It dissipated at the markers after I Burnt the ghosts that were tied to them. If there's a marker nearby, I can try to find it and Burn whatever ghost is there."

"Let's do that," Cross says, eyeing the now-empty basement, "and fast."

I nod. "We can start looking for it as soon as we finish getting the scene processed. I want to stop people from coming in and out as soon as possible. For now, I don't know where he's gone. The wards didn't trip, but he's not here right now. If Scene Reconstruction and Forensics can get their work done before he comes back, I won't have to wait long to Burn this guy."

"You still going to do this quid pro quo question-and-answer thing?"

The idea of it makes me uncomfortable, something about Steve's emotional response to my answers leaving me unsettled. "For now, yes. It got us his full name, which means we can have the ME verify his dental records and run a background check. The evidence points to him being our killer, and his personality isn't doing much to convince me otherwise. If he has a history of violence against women, maybe even an arrest record? It's a good first step while we wait for the evidence to be processed."

"Okay. Let's call in the name and start running records on him. You okay with staying at the scene in case he comes back?"

"Yeah," I say as I glance at the dark energy still gathering on the floor. "But let's make it quick."

Cross turns and heads up the stairs. Alone in the basement, I can't help but focus on the painful sensation of the dark energy as it pulls against me. Though I'm not standing in any one stream of it, there's a pervasive sense of wrongness permeating the room that leaves me in a cold sweat. In Second-Sight, my body is covered in red and blue-white flames of power. Small flashes of green appear along the tips of my fingers and hands. I turn my hand so my palm faces upward, watching the swirl of colors as they arc and stretch across my skin.

They're changing again, Priya says quietly. *Your powers, I mean.*

Yeah, I think so. I turn my hand back over, unnerved, and tuck it into my pocket before looking at her. She's still waiting in the doorway, unwilling to enter the basement. *You going to come in here, or no?*

She shakes her head. *Not a chance. It's wrong in there, and I know you can feel it, too.*

It is, I say as I pace around the basement again, taking in the evidence markers and the bloodstains that have set in the concrete. *You're going to make it hard for me to do my job, you know.*

My apologies, she says. It's a bit sarcastic, but there's a thread of guilt there, too.

Can you go outside instead? Stick to the exterior walls while I move around down here?

Relief whips through me, an echo of her emotion. *That'll work.*

Priya disappears a moment later, and I feel our bond stretch as she makes her way to the side of the house. The pull eases, and I'm finally able to investigate the scene with limited distractions.

In the bright light of the rigs, the most noticeable thing about the scene is the sheer amount of blood. While the pool in the center is by far the largest, there are smaller droplets covering the walls, ceiling, and support posts scattered throughout the room. Looking at the blood patterns, I get a feel for how the attack happened. There are signs of a struggle, blood smeared on the floor from where the victim and their attacker grappled. With the woman's broken nails and the blood coating their tips, she probably fought like hell against whoever it was. Arcs of blood splash against the walls and ceiling. Empty spaces indicate where someone stood and was hit with blood spray. Footprints go from scuffing up dust and dirt to smearing blood, until, eventually, their patterns are no longer distinct in the swirls of blood that cover the floor.

Taking it all in, I see what Cross was talking about in

Walker's office. Though there are bloodstained prints on the ground, there's no sign that the person wearing those bloody shoes ever left the scene. No transfer stains anywhere near either of the doors, just dirty concrete. I make a note to compare the tread patterns on the floor with the victims' shoes and hope there will be enough to indicate that Steve was the assailant. I doubt I'll get him to talk, not with how he's changing. And supernatural testimony is all well and good, but the physical evidence has to back it up. To end an investigation without a conviction will take a hell of a lot of proof that our ghost is also our killer.

I also look around the room for a good place to put down a Burning circle. With Steve's odd behavior and the dangerous energy that fills the basement, I don't want to run the risk of him Turning and me being caught unaware. Like I told Cross earlier, most spirits take a long time to Turn, giving Burners ample opportunity to put down protections before they actually send the spirit on. With how quickly Steve is changing—and the unusual way he's doing it—I want to be as careful as possible.

Unfortunately, there aren't many places where I can put the circle. I don't know how the energy will impact my rune work, and the blood complicates things further. There's a small space in the far corner of the room that might work, but I'm not going to be able to put chalk to concrete until after the scene is cleared. It leaves me feeling uneasy, but I make a note on my map of the scene and head toward the stairs, also noting the changes to the energy lines I made the day before.

I find Cross outside, talking quickly to an unsettled-looking man in a Tyvek suit.

"I promise you, the ghost is gone right now," he says, nodding toward me as I approach. "Detective Phillips is a Medium. She'll confirm."

"The ghost is gone," I say. "For now, at least. To be on the safe side, I'll stay on scene while your team finishes up processing."

Though still a little pale, he seems relieved to hear it. "I'll get as many guys down there as I can. I don't think anyone wants to stay inside that building any longer than they have to."

"What was he doing earlier?" I ask.

"Making noises, startling techs. Bumping into things or moving our kits around. It was annoying at first, but then he started pushing and grabbing us, and that's when we all got out of there."

"He was physical with you?" Cross asks, shocked.

The tech nods furiously, sensing a captive audience. "Yeah, he nearly made Gary fall down the stairs, it was the scariest thing. I thought that ghosts couldn't do that, you know?"

They're certainly not supposed to, Priya says, glancing at Cross, then me. *Especially brand-new ones.*

"If anyone starts feeling physical contact from the ghost," I say as I fight to keep my expression neutral, "I'll be here to stop him from causing any real harm."

"You don't know how much better that makes me feel, Detective," he says with a relieved smile. "Like I said, we'll get cracking as soon as I'm done talking with you."

"Then consider this conversation over," I say. "I don't know how long he'll be gone."

The tech's expression sobers, and he hurries toward the Forensics van still on scene, yelling out a series of names as he gathers the rest of his team together.

"You're going to babysit the scene, huh?" Cross asks as we watch the techs start to quickly mobilize.

"Probably for the best," I sigh. "I still don't understand where Steve's gone or when he'll be back, and he's definitely on his way to Turning."

"You want me to go looking for the marker?"

"Depends," I say. "Can you see the energy it's drawing in?"

Cross's eyes go unfocused, and after a moment, he nods. "Yeah, I can see it."

"Then you need to get a map of the area and find the closest cemetery. The last two markers were in fairly large ones. Seems like they might be connected."

"Oak Woods is nearby," he says thoughtfully. "You think that could be it?"

"It'd be a good place to start."

"What should I look for?"

I shrug. "Creepy-ass ghost ladies?"

Cross huffs out a quiet laugh. "Duly noted."

"More seriously," I say, grinning, "you want to follow the power. It'll get stronger as it approaches the marker, like it's being directed that way. Take the car, and if you see anything like that, you call me, and I'll head your way. I can catch a ride back to HQ and grab my car."

"Sounds like a plan," he says. He jingles the car keys in his pocket as he gives me a long, considering look. "You be safe, okay?"

"I'm always safe," I say, trying for carefree nonchalance. "There's nothing to worry about. I've got this guy under control."

Cross has the decency to not laugh in my face, but the corner of his mouth kicks up a bit as he fights back a smile. "You rarely have things under control, Phillips, but I trust you to handle yourself. Keep me up to date on what happens here."

"Of course," I say. "Now get moving. If we're going to stop this from getting any worse, we need to find that marker."

He salutes, then heads toward the car. I watch him walk away, his long coat swaying with each step.

You think he'll be able to find the marker? Priya asks.

I think it'll be good practice for him, I reply, *and it keeps him out of trouble here.*

You know he's safe with those wards.

And I also know that the rest of the people here don't have the luxury of wards and need protection.

Which is you, Priya says pointedly.

Which is me, I agree. *And since there are other things that need to be done, and Cross doesn't need to be here or be saved by yours truly, he can go find the marker.*

You sure you're not just putting him at arm's length?

I pause, considering. *No, not this time. Whatever's going on between us, that's not why I'm sending him out scouting.*

That's a lot of faith to put in someone who's newly Sighted.

It's Cross, I say as if that explains it all. Priya nods, a soft smile on her face.

What do we do about our friend downstairs?

I frown, eyeing the house. *I need to go through the scene with the techs anyway. I'll stay on guard, stick to Second-Sight, and if he shows up, we'll Burn him. Though I'd love to know why you don't want to be in the room with him.*

I don't really know, she says slowly. *It's almost instinctual. He feels like a predator to me, like if I turn my back or let him get close, he'll try to hurt me.*

Makes sense, I say. *He sets my alarm bells ringing, too. Even before he started Turning. Keep yourself safe. We'll figure out how to make it work.*

I spend the rest of the morning in the basement, walking through the room with the techs and keeping an eye out for Steve. It hurts to be in the basement, the energy so interlaced with the concrete floor that there's nowhere to stand that isn't filled with the stuff. It bites at my senses, small pinpricks of pain that leave me flinching as I move through the scene. It's exhausting, and my patience frays as the morning drags on.

There's thankfully no sign of Steve's ghost, but a persistent sense of unease permeates the area. Forensics is able to wrap things up quickly, finishing up their photos and evidence gathering a little after noon. Stomach rumbling, I help them move their supplies back into their van, speeding up the tear-down process to get people out of the space as quickly as possible. When the lead tech goes to tear down the inner perimeter tape, I stop him with a hand on his arm.

"Keep it up," I say as he stills. "I'm not releasing the scene until I get that ghost out of there."

"Understood, Detective," he says. I take my hand away and direct him to take the lead up the steps.

I hope you'll be back, Steve says.

I whip around to find him standing mere inches behind me. I take a cautious step back toward the stairs and wish I had my knife in hand instead of tucked into my boot.

I'm sure you have more questions, he continues with a crooked grin. *I know I do.*

His smile begins to deform, the corners of his mouth pulling farther and farther back until his face is split all the way to his ears. Blood seeps down his chin and drips onto the floor, and through it all, his eyes—a swirling mix of black, white, and gray—stay locked on mine. My heel knocks into the bottom step, and I stumble a bit. Steve's jagged, bloody grin widens.

Watch your step, Burner. Wouldn't want anything to happen to you.

Don't worry, I tell him as he drifts after me, stopping at the doorway. *I'll see you again real soon.*

He watches me as I make my slow, cautious way out of the basement. As soon as my foot crosses the line of wards, he disappears. Heart racing, I flag down one of the uniformed officers on scene.

"I need you to take me back to HQ." I flash my badge. "Now."

CHAPTER FIFTEEN

When I get back to HQ, I hurry to my desk and fall into my screeching chair, fumbling for my phone. It rings a few times while I start pulling up case notes, and then the line picks up.

"Detective," Banks says, sounding surprised. "Two calls in one day. I should be flattered."

"What have you learned?" I skim the notes filling my computer screen.

"You called me four hours ago," she says, annoyed. "I'm not that much further along than I was this morning."

"I need something *now*." A few heads turn my direction, and I curse softly before lowering my voice. "Look, I think there's another marker, and it's fucking with my case. I need something to go on, either to find it or to stop it from doing whatever it's doing."

"Another marker?" Her voice perks up. "Where is it?"

"I don't know yet, but I'm working on that."

"That sounds promising," she says, her voice barely hinting at sarcasm, "but you said it was impacting a case you're working?"

"I've got a ghost on scene who's Turning," I stress, "and he's doing it fast. As far as I can tell, it's because there's an overwhelming amount of energy trapped in the building where he died. It looks exactly like what I saw at the first two markers, and whatever this stuff is? It's not helping. I need any info you can get me about those bindings and what they're doing, and I need it yesterday."

"Give me thirty minutes," she says, her voice tempered with caution. "I may not have more information about the markers themselves, but I may be able to help you find another one."

"Fan-fucking-tastic, Banks." I lean back in my chair with a sigh. "If I don't hear from you, expect a call."

"I'm flattered by all the attention, Detective. You sure you don't want to get that coffee?"

"You have something useful for me in thirty minutes, and I'll even pay."

She laughs. "It's a date, then. I'll talk to you soon."

I hang up, then turn back to the preliminary reports from the day before, especially the medical examiner's. I see that the full autopsy isn't scheduled for a few more days, and I consider calling in a personal favor with Abramo to push it forward before dismissing the idea. For now, his prelim report is enough to confirm my fears.

When a ghost manifests after their death, the way they manifest is dependent on their cause of death. Gunshot wounds, stabbings, falls, accidents, blood loss from any of the above. Whatever the cause, it's visible when the ghost manifests. Steve died because of blood loss and knife wounds, but there's nothing in the ME's report about injuries to his mouth. All of the damage to Steve's body is isolated to his chest, arms, and hands. No damage to his face.

Which means the way that Steve's face split open like one of the worm creatures in *Beetlejuice* is a physical sign that he's Turning, instead of his death. And not a subtle sign, either, but a blaring red neon one. I curse again and call Cross.

"You have any luck finding that marker?" I ask as soon as he answers.

"No hello?" he asks.

"Have you?"

He sighs. "It's somewhere here, but I can't tell where exactly."

"You mean at Oak Woods."

"Yes. But I can't tell which direction this energy is going. Any chance you can join in the hunt?"

"I'm on my way," I say, grabbing my keys and locking my computer. "I'll meet you at the visitor's center."

"How'd things go at the scene?"

"Forensics managed to finish up, and I don't think Scene Reconstruction is going to need to come back. Just to be safe, I've kept the scene cordoned off. I don't want anyone wandering in there with Steve Turning."

"Good call. Anything else worth noting?"

"Other than him showing up as I left and splitting his face in two, no," I say as I head back out of the building.

"That doesn't sound promising," Cross says, tone dry.

I grimace. "It's not. I'll see you soon."

Oak Woods Cemetery isn't far from HQ. Nearly two-hundred acres of burial grounds, it's not only one of the largest but also one of the oldest cemeteries in the city. I've paid it a few visits in my day, Burning ghosts who refused to pass on after their funerals, so I'm familiar with the area. As I draw closer, I let myself drift into Second-Sight, watching as thick lines of dark red energy course their way toward the cemetery. Whenever the car crosses one, I flinch at the electric pain. Red, blue-white, and green flames lick over my arm, flaring whenever I get too close to the lines of power running toward Oak Woods. The flashes of color are distracting, and mixed with the lancing pain, I'm sweating and nauseous by the time I arrive.

Cross is waiting outside of the visitor's center when I pull up. I park and join him, pulling my jacket close against the wind. The cool air does help calm my stomach, and I tilt my head back a little, enjoying the soothing touch of an ice-cold January wind on my heated cheeks. The weather is turning, the sky going cloudy and gray with the promise of more snow. Tombstones and mausoleums stretch out to the horizon, and I'm slightly overwhelmed by the sheer number of graves. Though I can't sense many ghosts here, there's still energy pooled from the many years and the many dead. It stings against my skin, and I shiver.

"Hey," Cross says as I approach, his hands stuffed deep into his pockets. "You want to tell me what you meant about Steve's mouth? What the hell is going on?"

"He's Turning," I say.

"I mean, I understand that from what I've seen. But that doesn't explain what you're talking about."

"Long story short, he's getting really bad, really fast. It's good that people aren't going to be going in and out of that scene anymore, but we have to get this marker figured out, and I have to Burn him. It's too dangerous to let him stick around any longer than he already has."

"All right then. Let's get this taken care of." He pulls his hands from his pockets to blow warm air into them. "It's so cold out here, I wouldn't mind being done quick so I can get back inside."

I nod, my breath fogging in the air, and fall into Second-Sight.

"What were you able to find?" I ask.

There are thick lines of energy running parallel to the road we're standing on, and Cross points to one to the left of us, then to the right.

"They're moving in opposite directions," he says, "or at least I think they are. I don't exactly know what I'm looking at."

I watch the streams for a moment, judging the ebb and flow of power in them, and exhale. "You're right. Good job catching that."

"Thanks. Which way do we go?"

"If it's flowing toward our crime scene, then that's the one we want to follow," I say and take a step to the left, following the stream of power there. It twists its way through the graves, tangling in and out of tombstones as it meanders toward whatever end point it has. There's a stinging warmth across my body that feels as though I'm standing too close to a fire. The pain gets worse when I get closer to the stream, then fades as I move away. I clench my teeth against it, fighting to stay focused on the line of power.

"I think I understand how this stuff moves, but how can you be sure?" Cross asks. It's a genuine question, not a complaint, but it draws my focus away from the sting of the energy. Mind fuzzy and concentration broken, I have to fight my way back into Second-Sight before answering.

"If you keep an eye on it, there's a certain way that the energy shifts. If you watch for a while, you can see the way those shifts translate into a current, and then you track the flow. It takes time, though, and concentration."

"Keep practicing?"

"Keep practicing." I nod. "And let me focus. We're getting closer."

The energy slows down, and the tendril we're following thickens like a river reaching a delta. Eventually, the power ends in a massive pool in front of a towering white memorial. The reservoir of energy is huge. It stretches before us, at least fifty feet across. It's slightly ovoid in shape, with the sides bulging a little. I've never seen anything like it, and the pain of it is like pins and needles that never end.

In the center of the pool is a tall, white granite obelisk. Capping the top is a bronze statue of a soldier, gun by his side, looking out into the distance. The base is encircled with plaques embossed with barely legible names. Carved images cover the smaller, secondary base to the monument—soldiers rallying to battle, then falling only to return to a ruined home—and interspersed between all of them are runes and sigils, hidden within the text and images.

"Jesus Christ," I whisper, throat closing around the words as a wave of nausea rolls over me.

"Shit," Cross agrees, his eyes unfocused as he stares at the pool before us. "What the fuck do we do with *this*?"

"I don't know." I'm dumbfounded and shivering with cold and the ache brought by the energy. The binding looks similar to the ones I saw earlier, but it's hard to tell from this distance, and there's no way I'm setting one foot inside the borders of the pool.

My phone goes off, its ring echoing loudly through the cemetery. I startle and fumble for it, fingers cold and awkward, and check the name. It's Banks, and I pick up before pressing the phone to my ear.

"You owe me a coffee," she singsongs. "I can find that marker for you."

"You've got a bad habit of being late," I say. My voice sounds strangled. "We found it."

"But I bet you'd still like to know what it's doing," she says, still half singing.

"Banks," I say carefully, "I am looking at a literal metric fuckton of dangerous, dark energy right now. Can you cut to the chase?"

She sighs. "You can't simply enjoy the moment, can you, Detective?"

"Not this one, no."

"All right." She draws the words out. "Based on what you showed me at the other marker, these things are meant to gather the naturally occurring energy in an area. Once it's gathered, the binding holds it in to wait for something. I haven't been able to tell exactly what, though. It's incredibly hard to determine the reason for a binding. Runes, as you know, describe things, while the sigils describe action, so when you look at the entire—"

"Banks," I say, voice raised as I interrupt her. "Is that it? Nothing else?

"They're also channeling the energy," she says, her voice more hesitant, cautious, this time. "As we find more of these markers, we can plot out where the energy is being funneled. Right now, all I can say is that it is."

"What about the ghosts I saw at the other markers?"

"I'm still working on that angle," she says. "It seemed like the most important part was helping you find the thing, and you had to go and fuck that up for me."

"I'll still get you a coffee."

"Gourmet," she says primly. "I don't want you showing up with a cup from Dunkin'."

"Fine, whatever'll keep you working on this. Call me if you learn anything else, and plan on coming out to Oak Woods Cemetery as soon as you can. I need you to see this."

"Yes, Detective," she says before hanging up.

I stuff my phone back into my pocket, eyes quickly falling back on the pool of energy surrounding the obelisk. Body shivering with pain and cold, I tentatively step closer to the edge of the pool. A shock ricochets through me, and I clench my teeth against it.

"What'd she have to say?" Cross asks, watching me

carefully.

"Not much. Only that these markers are gathering energy for some reason."

"I could tell you that from looking at this thing," he says on an exhale. "What do we do?"

"Break it, I guess."

But how? Priya asks, floating toward the edge of the pool. She reaches out and her hand meets a barrier. She presses against it, then lets her hand drop, fingers trailing over the invisible wall before falling at her side. *It's warded like the last one*, she Sends.

"Do you see a ghost?" I ask out loud, mainly for Cross's benefit.

"I'm not seeing much of anything except for whatever that is," he says. "And you think this is what's causing Steve to Turn so quickly?"

"I think, whatever this stuff is, it's not good for anyone, Steve included. I don't know who's gathering this energy or for what purpose, but from what I've seen of it so far, it doesn't lead to anything positive."

"How'd you Burn the other two?" Cross asks. "I missed the first one, and I was out during the second."

I remember blood coating the first ghost, smothering him in a layer of red that was almost black. And the second, smiling at me as her form was covered in ghostly flames, laughing as she was Burnt.

"To be honest," I say as I wrap my arms around myself, trying to hold back the painful shivers that rack my body, "I don't really know how I did it."

"Did you draw a circle? Throw energy at something or someone?"

"I followed my gut," I say.

"What's your gut say?"

"To get the hell out of here."

Kim, Priya says quietly. I turn to look at her. She's staring at the monument, eyes trained upward. I follow her line of sight and freeze.

"Cross." I take a step toward him and grab his coat sleeve before pointing to the marker. "Are you seeing this?"

The soldier at the top of the monument shifts, the metallic skin shimmering in the fading light. Slowly, a figure steps out of the statue. He's wearing what appears to be a gray uniform, the sleeves frayed and torn, a huge bloodstain covering the upper left side of his chest. The brim of his flat, circular cap pulled low over his eyes, he steps off the edge of the monument to sink down, slowly. His gaze is trained on something I can't see, and he takes careful, precise steps toward the edge of the pool as if marching on a parade ground.

"As if this day couldn't get any fucking weirder," Cross says. "Is that guy a Confederate goddamned soldier?"

I nod, mouth gaping. "He's hundreds of years old," I whisper. "I didn't think ghosts could get that old without Turning. Oh my God."

We need to be very, very careful, Priya Sends. *There's no telling what state his mind will be in after all of this time.*

The ghost turns, his movements crisp, and starts

marching back toward the obelisk. Priya and I watch, fascinated, as he continues his patrol.

"Something isn't right about this," Cross says hesitantly. "Just… Stay here for a moment."

"What?" I turn as Cross walks toward the monument. He steps into the pool of energy, and his wards flare. The dark energy pushes away from him, repelled by the light coursing off of his body. I stagger after and reach out to grab him, but the energy closes behind him like the wake of a ship, and I'm forced to stop at the edge of the pool, helpless as I watch him move farther and farther away.

Meanwhile, the ghost stills in his marching, his head turning to follow Cross's progress across the ground. His stoic expression shifts into a frown, brow furrowed in confusion. The ghost takes a hesitant step, then another, until he's marching toward Cross with a deliberate, slow pace.

"Cross!" I yell, arms tightening around my chest. "Get back here! You're about to have company."

He turns, and his eyes widen as soon as he sees the ghost. Cross picks up his pace, his long legs eating up the distance between him and the small informational plaque in front of the monument. He scans it quickly, occasionally glancing up to gauge the ghost's progress, and then a grin splits his face.

"This isn't a monument for Confederate soldiers wounded in battle," he says, pointing to the dark stain covering the ghost's chest. "It's for prisoners of war."

The ghost stops at this, then looks between Cross and me before he sighs loudly.

Why did they have to put that damn sign up? he asks, groaning.

I freeze and look to Priya, who appears as confused as I feel.

What? I Send, glancing back.

The ghost rolls his eyes. *Great. You're a Medium. There goes my fun for the day.*

"What's going on?" Cross asks as he heads back toward me, moving in a wide circle around the ghost. "He doesn't sound like he's from the Civil War."

"No," I say slowly, "he doesn't."

Geniuses. I'm surrounded by geniuses.

You're modern, I Send.

No shit. He laughs. *You think a ghost would stick around that long? This thing was put up in the late 1800s. No way there'd be anyone even remotely coherent from that long ago.*

So, what are you doing here? I ask, feeling lost.

He grins a wide, happy smile that hints at mischief. *I'm scaring tourists.*

CHAPTER SIXTEEN

P riya laughs. *What?*

Yeah, he says, turning to face her. *It's not like I can drink beer or play softball anymore. This seemed like a good way to stay entertained and pass the time.*

His gray uniform falls away to reveal a baseball tee, dark athletic shorts, and a pair of shin guards that rest above worn and dirty cleats. His Confederate cap morphs into a battered and sun-bleached Cubs hat, and he twists it around so that the brim is pointed back. I can make out a dark, ugly bruise covering his temple from under the band of the hat. Eyeing the injury, I guess that it may be his cause of death.

How long have you been here? I ask.

Oh, not very long, I don't think. Time gets a little hard to track once you die, you know. No newspapers, no social media. There're the seasons, but in Chicago, even those don't necessarily make sense.

Do you know what year you died? Priya floats a little closer, clearly intrigued.

2009, he says. *Spring.*

You look pretty good for being gone six years, I say. *Better than I'd expect.*

He grins and gives me a quick once-over. *You're not looking too bad yourself, considering.*

Considering what? I ask, frowning.

You're going through the change, right? It always messes with people, but you seem to be handling it well. I bet this place is killing you right now, though. I remember it hurt to be around the focal points when it happened to me.

Priya and I look to each other, then back to the ghost. *When what happened to you?*

He laughs. *When I got my second Affinity.*

Mediums can't get second Affinities, I say to Priya, keeping the Sending focused so the other ghost can't overhear.

You got one, she says and eyes the blue, red, and green flames coating my body. *Maybe two.*

I thought it had to do with Baker, though, I Send. *This guy is saying it happened to him. Like it's normal.*

You ladies want to share with the class? He grins at us, floating closer to the boundary between the pool of energy and the rest of the cemetery. *It's rude to pass notes.*

What do you mean by focal points? Priya asks.

That giant thing behind me? he says with some confusion. *The point that's focusing all of this energy?* He laughs. *You really must be new to this if you're asking me that.*

When I don't answer and continue to look at him in stony silence, he lets out a heavy sigh. *They used to be better about training you guys. That's why you're here, right? Someone sent you to talk to me, to make sure this is all going the way it's supposed to? That the tears aren't getting worse?*

I go still at the words. A faint echo of a memory plays

through my mind, of Caroline Moore and Joseph Baker facing off over a fallen table, my grandmother stepping in to calm the situation, and talk of tears and Turning.

The ghost must notice the sudden tenseness in my body because his brow furrows, and he looks between Priya and me. His grin fades. *You* were *sent here. Right?*

Something drew me, I say, hedging, *yes.*

That's not what I said. He goes cold, his eyes flashing black for a brief moment. *Why are you here?*

Why is this energy here? I shoot back. *What's it doing? And what do you mean by tears?*

Priya glares at me. *Why we're here isn't important,* she says, drawing the ghost's attention back to her. *We need to know what's going on. You said they used to be better at training. Is there a group organizing these things, these*—she gestures toward the obelisk—*focal points?*

Nuh-uh, he says with a shake of his head. *You weren't sent here, and I've already said too much. If you're not already in the know, then you're not supposed to be, and I'm not going to be the one to change that.*

What about the change you mentioned earlier? Priya asks again, moving as close to the edge of the pool as she can. *You said what's happening to Kim happened to you.*

The ghost holds up his hands and retreats, backing toward the obelisk. *I already told you, I'm not saying another word. Now, why don't you grab your apprentice and get the hell out here?*

I'm not leaving until you answer our questions, I say, moving closer to the pool of power.

And that's not happening, he says. He puts his hands down, fists clenched, before coming to stand opposite me. His eyes start to glow white, and I taste burning ozone at the back of my mouth. *These things are secret for a reason.*

Then I guess we have a problem.

Kim, Priya cautions. *Let's take a step back, regroup.*

We don't have time to regroup, I Send back. *This guy has information that we need. He knows why these markers exist. He knows what this energy is doing. He even knows about my Affinity changing. We have to get answers from him.* I shoot him a glare. *One way or another.*

The ghost laughs. *You really don't know anything, do you? You're completely in the dark.*

Why don't you change that and tell me what's going on?

Like you told your apprentice over there that you're not just a Burner anymore? How many other Affinities have you gained at this point? I'd guess at least one.

I glance at Cross whose eyes are trained on the ghost, listening intently to whichever parts of the conversation he can hear.

He knows.

That's funny, especially considering how little you seem to understand about what's happening. And what about him? Judging from those wards I saw earlier, he's got his own set of shit to deal with. The ghost floats closer to Cross, who takes a small step back before stopping and squaring his shoulders. *She tell you anything about the ride you're in for?*

I can't hear Cross's response, but the ghost laughs and shakes his head.

If you really think that, you're an idiot. Look, he says, turning his attention to all three of us. *You seem like reasonable people, but it's pretty clear that you're all in over your heads. Best scenario is you turn around and walk away. I won't go after you, you don't come after me. We'll be like two ships, passing in the night.*

I need to know what you know, I say, gesturing toward the large pool of gathered power. *This stuff is dangerous. It's Turning ghosts. Whatever you're doing here, it's going to hurt someone.*

He huffs out a laugh. *You really think this stuff is making someone Turn? How do you explain me, then? I've been surrounded by it for six years, and I'm fine. Totally lucid, no signs of Turning.*

I… I frown. I don't know. But at every one of these I've been to, there's been a Turned ghost, and I've had to Burn them.

He freezes. *How many have you found?*

Now look who has questions.

You destroyed them, he says, voice going icy. *You have no idea what you're messing with here.*

But you do. So why don't you start talking?

He opens his mouth to speak but stops himself. Glancing first to Priya, then to me, he flits back and forth between the two of us before stopping in the middle. Slowly, he moves backward toward the monument, his hands clenching and unclenching as he goes.

"What are we going to do, Kim?" Cross asks, dragging out the words as he keeps his eyes trained on the ghost, who finally fades into the obelisk and out of sight. "You got a plan for this?"

"No," I say before cursing. "I told Banks I'd wait for her before touching another one of these things. And it seems like our fake Johnny Reb here knows a hell of a lot more about what's going on than we do."

Cross walks to me, passing through the pool of energy as if it's not there. I shiver as I watch it part around him.

"You don't feel that?" I ask when he finally stops in front of me.

He shakes his head. "Other than the cold, I'm not feeling anything."

Remind me to reapply my wards when we get home, I Send to Priya before I'm racked by another wave of pain. Cross puts his hand on my shoulder and gently rubs my arm until it passes.

"You going to be okay?"

"I'll be fine," I say as he pulls his hand away. "Banks needs to get her ass here, pronto. And we need to figure out how to get that asshole"—I gesture toward the monument behind me with my middle finger—"to spill."

I pull my phone out of my pocket and text her for an ETA. After a moment, she replies that she's on her way and about twenty minutes out. I curse softly.

"Let's go wait in the cruiser," Cross suggests. "It'll at least be warm."

I nod and fight back a shiver. He leads the way, keys jangling in his hand, and we head toward the visitor's center. I feel eyes on my back, and when I glance over my shoulder, I catch the ghost peeking out from the monument. He freezes and disappears back inside the carved stone in a blink.

I don't feel his eyes on me again.

Cross is already climbing into the car and turning the engine on by the time I come around the side and clamber into the passenger seat. Heat turned on full, blowers maxed out, he leans forward to hold his hands in front of one of the vents. He pulls them back within moments, letting out a frustrated sigh as he falls back into his seat.

"Engine's gone cold," he says.

"You think maybe we should talk about the ghost instead of the climate control?"

He has the decency to look chagrined. "It seems like there's a pattern with them, at least. Wherever those markers are, there's always been a ghost tied to them."

"He called them focal points," I say, wondering. "But focal points for what?"

It's got to be more than just that pooled energy, Priya says. *Andrea said that they're directing, not simply holding it. I think the different markers could be connected, like guideposts or something.*

"But guideposts for what?" Cross asks.

"We'll find out more when Banks gets here," I say. "In the meantime, we have to figure out what we're going to do about this guy."

"What do you mean?"

"I mean, am I Burning him or what? This energy isn't safe, and whatever those 'focal points' are doing isn't good, either."

You're sure about that? Priya asks, her tone uncertain. *He's definitely not Turned, and the two other ghosts we found? I don't know that they were truly Turned, either.*

"What do you call them, then?"

That first guy seemed like an asshole. And the woman… Priya's voice trails off. *She wasn't safe, but her behavior still seemed different from that of a Turned ghost.*

"She tried to choke Cross," I say.

He reaches for his neck but stops. "She didn't hurt me that much," he says with a shrug.

I roll my eyes. *Men.*

"So, what? We leave this shit here?"

"Do you want to know what I think?" Cross says. "I think we get that guy to talk. Like you said, he knows way more than we do about what's happening. He's been stuck here for six years, right? He already admitted that he's getting bored. We could probably do some kind of information exchange. He's a Cubs fan. Maybe we can tell him how they did this season."

"They finished last in the division," I say, annoyed. "I don't think he's going to be happy to exchange his supersecret info for that nugget of trivia."

"He's *bored*," Cross persists. "Two homicide detectives, one of them a Medium? We've got to have something worth trading."

It's not a bad idea, Priya agrees. *He has information that we need. We should figure out how to get it from him.*

"If it's all about what we don't know, why don't we start with what we *do* know. One," I say, ticking the number off on my finger, "we've been running into more and more ghosts who are Turning instead of passing on.

Two"—another finger—"this energy has suddenly started cropping up all over the city. Three, it's all over our crime scene and the spirit there *is Turning*. How does that not add up to something that needs to be dealt with?"

"Johnny Reb said something about that, didn't he?" Cross asks, looking between me and Priya. "That someone would have sent us to make sure everything was doing what it's supposed to be doing. If it's not, maybe it has something to do with the increase in Turned ghosts you're seeing."

He knows what's going on, Priya reiterates. *I know you're freaked out about the power, but we need to find a way to work with him.*

"So, how do we get him to talk? Cubs trivia notwithstanding, how do we bribe someone who's dead? It's not like he needs money."

Quit your bellyaching, Priya says. *Once Banks gets here, we'll figure out a plan.*

"While we're on the subject of Turned ghosts," Cross says, "let's talk about Steve. Did you have a chance to read the ME's preliminary reports?"

I nod. "We'll need the full autopsy before we can say for certain, but it's looking like he's our perp. But why were they in that basement?"

"And, more importantly, who's the woman, and why did Steve kill her?" Cross looks at me and cocks his head. "How likely is it that you can get Steve to tell you what happened?"

"I don't know," I say, thinking back to the way his mouth split open, hinging his entire face in two. "He's losing his grip on reality pretty fast. I'm not entirely sure whatever he tells us from this point on would be considered admissible."

Cross sighs. "I never paid enough attention to this shit at the Academy. You don't think he'll give us a confession?"

"Oh, I think he'll confess to something," I say, "but I don't think there's any guarantee it'll be accurate. Let's assume he knew the victim and had a motive for the killing. If that motive had any kind of logical basis, that logic will get twisted the more he Turns."

"So, no admissible confession is what you're saying."

"Probably not," I agree. "But it seems like there's enough physical evidence that we won't need it."

The car falls silent except for the rush of hot air from the vents. The windows are starting to fog, though the windshield is still clear from the defroster. I stare through the condensation, tracing my eyes up and down the long lines of graves, wondering at the mess this has all become.

"You're still going to try, aren't you?"

Cross's question breaks me from my reverie. "Still try what?"

"Getting him to confess."

I think about it for a moment and shake my head. "Probably not, no."

"Why?"

"Honestly?" I shrug. "I don't think I'm going to have to try that hard to get him to talk. Steve… He wants to talk about death. If he killed that woman, he'll want to tell me all about it."

Before he tries to kill you, Priya says matter-of-factly.

"Why are you so bothered by him?" Cross asks, turning to face Priya. "I don't get the sense that this is how you normally respond to Turned spirits."

"It isn't," I say, shifting my focus to my ghostly partner. "And you've never actually explained yourself."

He's like a rotten tooth, Priya says, *or a wound that won't heal. He feels gangrenous to me. Putrid. Even before he started Turning, he was decaying from the inside out. The changes he's undergoing now? I think it's that corruption finally breaking through. He was human before. Now, he's turning into something different, something predatory.*

"Still doesn't explain why you won't go into that basement."

Infection, she says simply. *I can't risk him trying to take me down with him. There's a power to him that I don't understand. Maybe it's from that energy. Maybe the ghost in the monument can tell us more. Whatever the case, I won't get close to Steve. Not unless I have to.*

"Hopefully, you won't have to," Cross says reassuringly. "I'm sure our Burner extraordinaire will take care of him, no sweat."

"Your support is noted and appreciated," I say, leaning back in the seat and kicking my feet up on the dashboard. "But we'll have to play this very carefully, whenever we decide to get rid of the guy. He was unpredictable before. That's only going to get worse the longer we wait."

Cross looks out the window and grins. "Then we

should see what Ms. Banks has to contribute to the conversation." He tips his chin toward my window. "I think she just pulled up."

I turn to see he's right. Banks climbs out of her black two-door car, all elegance and sophistication in a long, black coat that hits right above her knee. She waves at me, a quick wiggle of her fingers, but the black leather gloves she's wearing make the movement into a challenging, rather than a childish, motion. I sigh heavily and reach for the door while Cross laughs.

"You seriously don't like her, do you?" he asks, and I can hear the smile in his voice.

"At least the feeling's mutual."

"I wouldn't be too sure about that," Cross says as he turns off the car.

I laugh. "Oh, I'm certain of very few things in life, Cross." I open my door. "But I can say with absolute certainty that the woman doesn't like me one bit."

CHAPTER SEVENTEEN

I step out of the car and nearly bump into Banks who has her hand stretched out to me, a paper coffee cup clasped in her gloved fingers. I pause, confused.

"I know you said you'd buy the coffee," she says, giving the cup a small shake, "but with how cold it is today, I couldn't wait. Figured I'd bring you one, too."

When I continue to stare at the cup in her outstretched hand, she sighs and starts talking in a slightly raised voice. "Why, thank you, Ms. Banks. How considerate of you. I will be certain to return the favor in the near future. Why don't I show you the only thing you'd come out to a cemetery on a Tuesday afternoon in the freezing cold to see?"

I snatch the coffee from her, and she grins widely. Cross walks around the side of the car and stands awkwardly to the side as I finally close the passenger door. Banks gives him a long, considering look from head to toe. Clearly, she likes what she sees because her smile turns coy and calculating.

"And who might this be?" she asks me, batting her eyelashes at Cross. "I don't believe you'd mentioned a partner before. Certainly not one this handsome."

Cross grins. "Detective Riley Cross." He shakes her hand. "I've heard an awful lot about you, Ms. Banks."

"I'm afraid I can't say the same," she says, her tone colored with remorse. "And that is a damn shame, if I do say so."

"Don't let me stop you," he says, grinning so wide I could put my whole fist in his mouth if I punched him in it. I glare at him, then at Banks.

"I wasn't aware you'd be joining us today," she continues. "Detective Phillips didn't make me aware that you were involved in her... off-duty responsibilities."

Shit.

"I was interested in what she does when she's not working," Cross says without any hint of concern. "She was kind enough to drag me along."

"Well"—Banks turns her eyes to me—"this should be an edifying experience for you, then. Detective, if you'd lead the way?"

I nod and turn my back on the two of them as I head toward the monument. Priya cackles.

She thinks he's cute, she says, in a teasing tone. *What're you going to do about it?*

Nothing, I say. *It's not my business.*

You want it to be your business.

But it's not.

But it could be.

Priya. This is not the time.

All right, all right. Fair point. She grins. *I couldn't help myself. I'm sorry. The look on your face, I swear.*

I can find a new partner, I warn her.

No, you can't, she says, still grinning. *Let's get focused, shall we?*

I wasn't the one who… I sigh. *Okay, focused.*

"You should be able to see it by now," I tell Banks, who's trailing behind me by a few steps. "It's that large monument." I point. "Hard to miss."

"I hate that thing," she says with a groan. "Whoever thought it would be a good idea to put up a monument to dead racists on the South Side of Chicago was an idiot."

"It was a different time," Cross says with a wince.

"I'm pretty sure they knew what they were doing." Her voice is thick with annoyance. "So, this is our third marker, huh?"

I nod. "I can't get too close to it. Whatever this energy surrounding it is, it causes me problems."

"I can see that," she says, eyes slightly unfocused as she looks from the monument to me. Her eyes widen, then turn calculating. "I don't know that I've ever seen that particular display of power, Detective. You continue to intrigue."

"Can you go take a look at it?" I ask, brushing off her comment. "See if it's anything like the other one?"

"Absolutely," she says. "Detective Cross, would you care to join me? I'd be happy to educate you on the finer points of bindings if you have an interest."

"Don't mind if I do." He shoots me a smug grin.

Together, Cross and Banks walk into the pool of energy. Cross's wards go off almost immediately, casting him in a soft, golden glow. Banks turns to Cross, eyebrows raised, and he gestures first to the obelisk, then to me. When she turns to face me, I smile, though it's tight and forced like a grimace. She shakes her head and turns back around.

Banks may have been surprised by Cross's wards, but they're not nearly as intense as the first time he walked into the pool. Looking at the softer glow emanating from him, a sudden twist of fear takes hold in my stomach.

He's fine, Priya says gently. *I think the wards are learning, like the ones you put up around the crime scene. There's some intelligence there.*

I don't know if that makes me feel any better.

They'll both be fine, another voice says from off to my right. I jump and spin, hand reaching for my gun. *You know that won't work, right? Already dead?*

It's the ghost from the monument, floating casually nearby. I drop my hand—slowly—and scowl.

Don't you have something better to do with your time? I ask. *Like tell me what the hell is going on?*

No, he says nonchalantly. *Scaring you seemed the better choice.*

Do you have a name or something? I ask, irritated as I watch Cross and Banks slow at the base of the monument. *I'd like to know who I'm cussing out.*

Frank, he says. *And it's not that I don't want to help you out, it's that I can't.*

That's bullshit.

There's a reason this shit is secret. You ever think about that?

I frown and shiver as another wave of pain washes over me. *Seems pretty stupid to me right now.*

I can feel him looking at me, but I refuse to take my eyes off of Cross and Banks. They're bent down near the base of the obelisk, Banks pointing at something while Cross nods attentively.

That's the pain talking, Frank says. *If you put up a shield, it'll help. Doesn't have to be a powerful one. Any barrier will make it better.*

I glance at him out of the corner of my eye, and I'm surprised to see a mix of compassion and sadness in his face. Pulling my eyes away before he notices, I gather power and put up a light shield. The relief is almost immediate, and my body sags with it. Muscles aching from being held tight for too long, I roll my shoulders to ease the discomfort. After a long, careful stretch, I look back at Frank and sigh.

Thanks, I Send begrudgingly. *I guess.*

Like I said: want to help, can't. He turns to face Cross and Banks. *You want to tell me what they're doing?*

You want to tell me how you got another Affinity?

He rolls his eyes. *Anyone ever tell you you're a stubborn ass? More than once.*

He laughs. *Look, you seem like a nice kid—*

Kid? We're the same age.

I was your age when I died, he says firmly. *I'm older now.*

Six years does a lot to age a man? I frown. *Don't patronize me.*

It's not the time. It's the responsibility. He gestures with his arm toward the pool of energy and the obelisk. *There's a lot riding on this that you don't understand, kid, and your friends there aren't going to be able to shed much light on it. Trust me on that.*

I think you underestimate how much of a stubborn ass I can be, I Send before strengthening my shield and pushing forward into the pool of energy. The pain of it lances through my body in an electric wave, but I grit my teeth and keep going.

You're also a bit of an idiot, aren't you? Frank says as he floats next to me.

I ignore him, pushing forward until I've joined Cross and Banks at the base of the monument. They're still hunched down, and Cross looks up as I approach. There's a slight hollow in the pool of energy around Cross—his wards keeping it at bay—and I take a step closer. He shifts his body so that I can stand next to him comfortably, and I sigh softly as the force of the energy against my shield lessens. I catch Banks looking at us but ignore it.

"What've you learned?" I ask, meeting Banks's eyes as she glances between Cross and me.

"First," she says, "this is way different from the other marker you showed me. The structure of the binding is similar, sure, but the execution is leaps and bounds more complicated than the last one."

"Explain it to me like I'm five," I say, a headache quickly growing, "and an idiot."

"If these are batteries, then the last one was a lemon with some wires stuck into it. This is lithium ion."

"What's that mean?"

"It means," Cross says, "that this can store more of whatever this power is and for longer."

Banks nods. "On top of that, there's no channeling. Based on the size and complexity of the rune work here, I think this—or another site similar to this one—is where the other markers were pushing their energy. It's all one circuit, but this seems to be the primary storage."

Seems like they're shedding plenty of light on the situation, I Send to Frank.

Fair enough, he agrees. *But you're still missing the big picture.*

"How do we unplug it?" I ask, and Frank's eyes flash white with surprise. He starts pulling in energy, his clothes whipping around him as an unseen wind kicks up. Eyes filled with white flames, he seems to grow with the power as he turns to face me, fists clenched.

There's no way I'm letting that happen, he says. His voice echoes in my head, and I flinch as it kicks my headache into high gear.

Priya whips into being beyond the barrier, her hair a riotous halo around her face, her eyes sparking white as she flies back and forth, unable to move forward. The energy coiled within my gut springs to life in the form of multicolored flames that course over my body. They wash away the pain with a warmth that I feel in my bones. I pour that same power into my shield and watch as its surface sparkles with blue, red, and green energy like a prism refracting light. Where the dark energy comes into contact with the shield, it evaporates, fading into an ephemeral cloud of fog that dissipates with the cold winds whipping through the cemetery.

Frank eyes the shield, the flames of power licking up and down my body, and Priya's vicious expression, then backs down, energy flowing out of him in a slow trickle until his shoulders slump and he shakes his head.

We both want the same thing here, he says. *And while I don't think you'd actually be able to undo any of this, I don't want to risk you trying. I'm not a killer, but I'll do whatever's necessary to protect this place.*

You touch my partner, Priya threatens from the boundary between the energy and the rest of the cemetery, *and you'll see what I'm willing to risk.*

That's very admirable, but there's no need for threats, all right? If you promise to leave this place alone, I'll answer some of your questions. He holds up a finger as soon as I open my mouth. *Not all of them, and I can't promise my answers will make much sense, but I'll tell you as much as I'm allowed. You have to promise me that you won't touch the focal point.*

It's not only up to me, I say, turning to Banks and Cross. They're both looking at Frank, bodies tense.

"Should I be worried, Detective?" Banks asks slowly.

"Not yet," Cross replies. "She gets pushy when it's time to be worried."

"He's offering to give us some answers if we leave this marker alone," I say. "I'm not sure it's a good call."

"Well," Banks says carefully. For the first time, her voice is hesitant, subdued. "I don't think it would be a good idea to simply turn this thing off."

"What do you mean?"

"I mean…" She pauses and bites her lip, thinking, then

perks up. "Have you seen *Ghostbusters*?" When I nod, she continues. "You know when they shut down the containment unit and everything goes to shit? I think it could be like that."

I like her, Frank says with a quick grin.

I don't remember asking your opinion.

"What are our other options, then? Can we disable it without pulling the plug?"

I feel Frank start to gather energy again, and I sigh. *Stop that.*

Not until I'm sure you aren't going to do something stupid.

I always do something stupid, I say, *but I'm not going to do anything stupid right now. We're talking, for Christ's sake.*

"No, I don't think so," Banks says, her eyes wide as she stares at Frank. "It's either on or it's off. There's no middle ground."

See? I say, and Frank lets the energy go again, his expression a little chagrined.

"You think we could take him?" I ask Cross, nodding toward Frank.

I'd like to see you try.

Cross looks uncertain. "I don't know, Phillips. I think you could probably do it, but I'm not entirely sure you should. He seems lucid, and if he's willing to talk... I don't see what we gain from it."

I look to him, then to Banks, then to Frank. With a nod, I start heading out of the pool, my senses still sparking with pain.

"Then let's start talking."

CHAPTER EIGHTEEN

I step out of the pool of energy and let my shield drop with a rush of relief. Cross and Banks are close behind, and Banks makes sure to keep Cross between her and Frank. As soon as we clear the boundary of the pool, Priya rushes to my side, flipping Frank off before trying to herd me farther away from the marker. I let her take the lead, watching as Frank stays close to the boundary, unable to move past the edge of the pool.

Where are you going? he asks, watching as we move farther away from the marker. *I thought you wanted to talk.*

We'll be back, I Send, giving him a pointed look. *Don't go anywhere.*

He eyes the edge of the pool, pressing his hand up against the invisible barrier between it and the rest of the world. *I don't think I've got much of a choice here, kid.*

Then we'll see you in a minute. Go see if any other tourists showed up.

He flips me off, and I return the gesture before turning back to the rest of the waiting group. We cross a small utility road and stop near the base of a bare tree, Banks farthest away from the marker, though it's still in sight.

I give her a look, eyebrow raised, and she flushes.

"I'm not warded," she explains.

I'm surprised, and my expression must show it because she ducks her head a little, suddenly bashful. "Considering how much you like runes, I figured you would be."

"I'm better with the theoretical, rather than the practical," she says, and her blush deepens.

She can't scribe? I ask Priya, slightly stunned.

Taka said she was Sighted, but he didn't say anything else about her abilities. Maybe that's why she's so fascinated by all of it.

"It's smart of you to stay back, then," Cross says, coming to stand next to me. "This guy seems reasonable enough right now, but there's no telling what he might do."

"Where do we want to start?" Banks asks, her usual self-confidence coming back quickly. "If he's going to answer questions, we need to make sure we're asking the right ones."

"I don't know if he'll give it to us straight," I say. "So, while he's talking, we'll have to pay close attention. He's likely to be evasive, and we can't let that trip us up."

"So, we start with the marker," Banks says. "Get him to tell us as much about it as he can."

"And what that power is and what it's being used for," Cross adds with a nod. "It's all tied together, so whatever information he can give us about it will help."

You need to ask him about your powers changing, Priya says quietly. *The rest of it is important, yes, but we can probably figure it out on our own, though it'll take time. That's not the case with what's happening to you.*

"Sounds like we have a place to start." I meet Priya's eyes and give her a small nod of understanding. "You two stay close, but Priya and I will do the questioning."

"Hold up." Cross frowns at me. "You can't go near that pool of energy without looking like you're going to throw up. That means you're going to be distracted and you're going to get sloppy. If we have to listen carefully, we also have to think carefully about what we're asking."

"I'll be fine," I say. He rolls his eyes.

"I'll take the lead on questioning, and you do follow-up. Trust me, it'll work out better."

I take in his earnest gaze, the certainty and confidence that he exudes, and after a long moment, I nod. "Okay. I trust you. But if he says something that seems odd to me, I'm going to jump in."

"That's fine," he says with a soft grin. "I'd be surprised if you didn't. So, the plan is markers first, then the energy, then any kind of follow-up. Let's go."

He takes purposeful strides back toward the obelisk, and I follow after him a little slower, not quite as confident as he appears to be. Banks stays close to my side, her expression contemplative as she stares at me. I raise an eyebrow, and she glances away, cheeks darkening.

"You got something you want to say?" I ask when I catch her looking at me again a moment later.

"Detective Cross," she says as way of introduction. "What's going on there?"

"What do you mean?" I ask, playing dumb.

"I mean I'm getting a vibe from you two." She smiles

as the heat creeps into my cheeks.

"A vibe. Very scientific."

"I write for the society pages. I've learned to read the tension between two people." She pauses, gauging my response, then smiles. "You're interested in each other."

"That's none of your business," I respond, eyes trained on Cross's back. If I make eye contact with Banks, I'll end up regretting it.

"I think it *is* my business," she says wryly, "since I've been trying to get you to agree to a date with me for the last three days."

"Wait, what?"

She laughs. "Really? You hadn't noticed?"

"You've been doing what now?"

"Why do you think I've been asking you about coffee incessantly?"

"I hate you," I say, stunned into rudeness. "I thought you hated me."

"That's a bit harsh," she says with a wince. "And, for the record, I don't hate you."

"I mean... I don't *really* hate you. Just... You tried to blackmail me for information about a series of murders. That's not what I'd call a great first impression."

"Your first impression of me was as a wrong number," she says wryly. "You probably thought I was going to be an overweight white guy. I'm obviously a much more pleasant surprise than that."

"Maybe, but you get my point."

"I get your point," she says. "I thought you were cute,

and the whole slightly gruff cop thing? It works for me."

"I'm not… I don't…" I fumble for words. "What?"

She brushes past my awkward question. "For what it's worth, I'm sorry. I knew I was pushing about the Mediums, but there's clearly more going on with those deaths than what was in the papers."

"If you swear it's off the record," I say slowly, "I can maybe answer some of those questions for you. But"—I hold my hand up, stopping her—"there are things I still don't understand about what happened, so I may not be able to answer everything."

"You sound like the ghost," she says with a slight grin.

"If I'm going to tell you about those deaths, you have to do something for me, though," I say.

"I thought I was, since I've taken the time out of my busy schedule to help you with these runes."

"You have to do one other thing for me," I amend. "You need to let Taka know I'm playing nice. He won't believe me if I tell him."

She laughs. "Taka dotes on you. He'd believe you if you said the sun set in the east and rose in the west."

"That's a bit much."

"Only a little," she says, her smile softening. "He's really proud of you. But if it'll help, I'll tell him."

"Thank you," I say.

"I get why you didn't pick up on things." She nods her head in Cross's direction. "Do you want to tell me what's going on between you two?"

"Absolutely not." I shake my head.

"I didn't think so," she says with a laugh.

I'm scowling when we finally approach the edge of the pool. Frank is waiting at the edge, arms crossed, fingers tapping impatiently against his sleeves.

"For the benefit of everyone," Cross says, gesturing toward our small group, "I'm going to ask questions out loud, rather than by Sending. If you could make sure to Send so that everyone hears your answers, that would be best."

Whatever you say, Apprentice, Frank says with an over-the-top eye roll. *Don't expect this to be that useful.*

"What can you tell us about the marker?"

First, it's not a marker. It's a focal point. Second, that's it.

"You don't hold up your end of the bargain," I say, taking a threatening step forward, "and I won't hold up mine."

If you want a fight, I don't have anything pressing on my schedule, he Sends, flaring with a sudden rush of power. *Kicking your ass would be a great way to end my day.*

"That's enough," Cross says, stepping between us. "Why are they called focal points? What are they focusing?"

The energy that you can clearly see here, Frank says, his eyes sparking white before they shift back to a more normal, muted gray.

"Phillips," Cross says, turning to me, "remind me what this stuff is again."

"Supernatural energy fills the world. It's more common in some places, less common in others. It generally gathers near the dead, but it can collect wherever something draws it in." I eye the obelisk. "This focal point would appear to be one of those things."

"Is there any use for it?"

"Other than helping to boost a Medium's powers, no, not that I'm aware of."

Cross turns back to Frank. "You mentioned a group earlier, people who trained others in how this all works. Are they using these focal points to gather this energy?"

No, they're using them to get free cable.

"I'll take that as a yes," Cross says with an annoyed exhale. "What are they using it for?"

For reasons. Ones I can't tell you.

I interrupt. "Is it about the tears?"

Frank tries to hide it, but he stills at the question, his face going tight as he fights to control his expression.

"It is," I say slowly. "But what kind of tears? What's getting torn?"

He doesn't respond and simply stares at me.

"Next question," Cross says, drawing Frank's attention back to him. "Why are you here? If these are giant batteries for Mediums, why put a ghost on guard?"

To keep people away who shouldn't be putting their noses where they don't belong.

"You're doing a great job," I snipe. "Keep up the good work."

Cross glares at me. "Not helping, Phillips."

"Sorry," I say, meaning it a little bit.

"Isn't there a risk in having you or any other spirit watch this place?" Cross continues. "What's to stop you from using this power yourself?"

Frank waits a beat, then lets out a long sigh. *Because I'm not just any ghost.*

"He was a Medium," Banks says suddenly. Cross and I start, then look at her. She glances between us and back to Frank. "He's not just any ghost, he's the ghost of a Medium. What Affinity?"

I was a Burner, he says, giving her a gentle smile.

"And what else?" I press. "You said you got a second Affinity. How?"

Can't tell you that, he says as Banks looks at him with wide eyes.

"That's not possible," she says with a shake of her head. "You get one Affinity. That's it."

"No, it's not," Cross says slowly, looking at me. I shake my head no, but he continues. "Phillips can Read now."

"Congratulations on your literacy," Banks says with a confused frown.

"No, Read-Read. Phillips, tell her."

I glare at him. "I don't know what you're talking about."

Yes, you do, Priya says gently. *He's already let the cat out of the bag, Kim. Between what Cross has already said and what Frank's been "not really telling us," she's going to figure it out.*

"You have another Affinity?" she asks, gray eyes wide. *Told you.*

"It's complicated," I hedge.

"No shit."

"It's not important right now," I say, turning back to Frank. "How did you get a second Affinity?"

I already told you, he says stiffly. *I'm not saying anything about that.*

"Do you know what this symbol means?" I ask, pulling a pen out of my jacket pocket and drawing a circle, quartered by a cross with one arm longer than the rest, and showing it to him. "What is this?"

Burner, he says, his tone somehow reverent. *It means Burner.*

"I fucking knew it." I close my hand over the rune and turn to Cross. "I bet all of those symbols had to do with the Affinities."

Banks takes my hand and unfolds my fingers, looking at the design. "It was all over that first marker you showed me, and I noticed it on this one, too." She lifts her eyes to Frank. "You were a Burner. Is that why the symbol is used here?"

Frank nods, the motion quick and a little jerky.

"So, there's a group of Mediums out there creating these focal points and protecting them with the ghosts of other Mediums. I'm going to assume that you," Cross says, tipping his head in Frank's direction, "were a part of said group, rather than a random guy they picked up off the streets. The energy gathered at these points is being used to presumably stop some kind of tearing from occurring. And whatever Phillips did with the other focal points was a bad thing. Does that cover it?"

It certainly sounds good, Frank says.

"And you can't tell us anything more than that?" I ask, moving closer to the energy though it sends pain ricocheting through me.

Frank gives me a sad, somewhat pensive, smile. *Sorry, kid.*

"Not even why this shit hurts me and apparently no one else?"

He meets my eyes, and when I wince as pain whips through me again, his shoulders sag. *All right, all right. It's because of how your connection to the afterlife is changing. You're more sensitive, more in tune with it right now. Once your powers stop changing, you won't notice this stuff as much.*

"And how long will that take?"

It depends, and I'm not saying that to be cryptic. Each Medium who goes through this experiences it differently. For me, it was a couple of weeks, no more than a month.

She's been dealing with this since November, Priya says somberly. *What does that mean?*

I don't know, Frank responds. *Probably nothing good.*

"What's he saying?" Cross asks, breaking my concentration. "He's not broadcasting whatever he's saying to everyone."

"It's nothing," I say, shooting Priya a glare when she opens her mouth. She closes it, but I can feel her displeasure down our bond. "I don't think we're going to get anything else out of him today."

"What about the ghosts Turning?" Cross asks. "There have been more, haven't there?"

How many? Frank asks.

"At least six since November, seven if you count the one that's Turning as we speak."

Be careful, he Sends, and the command echoes painfully in my mind. *If they're Turning that frequently and quickly, it's a sign that my friends aren't keeping up with their work.*

"These tears are getting worse," I say. He meets my eyes and gives a quick, almost imperceptible nod.

"So how do we help?" Cross asks.

You stay out of it, Frank says firmly. *Like I've said about a million times already, this is over your heads. You find any more of these*—he points to the marker behind him—*you leave them alone. Don't touch them, don't look at them, don't even think about them. My friends and I will figure this out.*

"Are you going to see these 'friends' of yours soon?" I ask. "It sounds like you're still in contact."

Again, he says, *none of your business.*

"Fine," I say with a shrug. "What do we do about this energy if we find it and it's not around a marker?"

He frowns. *You shouldn't find it except around a focal point. It dissipates naturally unless it's contained.*

"Contained by what?" Cross asks.

Natural boundaries. Fast-flowing water. Wards, sometimes, if they're strong enough.

Shit.

"How strong?"

If a couple Mediums were working together, that would probably do it. It's nothing a single person could put together on their own.

My shoulders start to relax.

Unless there's a lot of blood, he says, causing the tension to come right back. *Blood makes things less predictable, less controlled.*

Cross shoots me a look, and I shake my head. Now's not the time.

And that's all I'm going to say, Frank says as he starts to float toward the obelisk. *Keep your noses clean and stay out of this.* He eyes Cross and turns to me. *You've got enough to worry about already.*

With that, he disappears into the marble monument.

"I think we need to get back to our crime scene," Cross says quietly, his expression serious and slightly concerned.

"What about me?" Banks asks, looking between us and the monument.

"Here," I say, pulling out my notepad and writing on it. "This is the address for the other marker I found. When you have time, take a look at it. I want to know what's different between these three. It might shed some light on what they're doing and why."

"You don't believe this guy?" she asks sarcastically. "I'm completely surprised, Detective. You're usually so trusting."

"I don't know what to believe right now," I say with a bit more honesty than I intend. I tear the paper out and hand it to her. "Until we have all of the facts, I'm not willing to say what is or isn't true here."

"I can respect that," she says with a nod. "I'll stay in touch. Good luck with your case and let me know when you're going to buy me that coffee."

With a quick, small wave, she heads back toward the visitor center and her car.

"What are we going to do?" Cross asks. "At the crime scene, I mean."

"We need to see how Steve's doing," I say, thinking about the powerful wards, bound together with runes I found on one of the markers surrounding the house. "And fast."

CHAPTER NINETEEN

I t's a gray, cloudy day, one in the seemingly endless string of gray, cloudy days that make up winter in Chicago. The roads are dirty with slush and road salt, and Cross struggles to keep the windshield clear as we drive away from the cemetery. The whole world looks and feels dull and monotone, and when we reach the house at Sixty-Fourth and Wolcott, that sensation only increases. Some of it can be blamed on the weather, but there's a sense of desolation and defeat that seems to ooze out of the brick-and-mortar of the building.

"I don't remember it being this depressing," Cross says as we head toward the back basement steps.

"Something's amplifying it," I say quietly. "And since the only person, living or dead, who's here right now is Steve, I think it's safe to say that things are not going well down there."

Cross eyes the darkened stairs carefully. "What are we going to do about it?"

"*We* aren't going to do anything." I bend down to pull my knife from my boot. "*I* will go investigate."

You're sure that's a good idea? Priya asks.

"Probably not," I reply, "but I'm not putting the two of

you in harm's way if I can avoid it."

"You know that part of my daily job responsibilities is to put myself in harm's way if I have to."

"You don't have to." I glance up fast enough to catch Cross rolling his eyes.

"I'm not going to let you go down there by yourself," he says, taking my arm as I start to head toward the stairs. I let him stop me and turn as he gently tugs me closer. "I've got your back, same way you have mine, and it's safer for all of us if you're not alone with a ghost that's in the process of losing its mind."

"I'm not saying you're wrong," I say, "but I think some of what's happening to Steve is my fault."

"Your fault?" Cross looks annoyed. "Phillips, you need to stop it with this weight-of-the-world nonsense. Not everything is your fault."

I give him an exasperated look. "I know not everything is my fault, but in this particular case, I think some of it might be."

"Why?"

"Because I put up incredibly strong wards around a place that was filled with blood and energy, and I locked it all together with a series of runes from one of those focal point things."

Cross blinks at me, then lets his head fall back, eyes closed.

"And judging by how much energy is in this place now," I continue as I look around the yard in Second-Sight, "I may have created another focal point by accident."

Cross's head snaps up, and his eyes go unfocused as he drops into Second-Sight. He sees what I've been watching for the last few minutes. The lines of energy have thinned, no longer filling the backyard, but rather than dissipating, they've pooled in and around the house. There's a thin layer of the energy coating the ground around the foundation. It shifts and oozes, trying to move away from the house, to go back to where it started. But wherever my wards are, they stop the power from leaving. It sloshes up against the invisible barrier in thick, slow-moving waves of deep red. It moves like a living thing, trying to escape, and it makes me shiver.

Cross groans. "This is why you don't just *try* things."

"Look," I say, frustrated and more than a little scared, "this ghost was weird to start with. I needed to ward the house, so I warded the house. I didn't realize that this could happen."

He runs a hand over his face and breathes out slowly. "I get it, I do, but no more throwing things at a problem just to see what sticks, okay? Especially with ghosts."

"That's the other thing," I say, and Cross stares at me, unblinking.

"What other thing?" he asks in a monotone.

"I think Steve might be tapped into this stuff now."

"Why do you think that?"

"Because of what Frank said," I say slowly. "That he's not just any ghost."

He frowns. "You think it's important that Frank's a

Medium."

"They all were Mediums," I say. "And since Steve probably isn't one…"

Cross eyes the dark energy pooled around the house and sighs. "A Medium wouldn't misuse this stuff."

"But a Mundane person might," I say with a wince.

"Well done." He shakes his head and sighs.

"Yeah, go me. In the meantime, I'm—*we're*—going to have to figure out what to do about all of this."

"Were you able to get a binding circle put down earlier?" Cross asks.

"No," I say with a shake of my head, "but not for lack of trying. There was only one decent spot to scribe, and Steve forced me to leave before doing it."

"You think you'll be able to do it now?"

I eye the pooled energy that trickles down the basement stairs. "Maybe?"

"You don't sound very confident."

"I don't *feel* very confident." The joke falls flat, my voice shaking enough to hint at my growing fear.

"What about taking down the wards?" Cross suggests. "That'll stop holding the energy in."

"And it'll stop holding Steve," I say. "I can't let him out, not with how quickly he's Turning or with the way he's possibly misusing all of this power."

I don't like how this feels, Priya says. *Whatever is happening to him, it's getting worse by the second. It's like I can smell the rot coming out of there.*

"There's only one way to figure out how this is going

to play out," I say, finally pulling my arm out of Cross's grasp. "We're going to have to go down there."

"I don't like it."

"Neither do I, but we don't have much choice. Let's confront the guy, see if we can get anything useful out of him, and Burn the motherfucker."

"While you're busy doing that, what do you need me to do?"

"Watch my back and drag me out of there if anything goes sideways. I'm banking on your wards being strong enough to keep you safe, and I need someone to be backup for me down there."

He nods. "I can do that. What do we do if things go bad?"

"Run like hell and hope he doesn't come after us," I say with a nonchalance that falls flat. "But I don't think it'll come to that."

"Then let's get it over with," Cross says, cracking his knuckles. "I don't like how any of this feels, and there's no sense in delaying it."

He's right. The longer we wait, the worse Steve will get.

I nod and start pulling in power and dumping it into my reserves. After a moment, I close my eyes in concentration. The energy swirls deep in my gut, warming me from the inside out. My skin tickles and stings, and when I open my eyes, multicolored flames are licking up and down my arms and cascading over my hands. Slowly, they grow in size and speed until there's a firestorm of power swirling close around my body.

"That's impressive," Cross says, his eyes wide.

"Thanks. I made it myself."

He laughs, though the sound is a little choked.

"You ready?" I ask. His shoulders stiffen, his back going rigid and straight, and he nods.

I turn around and, with a deep breath, head toward the basement stairs. As soon as I cross the line of my wards, pain rockets through me. I clench my teeth against it and cold sweat breaks out over my body. Cross is by my side in an instant, his hand warm and comforting where it grips my elbow.

"I'm all right," I gasp out. My eyes water and I quickly wipe the moisture away. "I'm fine."

"You don't look fine," he says, eyeing the darkened doorway leading into the basement, "and I don't think this is the best place for you to be vulnerable."

"I need a moment. I promise."

He doesn't look convinced, but he does let my elbow go and takes a step back. After a beat, the pain lessens, or I get used to it. Either way, I'm able to catch my breath, and I start heading down the stairs again.

Without the lighting rigs, the basement is dim and it's difficult to see. With the overcast sky above, the light that makes it inside is thin and fades as the clouds overhead shift and move. On top of that, a supernatural darkness seems to crawl out of the corners of the room, covering the deeper hollows with a blackness that seems impenetrable. Cross pulls his small flashlight out of his pocket, and I regret not having the heavy-duty Maglite from earlier. The thin beam cuts through the basement, but it fails to do much against the encroaching darkness. Energy seeps in through the walls, down the stairs, and in from the side entrance. Spread across the floor like a wet carpet, it shifts with invisible currents and grows deeper as I watch.

After a moment, something tugs at the edge of my senses. I slowly scan the basement. A figure shifts in the darkness, and I freeze as Steve moves out of the shadows.

In the short time we've been gone, his physical form has deteriorated further. His mouth is still cracked and split at the corners, blood trickling down his cheeks to drip slowly off his chin. Clothes that were torn and ripped before are now falling off his body in strips, and the flesh beneath is putrefying, deep purples and reds that ooze with blood and offal. He takes slow, careful steps toward us, the trail of blood he leaves behind him lost in the inch of black-red power that covers the basement floor.

Detective, he Sends, and his voice is like sandpaper against my mind, the sound rough and painful. *Welcome back.*

This is bad, Kim, Priya says.

Steve tilts his head like a hunting dog hearing prey. *Who's that?* he asks as he continues to move toward us. *I hear someone new.*

Don't Send again, and get yourself hidden, I tell her firmly—focusing the Sending as tightly as I can so that she's the only one to hear it—before turning to face Steve.

It's just me, I Send, *and my partner. We have some questions for you.*

I bet you do, he says with a bloody grin that tightens the ball of cold dread in my stomach. *You must have so many.*

Why were you here? I ask.

He laughs. *Why are any of us here? That's not the question you want to ask, Detective. Why play games?*

I'm not the one playing games, Steve, I say. *Answer the question.*

I was here because she was here. He moves smoothly through the energy, pacing toward the base of the stairs where Cross and I stand, his movements slow and deliberate. *I've made some friends while I've been here, you know. They have interesting things to tell me about you, Burner.*

He lingers on the Affinity, and I watch his tongue as it darts out of his mouth as if to taste the word.

Did you know the other victim? I ask, forcing myself to stay with my original line of questioning.

He clucks his tongue at me and takes another step forward, his foot splashing soundlessly in the energy covering the floor. I watch as the liquid parts around him, then creeps its way over his decaying skin.

Don't you want to know what they say about you? He starts to hum, the tune off-key but still familiar. *Burner, Reader, Healer, Speaker.*

I turn to look at Cross, whose face is white and tight with worry.

"That's the song that woman was singing," he says softly, the sound of his voice amplified in the silence of the basement.

Steve starts to laugh. *They've told me about you, too.* He

turns his black eyes to Cross, bloody mouth wide open. *So many things.*

Why did you kill her? Cross asks, and I curse as I whip around to look at him.

Steve grins, and his teeth are coated with blood. It drips out of the corner of his mouth, staining his face. *I did tell you this was my murder, didn't I?*

"Goddamnit," I say under my breath. "You're supposed to fucking *de*-escalate the situation."

Steve laughs. *I'd seen her here a few other times. Never for long, but always poking around. Sometimes by herself, sometimes with others.*

You were stalking her, I Send, drawing the ghost's attention back to me. *Why?*

Because she was like the rest.

A shiver crawls up my spine. *The rest?*

My others, he continues. *They knew what they were doing. That they were tempting me. Teasing me. I found them, of course I did, and then I followed. And when it was time? They knew it. Just like you will.*

"That's not good," Cross whispers.

"Yeah, no shit," I say, hushing him.

How many?

Why does that matter? They all deserved it.

The energy is covering his leg to the knee now and slowly making its way up his other leg. He idly brushes at it with his hand, and I watch as it coats his fingers and slowly creeps up his arm.

Just like you, he Sends before taking another step and

stopping in the middle of the basement. *Just like the rest.*

The light flickers and he's gone.

Steve? I ask, reaching out tentatively. There's no response, no sense of him in the basement.

Shit. Shit shit *shit.*

"He's gone. Fuck, he's gone."

"What do you mean?" Cross asks, eyes unfocused. "He was just here."

"He's gone now. *Shit.*"

I scramble up the steps, reaching for the line of wards that block the exit. They crackle against my fingertips when I slam my hand against the concrete, still as strong as they were a minute ago.

"He's still inside," I say, turning to Cross who's at the bottom of the steps, looking worried. "I'm going to have to Burn him. There's no other option. He's too far gone. And you need to get out of here."

"What do you need me to do?" he asks as he joins me at the top of the stairs.

"Get the hell out of here. Call Dispatch. See if there are any other Burners who freelance with the CPD. I'm going to need backup, and fast." I walk into the center of the yard and start pacing, my hands shaking as I run them through my hair.

Cross frowns. "You never need backup."

"Well, I need it now. Go make the call."

"Wait, wait," he says, taking the last few steps into the yard to join me. "How serious is this? Can you wait until someone gets here?"

"You remember the creature that Baker turned into?" I ask, shrugging out of my jacket and quickly rolling my sleeves up so that my forearms are bared. The air is so cold, it stings against my skin, but I ignore it as I start pulling more power into my body. "Like that, but probably worse."

Cross goes a little pale but steadies himself. "Then there's no way I'm leaving you here by yourself."

"While I appreciate the sentiment," I say, "you're going to get in my way. I'll worry about you, instead of Steve, and I can't afford to be distracted."

"And I can't leave you in there by yourself."

His expression is stalwart, unbending.

Priya, can you stun him? I Send. A ripple of annoyed amusement comes down our bond.

Not that I would *do it*, she says, *but I also* can't *with those wards you put on him. He's locked up tighter than Alcatraz.*

Cross points his finger at me. "Don't you dare sick Priya on me. You need backup, and that's me."

"We still make the call," I say as I turn toward the street. "And you stay behind me, or so help me, Cross…"

"Yeah, yeah," he says, hurrying past me to the Interceptor. "I got it."

He makes the call to Dispatch as I scrounge through the car for supplies. I've got two pieces of chalk in my jacket, my knife in my boot, and little else. No additional chalk if I run out of it while scribing, no added protection in the form of warded clothing or items. My personal wards are still fairly strong, but I take a moment to reup them. I use blood—a prick on my pinkie finger that brings up a bead small enough to rewrite the final linking sigil—and reenergize the entire warding. I'm not as heavily warded as Cross is, but it's better than it had been.

I'm still not sure it'll be enough, but beggars, choosers.

When Cross and I turn back to the house, I freeze. The energy around the house is glowing, a sickly light that beats against the wards surrounding the building. The colors meld in a few places, and as I approach a patch, I sense a growing weakness in the warding. I swallow, my throat suddenly dry.

"Stay behind me," I say again, knife held tight in my hand, and I head toward the stairs.

CHAPTER TWENTY

I make my way down the steps carefully, eyes glued on the softly glowing entrance to the basement. There's no movement beyond the doorframe, just the pooled energy motionless in the center of the room.

As Cross and I pass the threshold into the basement, the darkness from the corners of the room rushes in, blocking out what little light there is. My body tenses. I flip my knife to rest against my wrist and press a hand to Cross's chest to stop him. As the light continues to fade, the energy trickling through the walls stops as if a tap has been turned off, leaving only fading trails behind. The well of power in the center of the room shifts and churns. It turns into a shimmering, twisting mass of power that grows until it fills the center of the room, dark light arcing from its surface in sickly tendrils.

Slowly, something rises from its center. At first, it's a sluggish mound of power, a heap of bloodred sludge that expands upward. As it stretches, the top of the mound turns into a faceless approximation of a head. It rotates, the line of energy connecting it to the main shape thinning and shifting until it can't support the weight anymore, and the head tilts crazily to the side, two dark holes opening in the place of eyes. They close, as if blinking, and fill with a dark light that oozes from the sockets, dripping down the face to where it splits into a gaping maw.

Arms peel off from its sides, ending in thin, three-fingered hands that reach toward us. I hastily throw up a shield, pouring my own power into it until it's a flaming blue-white barrier between us and the creature that makes its steady way closer.

Burner, it says with Steve's voice. *I thought you left me all alone down here.*

I gag as the Turned spirit touches my barrier. Though its fingers don't come into contact with me directly, I can feel them against my mind, a slimy, rotten sensation that makes my gut twist and my head ache. There's a sudden flash of light and the smell of burning ozone as my shield flares in response to the touch, and what used to be Steve screams, angry and injured. It hisses as it recoils, pulling its hand back as it throws a wave of power from the ground over us. Coated in the noxious stuff, my shield struggles to stay up.

Priya! I yell, swallowing back terror and pouring more energy into the shield. *What do we do?*

I don't know, she says. Her voice is strained and distant.

I need you here, I Send, though it's a struggle, as if the energy around us is muting our connection.

After a moment, I feel her agreement echo down our bond. She comes whipping through the wall to crash into the barrier between us hard enough for my feet to slide on the floor. I blink, dropping the protection long enough for her to duck inside its protection. When I move my head to see her out of the corner of my eye, her hair is whipping around her face in an unseen wind, bright white light sparking from her eyes like a thunderstorm as she pours her own energy down our bond to strengthen the shield. *We can't leave this thing here.*

Tell Cross to get out, I Send, unable to speak or risk throwing up.

He's not going to like it.

He doesn't have a choice, I Send as I pull my knife back and cut my arm. Blood pools on my skin, the sting of pain and heat a familiar burn.

Cross startles behind me, but I force myself to ignore him before bending down to scribe. I place as many runes for protection as I can remember in a curved line before me, then hastily tie them together with sigils for control and containment. The creature screams again and throws itself against my shield, clawing at the barrier like a rabid animal desperate to attack. The energy making up its body chews at the thin wall of light between us, and I break into a sweat as I try to split my focus between scribing and holding the Turned ghost at bay.

I need another minute, I Send to Priya, hoping that she still has power enough to bolster my rapidly emptying stores.

You won't get away from me, the spirit yells, its approximation of a mouth gnashing as it Sends the words. *You'll die here, Burner! I'll bathe in your blood, same as the others. They were mine,* mine, *and now you will be, too. You're* MINE. *They promised!*

My hands are shaking, blood and dust making my fingers hot and tacky as they drag across the dirty floor. I can't hear Priya or Cross over the creature's screams and the pounding of my heart. I finish the last rune, and there's a flash of light. Energy snaps into place around the marks. As the warding takes ownership of the shield, powering it for me, I sag a little, leaning forward as blood continues to drip down my forearm. Cross places his hand on my shoulder and crouches down next to me, offering his hand. I wave him away, catching my breath for a moment.

The reinforced barrier only makes the creature angrier, and it gathers the pool of power circling its feet into a swirling maelstrom of energy, filling the room with lashing waves of caustic power. When the corrosive force crashes into my now-bolstered shield, the wards flicker, and I rush to my feet—Cross rising with me—and hold my breath tight in my lungs as I wait for the marks to fail. Instead, they steady, flashing with blue-white light that moves from the marks to cover my body in bright flames of power.

At last, I turn around to face Cross, his feet right inside the barrier, his eyes wide as he looks between me and the creature. The wards on his body are shining golden bright, cutting through the unnatural darkness that fills the basement. In the places where his body is closest to my shield, the blue-white light takes on a slightly golden glow that fades as he takes a step closer to me.

"What do we do?" he asks, looking back to the creature as it rages on the other side.

"You get the hell out of here," I say, turning back to the creature as it rampages around us, its fingers scrabbling against the barrier between us in sparks of light that nearly blind me. "And you make sure no one else comes in."

"Kim," he says, grabbing my arm. His fingers sting against the cut there and slip a little in my blood. "I'm not leaving you with that thing. Those wards outside, they'll hold him." Cross looks back to the creature as it stalks around us and pales. "They'll hold him, right?"

Such a pretty thing, the ghost slurs, its voice gurgling as more red-black power pours from its mouth to drip onto the floor. *I wonder how your screams will taste.*

"We can't both get out of here without him attacking," I say quietly. I put my hand on top of Cross's, the cold metal of my knife pressing into his skin. "And he only wants me. I need to know you're going to be okay."

There's a flash of light behind me, and I feel one of the wards fail. Energy is pulled from my body in a sudden rush, the shield needing power to stay in place. I grit my teeth, and my body grows colder.

Not a good sign.

"I'll be fine," I say, squeezing Cross's hand again. "And I'm sorry."

His eyes widen, and I plant my booted foot in the center of his chest. I put all of my weight into the kick, throwing him out the basement door, which slams behind him as the creature that used to be Steve starts to laugh.

Burner, it says, his voice almost singing. *Maybe I will play games.*

All right, you son of a bitch, I Send as I turn around, drawing power into my body in a flaming mass. *You want me, come and get me.*

I let the shield fail, watching as it collapses around me.

The Turned spirit screams with a mix of elation and laughter, then charges. I spin away, slashing at its form with my knife. The silver cuts into it, leaving a gash of darkness that slowly heals. The creature chuckles.

You think you can hurt me? it asks, moving swiftly around the perimeter of the room, the energy trailing after it in a low wave. *I'm already dead, Burner. There's nothing left for you to do.*

Yeah, fuck that, I say, dropping low as he charges for me again. I throw a bolt of energy from my hand, watching as it blasts a hole in the center of the creature's body. Again, the deep red power flows into it, sealing the gap.

The Turned ghost starts to laugh loudly, the sound echoing through my mind and the basement. *The others didn't fight,* he says, voice giddy. *Only the last one, and you.*

He darts toward me, whipping his hand at my face. I duck, and his fingers tear through my shirt and into the muscle of my shoulder. It stings, the red-black power from his hand now coating my skin. The blue-white flames of power flare around the injury, burning away the noxious energy in a wave of clean light. Blood seeps out of the cuts, staining my shirt and making it stick to my skin.

Used-to-be-Steve laughs again. *How fun,* he Sends. *I wonder how long that will last.*

He speeds toward me again, and I throw another hasty shield up. With a crash, he ricochets into it, pushing my feet back on the ground with the force of his hit. Cackling, he rams into it again, pushing me back inch by inch until my foot hits the cinder block wall behind me. Teeth gritted, I flare my power, and the energy crackles around me, throwing blue-white sparks that make the ghost hiss and scrabble backward, gaping maw twisted into a grimace.

How the fuck am I going to Burn this guy? I Send to Priya as I take a quick moment to look around the room. Not-Steve paces in front of me, gauging my response. There's no way he'll lay off me long enough to let me scribe a proper circle. I glance at the blood still coursing down my arm and feel Priya's unease down our bond.

You're not thinking what I think you're thinking, are you?

…Maybe.

Kim, she Sends, voice tight, *you nearly killed yourself doing it with Baker's ghost. And we still don't understand what happened when you did it to that guy at the first marker.*

I don't have time to scribe a circle, I say, tensing and releasing my clenched left hand so that the blood pours faster from my forearm. *And we know it'll get rid of the guy.*

You sure about that?

It worked last time, I hedge.

You think *it worked last time. And that ghost wasn't nearly as far gone as this one is.*

Not-Steve runs a tongue of congealed blood over its lips, the dark light smearing around its face. The energy pool whirls around its feet, kicking up in waves and splashes to sizzle against my shield. I can already feel it starting to fracture at the edges.

We don't have time. I take a deep breath and switch my knife to my left hand. *We can't wait for another Burner, and it's not going to let us out of here.*

I don't like this, Kim.

I don't either. I press my right hand against the cut, smearing blood over my palm and fingers. *Watch my back, all right?*

She sighs and starts pulling power into herself. Her eyes flash white again, her hair billowing out behind her. *If you get yourself killed, I am* not *hanging out with you in the afterlife.*

I grin. *You'd get bored without me.*

That's one word for it.

I switch my knife back to my right hand, squeezing my left until blood runs down my wrist and over my palm. Both hands bloody, knife pressed against my forearm, ready for attack, I shout, "Yo, Steve!"

The ghost turns its head, the too-thin neck twisting under the weight, and faces me. Its empty eyes stare at me, mouth open and grinning.

Is it time to play, Burner?

"Fuck you," I say before dropping my shield and charging it.

I must catch it off guard because it doesn't move and stands still as I rush forward, left hand out, knife ready in my right. The blade slices into the creature, its semicorporeal body slowing the motion for a moment before my hand meets enough resistance to stop. Not-Steve turns its head again, staring at my clenched fist half-submerged into its flesh, then looks at me and starts to laugh.

There's a sudden, aching sense of *wrongness* as Not-Steve wraps its arms around me. I struggle, but it pulls me closer. My bloody palm pressed into its body doesn't seem to be doing anything. Pain lances through me with every movement, but unlike with the spirit at the first marker, my blood doesn't eat away at the energy. Instead, the opposite happens, the dark red power slowly creeping its way over my skin as Not-Steve draws me closer, mouth gaping.

You're mine, it croons as it presses its face against mine, a sickening caress that makes me vomit. It laughs as I heave and struggle against it, but as the dark power licks over my arms, wrapping me in a blanket that burns away my skin, I can't break free.

With a primal scream, I push the energy still gathered in my gut out in a wave. Multicolored flames flash underneath the dark energy, eating away at it to break free in huge gouts of fire. The energy flows down my arm, through my hand, and into the knife. The creature's skin parts, flames eating away at the edges of the wound in crackling lines. Slowly, the dark energy covering my body falls away, until I'm left in a small circle of clear space, panting and hunched over as Not-Steve flails at the fire still eating away at its body.

I grin, and a feral, predatory emotion whips through me. I smear more blood from my arm onto my hand and dive for the creature, slashing at it with my knife and blood. It falls back, screaming, mouth twisted in a grimace of fear. As flames coat my skin, I push it back, step by step, until it's cowering in front of me, body shrunken and falling to pieces as it burns away.

I'm not yours, I Send viciously. *And you're going to pay for the lives you've taken.*

The creature tilts its head up, sunken eyes wide and unseeing. It's pathetic, and revulsion twists in my gut as I stare at this thing that used to be human. I ready a binding net in my hands, power crackling between my blood-coated fingers as it forms. With a shout, I throw it at the Turned spirit and watch with satisfaction as it wraps around its body, tightening until its arms are pressed against its sides, unable to move. Lightning crackles over its bloodred body, and the creature twists and recoils in pain.

Time for you to get the fuck out of here, I Send before bending down to scribe a Burning circle. My chalk scrapes across the floor as the creature whimpers and continues to struggle.

As I finish putting the last rune down, something shifts within my gut. I look down to find my blood mixing with the chalk, the sigils and runes flaring and fading in an unsettling wave. The energy within me twists, then gutters. The flames on my body disappear, and I'm left in sudden darkness. Head whipping up, I see the binding net around Not-Steve shimmer, then fade as it's absorbed into the creature's body. As the light dims, the creature stretches. Its arms pull away from its body to reach for me. I stumble back, chalk falling from my fingers, and swing at the creature with my knife before falling back onto my hands. It crawls after me, dragging its body through the dark energy and absorbing it, growing with each shuddering pull forward.

As the once-clear space around me starts to fill with the dark power, it stings against my skin. I try to pull my own power again, to flare it over my skin in that protective coat of fire, but while my hands fill with flames, the rest of my body remains unprotected.

Distracted, I don't pull my foot away from the creature fast enough as it lunges for me. Its fingers wrap tightly around my ankle, and I scream as its caustic skin eats through the thick leather of my boot. After a moment, it starts eating into my skin, and I scream again.

Priya throws a ball of energy at the creature, body pulsing with white light as she pours attack after attack at the Turned spirit. Her barrage leaves it reeling, and I pull my leg away. Blood starts to pool in my boot, and I grit my teeth as I get back to my feet, though I'm unable to put my weight on the leg that the creature grabbed. I try to throw another shield up, but the creature lunges for me, wrapping its arms around my body. Its energy starts coating me again, and though I struggle, I'm weaker than before, and exhaustion sweeps over me as my mind goes blank.

Priya screams, beating against me and the ghost, but it's too late. The energy and Not-Steve's body cover me in a thick, heavy coat that eats away at my clothes and skin like acid. In a few minutes, my chest and head will be encased, and I know in a primal, visceral way that I won't be able to come back from it. Either the pain or the corrosive nature of the energy will destroy me.

I struggle one last time, a mammalian survival reflex kicking in, and I catch Priya from the corner of my eye, tears running down her face as she claws at the creature and power encasing me.

I'm so sorry, I Send, my mental voice barely a whisper. Her eyes flash up to mine, wide and bright, and then the power covers my mouth and my eyes, blocking out everything but dark, red light.

CHAPTER TWENTY-ONE

At first, all I feel is fire. It rolls over me in an unending wave, and though I open my mouth to scream, there's no sound. The energy burns, eating away at my skin and mind, wiping everything out except for pure, bright pain.

Please, I beg someone, anyone, *make it stop.*

Power flickers in my stomach, then fades, and I reach for it in desperation. It tickles at the edge of my senses yet fades again, leaving only desolation.

A sudden wash of golden light follows, and my suffering disappears in a rush. I blink my eyes open, trying to find the source of relief, and find Cross standing over me, arms spread wide as his wards flare with power. Golden light is all around us. A wave of energy pulses out of him, and it crashes into Not-Steve and the dark energy in the basement, pushing it all away in a tumbling crest that smashes into the walls. Where the light touches the Turned ghost, its body leaps into flame. It screams, mouth open and vomiting power in great gouts. Desperately, it tries to beat the flames from its body. Instead, they engulf it entirely, leaving a pillar of golden fire that grows brighter and brighter until I can't look at it.

Rough hands grab me under my arms and drag me back toward the stairs, and pain blanks my mind again. The last thing I feel before blacking out completely is the rough sandpaper of Not-Steve's voice in my mind.

We will see you again, Burner. Joseph promised.

───────

I come to in the backyard of the house. My jacket is lying on top of me like a blanket, and dead grass bites into my back. I turn my head with a groan and look down. My hands are bloody and raw where they peek out beneath leather. Slowly, I turn my left palm up and flex my fingers, the motion sending sharp sparks through my arm. I drop my head back onto the ground, groaning.

"Kim," Cross says, and his hand pushes my hair back from my face as gently as possible, though the touch sends another frisson of pain through me. "Fuck, I thought I'd lost you. EMS is on its way. You just hold on."

Swallowing, I try to nod but groan again. Everything hurts. My skin is on fire, like a skinned knee but everywhere. Raw and aching, I'm nearly overpowered by it. Where the creature grabbed my ankle, all I feel is a cold sensation that's as terrifying as the overwhelming pain coursing through the rest of my body.

I start to drift back into unconsciousness, and I fight against it. Power shifts in my stomach and I reach for it reflexively. Like a timid beast, it responds, slinking through my body and rubbing against my senses as if apologizing for its bad behavior. I welcome it with open arms and shudder as it floods back into my veins. Heat courses through my body, washing away the pain for a brief moment.

"Oh shit," Cross says on a whisper, and his hand on my face stills, then falls away.

I crack my eyes open, then widen them in shock.

My body is glowing with power, a grass-green energy that coats me from head to toe. It shimmers and shifts like light through the branches of trees and twines its way over my skin. Where it gathers, I feel something like an itch. As I watch, those places begin to heal, the raw open sores covering my skin turning an angry red, then yellow, then brown, before finally fading back to smooth, pink skin.

Agony shoots through my leg, and I arch off the ground, reaching blindly for my ankle. Cross holds me down, and I turn my head wildly to the side, watching as the bright green light flares around the ruined joint. Something cracks loudly, and I shout as the energy forces bone and sinew back together in a rush. The pain fades quickly, and I fall back against the ground again, panting and out of breath.

Rolling onto my side, I reach for Cross as I curl into a fetal position, breathing carefully as the prickling sensation fades. He takes my hand in his and leans his body over mine, shielding me from the night sky. His touch is gentle and comforting, and I squeeze his hand weakly as I catch my breath. The newly healed skin feels tight and warm, and it pulls painfully as he rubs his thumb over the back of my hand. There's another soft flare of green light, and even that discomfort fades, leaving only Cross's gentle touch.

"What was that?" His soft voice is close and intimate. I squeeze his hand again and try to sit up. "Whoa, now," he says before forcing me to lie down again. "You're staying put until the ambulance gets here."

"I don't need an ambulance," I say. My voice is rough, and it hurts a little to talk. I cough and try again. "I don't know if you noticed, but I'm better."

"Trust me, I noticed." He turns my hand over in his and shakes his head. "It looked like the top layer of your skin had been burned away, Kim, and don't get me started on that ankle of yours. This is…"

It's Healing, Priya says. She appears above Cross's shoulder and leans in through him to put her hand on my face. He shifts, shivering, and makes room for her. Slowly, she runs her fingers over my face, down my neck, and to my arms and the rest of my body. Sighing, she settles on the ground, confusion written all over her face.

"I guess that answers that question," I say quietly. I start to sit up, and Cross doesn't stop me, rolling his eyes at my stubbornness.

"What question?"

"How many Affinities I have now," I answer, pulling my knees up and leaning my arms on them. Cross's hand falls from mine, and I miss the comfort of it. "Seems we're up to three."

I pull my right pant leg up, and the fabric starts to fray at the touch. Rubbing it between my fingers, the weave falls apart as if eaten away. Beneath the cuff, the top of my heavy leather boot is missing. Instead, there's a ragged edge and a fresh pink scar around my ankle. I run my finger over the puckered skin and shiver.

"What do you remember?" Cross says as he settles on the ground next to me. I pull my jacket around my shoulders and hold it closed rather than putting it back on.

"Not a whole lot," I say, voice trembling a little. "He said something before you pulled me out of there, though. About Joseph."

"Joseph?" Cross looks to Priya, brow furrowed.

Do you mean Baker? she asks. *He can't mean Baker.*

"I think he meant Baker," I say. "He was talking about his friends earlier, too. I think..." I swallow, throat tight. "I think he might have been talking to ghosts that had already passed on."

That's not... Priya stills, eyes wide. *The tears?*

I nod. "I think that's what Frank was talking about."

"Can you two catch the rest of the class up?" Cross asks, looking between Priya and me with confusion and a bit of fear. "I'm a little lost."

There's a barrier between life and death, Priya says. *You cross it when you die or if you're Burnt.*

"It's supposed to be a one-way street," I continue. "You can't come back to the living world."

Unless something destroys the barrier.

"*That's* what's tearing?" Cross asks, his voice rising in surprise. "You think the barrier between life and death is falling apart?"

"Yeah," I say. With a groan, I try to stand but fall back, exhausted.

You need to take it slow, Priya says. *A Healing like that is going to take a lot out of you. You probably have ten more minutes before you're going to crash, hard.*

"And you're also not going anywhere until you're seen by a medical professional," Cross says emphatically.

"Priya was a doctor," I say with a hint of a smile. "Does she count?"

"A *living* medical professional," he says.

"We need to go talk to Frank again," I say. "I think he'll tell us more now. We'll have better questions this time."

"That's a great idea," Cross says, "but you're getting seen by a doctor, and then you're getting some rest. He's not going anywhere. It can wait."

"Are you sure about that?" I nod my head toward the basement. "I think what happened down there is pretty good evidence that it can't."

For that matter, Priya says, turning to give Cross a thoughtful look, *how'd you get inside? He had the door forced shut.* She looks to me. *I tried to open it, but it wasn't moving.*

"I pushed," Cross says with a shrug, "and it eventually gave."

"I think it has something to do with those," I say, waving my hand to indicate his wards, "and that Burner symbol on your chest."

He rubs at the space idly and sighs. "Yeah, probably. It lit up right before the door opened."

"Wednesday night dinner," I say, "is going to be very interesting."

Exhaustion starts to overwhelm me. I motion for Cross to help me to my feet, and he begrudgingly does. I stumble a bit and land against his chest. He wraps a warm, strong arm around my waist, helping me catch my balance.

"If I promise to go see a doctor tomorrow," I say into his shirt, "can you please take me home now?"

He sighs, and it stirs my hair. "You promise you will?"

After resting my weight on him for a moment longer, I push away and stand on my own. My legs are weak, and I lock my knees to stay up. The world goes a little gray at the edges, sounds go tinny, but I keep my feet and it eventually fades. Priya gives me a concerned look.

I'll be okay, I say, Sending the words along with a pulse of reassurance down our bond.

"I'll be fine tonight," I answer. "All I need is to get home and lie down. Like Priya said, I'm crashing."

"I want to see a note tomorrow," Cross says threateningly.

"Whatever you want, as long as I can go to bed."

Cross helps me to the cruiser after that, and I fall into the passenger seat. My eyes are drooping as soon as I have my seatbelt on, and I'm nearly asleep by the time we hit Sixty-Fourth Street. A heartbeat later, I'm out completely.

In what feels like seconds later, Cross shakes me awake. I blink at the dashboard clock, surprised to see a half hour has passed since we left. Yawning, I rub a hand over my face before unbuckling and wrenching the door open. I stumble a little as I step out of the car, and in a moment, Cross is out of the driver's seat and coming around to my side. He wraps an arm around my waist, helping to support me, and for once, I let him, leaning into the comforting strength and warmth of his body. He reaches behind us and slams the door shut, then helps me shuffle my way to the door.

"I didn't think you'd remember where I lived," I say.

"Priya told me how to get here," he says as he pulls the lobby door open. He ushers me inside and eyes the still-broken elevator. "Fifth floor?"

I nod, and he sighs. "Okay, let me know if you get tired on the stairs."

"You going to carry me up them?" I ask.

He gives me a once-over, green eyes coasting from my face to my feet, then back again. It's an assessing gaze—a quick gauge of my size and weight, nothing more—but it still makes me shiver.

"If I have to," he says at last. "But I'd prefer you make it on your own."

We finish crossing the lobby to the stairs. I shift my weight so I'm leaning on the handrail, Cross's arm still wrapped around my waist, and I start walking. My feet feel like lead, and he keeps pace with me, taking slow careful steps with my own. The walk up isn't taxing, not in any concrete sense, but my muscles and bones feel tired, like they've been pushed too far, too fast, too recently. I fight to stop my knees from shaking with each step, and though my legs burn as we keep going, I force myself to keep moving.

When we reach the fifth floor, I lean heavily on the banister, breath coming quick and heavy through my mouth.

"You could always move," Cross suggests as I catch my breath. "There are plenty of apartment buildings with working elevators."

I shake my head and cough out a laugh. "It's part of the charm of the place."

"I think tonight," Cross says, "you could use a little less charm and a lot more working elevator."

"Maybe." I push myself away from the banister, his arm catching me against him as I take a stumbling step forward. "Let's just get inside. We're nearly there."

We make our way down the hallway toward my apartment in silence. I fumble for my keys and jam them into the door. It swings open, and I slip out of his grip, tossing my keys onto the small table. I walk to the couch, flop down, and start wrestling with my ruined boots.

Cross is still standing in the doorway, eyes wide as he takes in my apartment. I glance around, confused. The place is pretty clean, at least for my standards. No dirty dishes, not that much junk mail lying about. I even took the trash out the other day, so it's not overflowing in the kitchen.

"What?" I ask him as he closes the door behind him. "Did you think I'd live in a sty or something?"

"No," he says. "I'm surprised. I expected worse."

"To be fair, it usually is messier than this," I admit, exhausted, before falling back onto the couch. I wave toward the kitchen and throw an arm over my eyes. "Help yourself. There's beer in the fridge and I think some orange juice."

I wouldn't drink that, Priya cautions. *I'm pretty sure it's past expiration.*

"Whatever," I mumble, starting to fall asleep now that I'm lying down. "It's fine."

I hear Cross rummaging through the fridge as I doze. After a moment, he comes back into the living room and joins me on the couch. I pull my legs back, knees bent and resting against the back of the couch to make more room. I shift my arm enough that I can see him. He's got a glass of water, which he sets on the coffee table next to me. He twists so that his back is leaning up against the other armrest, his knee resting on the cushion in front of him.

"Drink that," he says, nodding to the glass of water.

"You couldn't have brought me a beer?" I ask. He doesn't say anything, and I take the glass and sip. The water hits my mouth in a cool, refreshing rush, and I drink the entire thing in slow, careful swallows.

"Good," Cross says as I slide the glass toward him and lie back down. "You ready to talk about what happened tonight?" he asks, looking at my ankle and the disintegrating pant leg above it.

I fight the urge to hide it under my other leg. "Yes," I answer after a long moment. "I don't know that I can explain any of it, though."

"Let's start with something easy, then," Cross says with a groan. "Who's our Doe?"

"A Medium," I say with certainty. "We know that from the knife."

"You get anything more from Steve?"

"Other than a new scar, no. He was too far gone to be concrete about what he was saying, though he did mention there were more like her." I shiver, remembering the ownership in his voice when he spoke of his victims. "We're going to have to find them."

"We'll start in the morning," Cross says in agreement. "In the meantime, though, we still have our Jane Doe."

"She was in that basement for a reason. Now we have to figure out what it is."

"You think it might have to do with the energy that was down there?"

I groan. "God, maybe? I don't know. Do we have her picture?"

Cross nods. "Yeah, I can get a copy printed in the morning. You want to go canvassing?"

"I want to ask Frank," I say. "Maybe she's part of his group."

Do you honestly think he'll tell us anything else? Priya asks.

"I hope he will, especially if one of his friends ended up dead." I wiggle deeper into the cushions of the couch, fighting to keep my eyes open.

"What about your new powers?" Cross asks. "How are you feeling?"

"Tired," I grumble.

"Anything else?" He leans forward and gently grabs my right foot. I let him pull until my leg is stretched out, my foot resting in his lap. He twists it in his hands slowly, fingers running over the raised scar tissue encircling my ankle. "It doesn't look bad."

"It's itchy but fine otherwise. What about you, though? You busted in there like a knight in literal shining armor."

Cross rolls his eyes at my joke before setting my foot back on the couch. "I'm fine. Nothing happened to me."

"Something happened," I press. "Tell me what you did before you got through the door. What you were thinking, how you felt."

He meets my eyes, his expression serious and considering. After a moment, he lets out a long breath and looks away. "I was terrified. I thought you were going to die in that basement with that thing, and that I wasn't going to be able to do a damn thing about it. And then…"

I wait, but he doesn't continue. "And then?" I ask, pressing.

"And then I got mad," he says, shaking his head. "That's when everything"—he waves his hand toward his chest distractedly—"turned on, I guess."

"You saved my ass," I say quietly. "Thank you."

"You don't have to thank me."

"I think I do," I say. "I would've died in there if you hadn't… So, yes. Thank you."

"Consider us even, then," he says with a small grin. "You saved me from one rampaging ghost, I saved you from another."

I laugh, then yawn, unable to stop myself. Cross's smile turns soft as I fight down a second yawn.

"You need to go to bed," he says, starting to stand. "I'll see you in the office tomorrow?"

"I'm going to need a pickup," I say.

He raises his eyebrows. "You need me to carry you to bed?"

"What? No. I don't have my car."

Face turning scarlet, he coughs and looks away. Priya starts laughing, and we both glare at her. After a moment, I can't help myself and let out a soft laugh, too.

"You can give me a hand off the couch," I say, still smiling as I hold my arm out to him.

He takes my hand in his and pulls me up in a smooth movement. Legs still tired, I stumble a little, and he catches me. His other arm wraps around my back, pulling me closer, and our clasped hands fall against his chest.

"You sure you don't need help?" he asks, his voice suddenly low and gravelly. His hand flexes against my back, and I shiver, my heart racing. After a moment, I nod.

He lets me steady myself and pulls his arm away, letting his hand trail a path of warmth across my back as it retreats. I shiver again, and he squeezes my hand gently before letting it fall, too.

"We're going to talk about this?" he asks, his tone of voice forcing me to meet his eyes. Though there's a good foot of space between us now, I can still feel the ghost of his hands on me, warm and tempting. "Because I don't know how long I can wait for that conversation."

I nod again, my throat tight.

"Good," he says before reaching up to brush a lock of

hair from my face. "I'll see you in the morning. Try to get some rest."

I mumble something and let him out of the apartment, knowing that sleep will suddenly be difficult to find.

CHAPTER TWENTY-TWO

I end up falling asleep quickly, though it's far from restful. I'm haunted by the fight with Steve, with his final words, with the terror that overtakes me whenever I think of Joseph Baker. Shuddering awake around three, covered in sweat and panting, I end up tossing and turning the rest of the night, unable—or unwilling—to find sleep again. I flop out of my bed around six and take a shower, hoping the heat will wake me up. Instead, it gives me a long time to look at my body, and I wonder at the smooth, pale skin that was raw and bleeding last night. Even the cut on my arm is gone, a thin, fine line of scar tissue the only sign of injury.

I towel off and head to the kitchen to brew coffee and figure out breakfast. A quick check of the fridge tells me I need to go grocery shopping immediately, so I scrounge for the last few pieces of bread and pop them in the toaster. There's a little bit of butter in the back of my freezer, and I toss it into the microwave, setting the timer a bit too long. When I open the door, melted butter is pooled in the paper wrapping. Carefully, I try to take it out, but butter spills onto the counter when I remove it from the microwave. Sighing, I pour the rest of it over my toast and let it soak into the bread.

Off to a great start this morning, Priya says, startling me. What's left of the stick of butter falls out of my hand and lands on the counter with a splat. *Sorry.*

I sigh and scoop up the half-melted mess and drop it into the trash. *No kidding.*

You're feeling okay, though? No side effects?

Just tired, I Send with a sigh. *That Joseph comment has me shaken.*

If the barrier between life and death is weakening… Priya shakes her head, looking scared.

We'll figure it out, I say, trying to reassure her and myself.

And what do we do after that? she asks.

If that's truly what's happening, we'll help fix it.

She shakes her head. *I don't know if we're going to be able to get anything out of Frank, though. He seemed dead set—no pun intended—about not telling us more.*

He's not our only resource, I Send and take a bite of toast. *There's the diary.*

She frowns. *Comfort Bell's?*

It's the only other place I've heard about tears, I Send. *When Baker was confronting Moore, my grandmother mentioned ghosts Turning and tears.*

And you think Bell has more information about it?

I don't think it'll hurt to try.

You were barely able to read the diary before, though, Priya says, still confused. *How're you going to do it now?*

I sigh. *I'm not sure. I was going to… I don't know, ask it for help or something. If it doesn't work, we're not worse off than we were before.* I shrug. *If it does, we have more information to use when we talk to Frank.*

Priya floats over to the coffee table in the living room and settles down on top of it, eyeing the diary as I finish my toast and join her in the other room.

I hope it cooperates, she says.

We'll find out soon enough.

I take a quick minute to get dressed, throwing on black slacks and a white dress shirt and grabbing my shoulder holster, though I don't put the leather straps on yet. Instead, I set it next to the small table by the door and text Cross that I'm ready for a pickup. He sends back a thumbs-up emoji, and I put my cell down on the small table as well. With a deep breath, I turn back to the living room table and Bell's diary.

"Let's see how this goes," I mutter to myself before reaching for my knife.

Yet I stop.

I look back to the small table by the door, and while I see my gun and keys, my knife isn't there. Spinning around, I find my boots from the night before, but my ankle sheathe is missing.

Priya, I Send frantically. *Where's my knife?*

She looks up, eyes wide. *What?*

My knife. My Medium's knife. Where is it?

I don't… You had it last night. I thought you brought it home.

I shake my head. *It's not here.*

Could you have left it at the scene? she asks.

Fuck, I run a hand through my hair and curse again. *How could we have left it?*

There were slightly more important things to consider, she says, *like your life.*

How am I supposed to Read this thing if I can't draw blood with silver?

She pauses, biting her lip as she thinks. *Do you have a backup?*

No, I say dryly, *I do not have a backup.*

What about any silver jewelry?

Priya, I say, exasperated, *you've lived with me for over a decade. You know exactly how much jewelry I don't own.*

Did Sadie leave you any silverware?

You're hopeless, I say and look at the diary again. *This is hopeless. Shit.*

You'll have to wait until Cross gets here, then go to the scene to get your knife back. She swirls around me, kicking up a cool breeze that's meant to comfort. *Bring the diary with you. You can Read it there.*

I sigh and snatch the book from the table. *I hope no one's walked off with the damn thing*, I Send angrily. *I can't believe I forgot it.*

You'll have it back in no time, Priya offers in sympathy.

I nod, trying to get my temper under control. It's an annoyance to be without my knife, but Priya's right: it's far from the end of the world. Still, now that I know it's missing, I feel the lack of it like a limb. Ever since I was gifted the blade by my grandmother when I finished my apprenticeship, I've carried it with me wherever I go. To be without it now leaves me anxious and a little jumpy.

Cross arrives a few minutes later, buzzing up from the lobby. I stuff my gun in its holster, grab my keys and jacket, and hurry toward the stairs. Barely taking the time to get my arms through the sleeves, I jog down the steps, my footsteps echoing in the stairwell. I rush through the lobby and burst out the door, startling Cross from his perch near the buzzers.

"We've got to go back to the scene," I say quickly, shifting my coat so it settles around my shoulders. "I left my knife there, and I need it."

Cross hurries after me. "You look like you're feeling better," he says. "And good news, there's a MedCheck between here and the scene."

"I don't need a doctor," I say, pausing next to the car. "I need my knife."

"You promised."

"I've been Healing all night. I'm *fine*. Priya, can you talk some sense into him?"

She really is okay, Priya Sends. *I've been monitoring her vitals all night. There's barely any sign of trauma now.*

Cross frowns. "If you feel even a twinge of something, I'm taking you to the ER. No complaints."

"Fine," I say as I climb into the passenger seat of the Interceptor. "Let's go."

Cross speeds toward the crime scene. He doesn't turn the lights on, but he does whoop the siren a time or two when a driver ahead of us doesn't go fast enough.

Twenty minutes later, he screeches to a halt in front of

the abandoned house. I jump out of the car almost before it's completely stopped and hurry to the side entrance. Now that Forensics has cleared the scene, there's no reason to walk all the way around to the back, and I rush inside.

The basement is still dark, but it's a more natural darkness: the gentle muted gray of indirect sunlight and partially covered windows. I glance around the room, trying to keep track of where I'd been the night before and failing. After a moment, I catch a glinting light in the darkness and hurry over. My knife is resting on the ground, the silver tarnished except for where my hand was wrapped around the hilt. That section is bright and clear of discoloration. I let out a relieved breath and pick up the knife.

Wielding the blade for years has taught my hands the weight and feel of it, and I can tell immediately that something is off. Between the tarnish and the darkness of the basement, I can't see what's wrong with the blade. I rush to the exit, then hurry up the stairs, flipping the knife back and forth to see both sides. As soon as I get into the light, the problem is obvious.

The runes and sigils that were etched into the blade are nearly gone, some caustic material eating away at the silver so that the deeply engraved marks are almost indiscernible. The change is most evident in the places where my hand gripped the hilt last night. In the untarnished voids where my fingers were, the runes are unchanged, still as deep and clear as they were before. But where my skin didn't protect the metal, it's worn smooth. Whatever caustic energy made up Not-Steve's body ate away at the metal as easily as it ate away at my skin.

I shudder.

"You find it?" Cross asks as I walk back to the car.

I hold the knife up so he can see it. "Yeah."

"And here I thought *you* were beat up last night," he says, holding a hand out. I pass him the knife, hesitating only slightly before letting him take it. "Will it still work?"

"I don't know," I say, watching as he flips it over in his hand, peering down at the faded runes. He hands it back to me, his fingers stained dark by the tarnished silver. "There's really only one way to find out."

I walk to the still-active wards around the house and pull a piece of chalk out of my jacket. I scribe another series of runes, a continuation of the existing marks, and loop them back into the active wards. The knife still cuts cleanly through my skin, and blood wells on the top of my finger. I press it into the chalk, watching as the symbols flare briefly with power. A weaker version of the warded barrier comes to life. It flickers and sparks with light, dimmer than the original wards, but it stays.

"That's a relief," I say as I stand.

"Everything okay?" Cross asks. "Those don't look nearly as impressive as the others."

"It'll do for now." I tuck the knife into its sheath on my ankle. "I'm going to have to get the runes redone soon, though."

"Let's get going, then," Cross says, turning back to the cruiser. "We've got a ghost to interview."

"Not quite," I say as I follow him to the Interceptor. "I'm going to try to read this thing, see if I can get any more information from it."

He opens the driver's side door and leans his arms against the frame. "What do you need me to do?"

"Sit tight and look pretty," I say with a smile.

"Look pretty?" He climbs into the car. "I'll do my best."

"If it works, I'll let you know what I find out."

I get into the car and kick my feet up on the dashboard, knees bent as I wedge myself into the seat. With a slight tug, I pull the diary from my pocket and lay it across my knees. Squeezing the tip of my finger to get more blood to well there, I look at Cross.

"Here we go," I say, pressing my thumb to the leather cover. I close my eyes and reach for the diary. *I need your help*, I think, forcing the thought into the leather cover along with my blood. A sharp tug blossoms in my stomach as the Reading starts to drag me under. Exhaling slowly, I fall into it, swept away by memory.

———

It's dark, night having settled around the city like a warm blanket hours before. Lights twinkle outside your window, distant skyscrapers reflecting starlight back onto the city in a mirrored image of the sky. It's early May, and you've left the windows open. Sweet, cool air breezes through the house, errant gusts of wind tangling with the curls hanging against your forehead in gentle, cool caresses. Your ghost partner, John, sits in the wide bay window in the living room, his ghostly head resting against the glass as he looks out over the street.

You're sure this is the right thing to do? he asks you, eyes still trained on the window.

Yes, you send with absolute certainty. *There aren't any other options.*

He nods, and you look back to your hands clasped before you. Their wrinkled surface sometimes catches you by surprise. You still feel young, like age has transformed your body while leaving your mind intact. But you know better. This entire experience has aged you in ways that you didn't consider when you started down this path. Now, the only choices left to you are to move forward, to continue to feel the weight of time—and your choices—on your shoulders.

You've left these messages, these memories, many times over the years, your diary clenched tight in your hands. Never again did you use the mirror, though. That experience left you unsettled for days and unable to meet your reflected eyes. Tonight, you're looking for comfort more than anything. You're in your favorite chair, and as you stare at your hands, flexing them slowly to watch the wrinkles fade and reform, you start thinking.

We didn't know what was happening at the beginning. Sadie was the first to notice the changes, that ghosts were Turning more often, that it was happening more in certain places around the city. She's an incredibly talented Burner, and it is no surprise that she was the most in tune with the ghosts around us. That first breach… the feeling of it was like sandpaper against my mind, a slow, dragging wound that started as a burn and turned into wild, screaming pain.

Caroline was still hesitant to believe what our senses were telling us, though. We spent months going back and forth, trying to come to an agreement about what was happening and why. And through it all, the hole had grown bigger, the ghosts more untamed and violent.

Our first thought was that it had to do with Joseph's experiments, his attempts to unlock additional Affinities. The two started at the same time, and as the natural boundary started to break down, it made sense to us that Joseph's attempts to break his internal boundaries were related.

She—we—Bound him for that, locking him away both literally and metaphorically to prevent him from doing any further damage. We felt right in those actions, justified. We stopped a great evil from growing in the world and saved those we were tasked with protecting. But when the tears didn't stop, when they continued to worsen, we knew we were wrong.

Shame and regret sweep over you, and you have to close your eyes against the emotions. Tears prick the corners of your eyes, and you squeeze the lids tightly shut to stop them from falling. Your part in Joseph's Binding haunts you even though it's been years since the event. On the bad nights, you can still hear him yelling as you stripped him of the powers that made him a Medium. It sounded like his soul was being ripped from him, a bone-deep pain that echoed throughout the darkened room so that you felt his suffering as your own.

The tears grew worse and more common. Day by day, we could see the barrier weakening. And Caroline, in her usual, strong-willed way, found a solution of sorts. Focal points to direct the energy away from the weakened places in the world and to corral it for later use. It was a kind of treatment for the disease. And though it works, stopping the decay from growing worse, I can feel the rot beneath it. We may be managing the symptoms, but the sickness still lingers.

You look up from your hands to John sitting in the window. His soft glow reflects off the glass in Second-Sight, the picture he makes one of peace and contentment. But you find yourself unable to feel any of that same emotion. Instead, there's a bone-deep worry that dogs you with every breath. You caught a flash of black in his eyes the week before, a moment that left you shaken for hours after. The weakness of the barrier, you know, was manifesting itself in the world. You should trust him. He is your partner, after all, but you find yourself doubting that bond and its power. He turns his gaze to you, eyes gray and steadfast, and you fight a shiver.

There must be more we can do, you think. *But I don't know what.*

You stand up and head to the window, your reflection looking back at you from the glass. You are old and tired, and it shows in your white hair and wrinkled skin and clouded eyes. The windowpane is cold beneath your hand as you press your palm to it.

We are missing something, you think, *something vital and necessary, but we have gotten no closer to finding it in the decades since we started creating focal points in the city. And though we talk, endlessly, about what the cause is and what possible solutions there might be, we are no closer to solving it today than we were that first night when Sadie brought the problem to our attention. I can only hope there's something more that can be done when you Read this, something that we missed in the interim between now and then.*

You close your eyes and lean your forehead against the window. The cold is soothing, centering, and when you pull your head back, there's steel in your eyes and bones.

"It's time," you say, turning to John.

Silently, he joins you as you move to the back room of the house. There's a small desk set beneath a window overlooking the backyard. You watched your children grow and play in that yard, watched your grandchildren do the same. The maple tree that towers over it all started as a sapling, planted by your husband the day you moved in. Time's hand lay, once again, upon your world.

You pull the chair back from the desk and settle into it, wincing as your bones shift. The side drawer opens soundlessly, and you pull out your knife. The metal is cold and heavy in your hand, but it warms quickly. You lay your arm on the table. The paper-thin skin parts at its first brush with sharp silver. Blood coats the blade, red and wet as you drag the knife from the crook of your elbow to your wrist in a slow, shallow pull. Blood spills from the wound, trickling over your skin to stain the desktop. Hand shaking, you lay the knife down and run your freed fingers through the red, swirling it into a simple mark that covers the entire surface of your desk.

When you finish the final line of the symbol, light bursts from the surface, green like grass in spring sunlight. It pulses softly, calling to something in the core of your body. With a breath, you follow that pull, letting it lead you into an unknown, alien world. John rests his hand on your shoulder, and for once, you can sense the touch as if it were real. It tightens, fingers pressing too hard into your age-softened flesh. Wincing, you turn, and you're met with black eyes and bloodred teeth.

It's time, he says, voice gravelly and warped. He pulls you toward him, his arms open and inviting like the shadowed doorway to a tomb.

And with another exhalation, you follow.

CHAPTER TWENTY-THREE

I fall out of the Reading like being dropped off a cliff. My body wrenches forward, and I fall against my legs. I'm thankful that I wedged my knees into the dashboard before handling the diary. Heart racing, I lean into them now, trying to catch my breath and understand what I saw.

"Welcome back," Cross says. He puts his hand on my shoulder, and I have to fight to shrug it off, still feeling another set of ghostly fingers pressed against my skin. I catch his gaze and find comfort in the jade green of his eyes. "What'd you find out?"

"Nothing good," I say as I finally get my heart rate under control. "I think she killed herself."

Cross takes his hand back and leans heavily against the door. "Well, shit."

"Yeah." I shake my head, trying to clear the memories. "There was a symbol. Hold on, I need to write it down."

I reach into my jacket, hunting for my notepad. I pull it out a moment later, along with a pen, and draw the symbol, a crescent moon within a larger circle.

"That looks familiar," Cross says. "It was on one of those books, wasn't it?"

I nod. "Pretty sure it means Healer. But I don't understand."

"What?"

"She scribed it in blood," I say, brow furrowed, "and then she let her partner kill her or help her pass, I'm not sure."

Her partner? Priya asks, shocked. *But why?*

"I don't know." I look at her, wondering at the color of her eyes and if they would darken like John's had at the end.

"I thought you said she killed herself," Cross interjects. "If her partner killed her, that's not suicide."

"It felt like she wanted him to." I shiver.

"Whether it was a suicide or not isn't important. Did you learn anything else or just see her death?"

I struggle for words. "There was more to it than that, but it's all jumbled up." I squeeze the bridge of my nose, pushing back a headache that blooms behind my right eye. "She said that Baker tried to gain additional Affinities. It's why they Bound him. They thought it was tied to the barrier failing."

"Since it's still failing, I think it's safe to assume he wasn't the root cause."

"No," I say. "Things kept getting worse. They created the focal points to stop it, but it's still tearing."

"Did she say anything about that or give you an idea of why you've developed additional Affinities?"

I shake my head. "No, nothing about that, only the tears and why they Bound Baker. Something about that memory bothers me, though," I say, fighting against a niggling sense that whatever I just saw wasn't intended for me. "In the first Reading, Bell was young. She was old in this one."

Cross frowns. "Maybe you skipped something."

"I think I did, but I don't know how to Read the other memories. The knife may have had something to do with it." My headache grows worse, and I wince. "I'll try to Read the diary again once I get my knife reinscribed. In the meantime, I want to go talk to Frank."

"He made it pretty clear that he didn't want to see us again," Cross says. "You sure it's a good idea?"

"You have that picture of our victim?" I ask.

He nods and pulls a small photo from his pocket. "Right here."

"Then yes, I'm sure it's a good idea. I've got a hunch."

"A hunch." He sounds doubtful.

"We know two things right now. One, that she was a Medium, and two, that there was power pooled here even before I trapped it with the wards. The only other people we know who are Mediums interested in energy like this are the people working with Frank, whoever they might be."

"And you think she might be part of that group."

"Bingo," I say. "And since Frank is still in contact with that group, he may know her."

"I still think we should be canvassing the area," Cross says, "but you've had worse hunches in the past."

"Your confidence in me is thrilling," I say.

He turns the car on and motions for me to put my seatbelt on. "I have enough confidence in you to drive over to Oak Woods. And maybe Frank will be willing to talk to us about how your powers are changing."

"Maybe," I say, looking at the diary laying in my lap. "Let's focus on whether he can ID our vic or not."

"And if that doesn't work, we can get back to canvassing."

I hum my agreement, and the car falls silent. As we pass buildings, I wonder at that final moment when John looked like a Turned ghost. It seems impossible. The bond between ghost and Medium stops the process of Turning, returns sanity and connection to the ghost while bolstering the Medium's powers. What could disrupt that enough to allow the Turning to continue, to complete? I look at Priya in the rearview window, watch as she stares out the window, her hair blowing softly around her face in an invisible breeze. She catches me looking and meets my eyes in the mirror. They're gray and steady, and I'm comforted when they turn up slightly at the edges, a reassuring smile crossing her face.

We'll find out who she is, she Sends. *I have faith that the two of you will figure it out.*

Thanks, I Send back.

Speaking of figuring things out, she says. The thought is laser focused, keeping Cross from the conversation. *When are you going to talk to him?*

Soon, I say as I fight a blush. *I said when things calmed down.*

Things never calm down around you, she says with a smile.

Maybe you shouldn't keep putting it off.

Maybe you shouldn't keep butting in.

She laughs. *What can I say? I'm a romantic.*

You're a pest, I say, but I'm grinning. I look at Cross, taking in the clean lines of his profile, the soft slope of his lips, the hard jut of his chin. Warmth grows in my chest, and my smile fades, replaced by some other ineffable emotion. *Don't worry, it'll happen.*

Good. I'm going to nag you until it does.

I wouldn't expect anything less, I Send, rolling my eyes.

She falls quiet and her expression becomes more serious. *You're sure that Bell's partner killed her?*

No, I say while also sending comfort down our bond. I don't mention Bell's fear or her uncertainty about whether her bonded ghost partner could be trusted.

Priya sighs. *That's good. I couldn't imagine…*

I know.

She quickly changes the subject. *What are you going to ask Frank when we get there?*

If he can help ID this girl, mainly. Half of the difficulty in solving a case is ID'ing the victim. Hopefully, once we're able to do that, we can figure out why Steve killed her.

And his other victims? Priya asks. *He said there were others.*

We'll send a DNA sample to the FBI, let them run it through CODIS. Hopefully, it'll hit. If not, we'll pass his info and MO off to the Cold Case squad and see if they've got any murders that fit.

Priya nods and falls silent again. Cross slows, and I look up, surprised to see that we're already at the cemetery.

"You guys done talking?" he asks, looking at Priya in

the rearview mirror. "I didn't want to interrupt."

"Yeah, we're all set."

"Good," he says as he pulls into a parking spot before the visitor's center. "Here's hoping Frank isn't angry that we came back."

"If you get your light show going," I say with a quick grin, "we should be fine."

He sighs. "Are we going to figure that out?"

"Maybe," I say. "It's Wednesday, which means dinner with Taka. Hopefully, he'll have some idea of what's happening with you."

"But probably not," he says.

"Probably not. You're somewhat of an anomaly."

"Speak for yourself," he says. "Miss Three Affinities."

I flush. "Birds of a feather, I guess."

"I guess." He grins at me. "Partner."

"Partner." I match his grin.

As we draw closer to the monument, though, our moods darken and turn more businesslike. The pool of energy surrounding the stone obelisk is still. It reflects the sky, ghostly echoes of clouds coasting across its surface. Frank is sitting at the top of the marker and leaning against the legs of the statue topping it. He leans forward, arms resting on his knees as he looks down on us.

You kids better get off my lawn, he says, and I roll my eyes.

"We've got some more questions for you," Cross says as he reaches into his jacket pocket for the photo of our victim.

I already told you, I'm not answering any more questions. Frank starts to sink into the stone, and Cross yells at him to stop. The ghost pauses, eyebrow raised.

"It's about a homicide," Cross says, holding the photo up. "We're wondering if you can help us ID our victim."

Frank frowns. *You guys are cops? And Mediums?*

"Homicide," I say, pulling my badge from where it's looped around my neck so he can see it. "Think you can help us out?"

I guess, he says, still sounding surprised. *I've been dead six years. My social life is a little limited.*

Frank comes down from the top of the monument and floats in front of Cross who holds out the photo of our victim. Frank stares at it for a long moment, then sighs.

Yeah, I know her, he says sadly. *Or at least I've seen her around. She comes through here to check on the focal point occasionally. Never caught a name, though. She wasn't much for talking.*

"Great," I say as Cross tucks the photo back into his jacket. "Is there anyone else we can talk to about her? Maybe another member of the group who can tell us who she is?"

Maybe, Frank says, and he suddenly looks nervous. *Look, I'm not supposed to be talking to you guys at all. I'm supposed to scare people away, keep them from the focal point, make sure that we're still channeling the energy appropriately. If someone found out that I was telling you things, I'd be in deep shit.*

"What kind of shit can you get into?" Cross asks.

The Burning kind, Frank says matter-of-factly. *And while I may be dead, I still appreciate being here instead of on the other side.*

"Any help you can give us would be appreciated," I say. "We don't have to tell them that you were our informant. Just because you're dead doesn't mean we can't keep this confidential."

So, nothing on the record? He still looks nervous, though it's eased somewhat. *You won't say where you got her name?*

"Absolutely," Cross says, pulling a notebook out from his jacket. "You give us a name, and we'll get out of your hair."

Frank looks between the two of us and turns to Priya. *I can trust them?*

You can trust them, she says. *They're good people and good cops. They'll protect you.*

Okay.

He takes a deep breath, though he's long since needed to breathe.

Ruth, he says. *Ruth Peterson.*

CHAPTER TWENTY-FOUR

M y first response is shock, then confusion.

"Ruth Peterson? The Seer? The one who's apprentice was found dead in a warehouse?"

Frank nods. *Yeah, she's running the whole operation. There are lower-level people whose names I can give you, but if you want to know who that girl was, Ruth's the person you want to talk to.*

"Thank you," Cross says and catches my eye, tipping his head back toward the cruiser. "We appreciate your help."

Frank starts to head back to the monument, then hesitates. *Will you... Is there any chance you might swing through again? Tourists are fun and all, but it's been... I don't want to say* nice, *but it's been different.*

Cross stops and tilts his head, considering. "Maybe," he says. "I could make it happen."

Frank grins self-consciously. *Okay then. Stay out of trouble, and good luck with your case. Hopefully you catch the bastard.*

"Yeah," I say, still trying to process Ruth's part in the bigger picture.

"So, Peterson," Cross says as we draw closer to the cruiser. "We've got her apprentice killed by Baker, and now another Medium killed who's associating with her. That's a lot of dead, young Mediums in her circles."

"She didn't kill them," I say, jumping to her defense out of habit more than anything. "With how active she is in the community, she's bound to run into a lot of Mediums."

"I wonder if she's using that community to recruit for her shadowy organization," Cross says.

"You don't have to make it sound so nefarious," I grouse before climbing into the car.

"It's a little nefarious," he says seriously. "This group is keeping a huge secret, one that could have a major impact not only on the Medium community but the world at large. On top of that, we've got a dead girl who may have been killed while doing work for that same group."

The car starts, the roar of the engine loud and unsettling. "So, what do we do about it?"

"We talk to Peterson," he says simply. "We ID our vic, and we find out definitively if Steve killed her. Then, we figure out what to do about these tears."

"And dinner with Taka," I say.

"He's friends with Peterson, right?" Cross asks.

I nod. "They've known each other for years."

"You think Taka has any inside knowledge about these tears?"

I balk at the idea. "No. Absolutely not."

"You're pretty confident about that."

"He'd never keep something like that from me," I say again, my temper rising.

"Don't get defensive on me," he says. "I'm just asking."

"Well, you can stop."

Kim, Priya says cautiously. *He's trying to help.*

I let out a slow breath. "Sorry," I say. "As long as we find out who our Doe is, that's all that matters. The rest…"

"We'll deal with it as it comes," Cross says. "Do you want me to contact Peterson for an interview?"

"No," I say quickly. "No, I'll call. She knows me as more than a cop, and with her apprentice dying a few months ago, I think it'll be better if I talk to her about another death."

"I agree. I'll follow up with Abramo on our Doe's autopsy. It was scheduled for this morning, so he might have something to tell us."

"And Steve?"

"I think they were holding off on scheduling his until after you interviewed him." He shoots me a wry glance. "I'll let them know they need to get it on the calendar."

We ride to HQ in a silence that's only slightly strained. The uncomfortable edge to it could be my imagination, yet for some reason, I can't bring myself to believe it. My immediate defense of not only Taka, but Ruth as well, seems to have put Cross on edge. I glance at him as he drives, wondering if he's doubting my ability to be impartial. As I mull the idea over in my head, I wonder about it, too.

Cross's suggestion that Taka could be involved, that he

might know a secret of this magnitude and keep it from me is antithetical to our entire relationship. He saved me as a kid, taught me about my powers and the supernatural world around me with blunt honesty. Before him, I was lost and confused, unable to understand what my senses were telling me. Even my grandmother wasn't able to make me understand like Taka did. He was my Mentor, in every sense of the word, and the thought that he might have *lied* to me about something this big…

I can't bear it.

The sound of the engine cutting off knocks me from my introspective haze. Looking up, I see that we're in the parking lot of HQ, Cross turned in his seat and regarding me with calm, understanding eyes.

"You'll be okay," he says. "It's a bit of a shock for you, I'm sure, but we'll make sense of it."

"Yeah," I say softly. "But I trust your gut, and if you think that Taka might have known something…"

The words are sour on my tongue, and I swallow around them, trying to banish their bitter taste.

"I haven't met the guy," Cross says, offering me a conciliatory smile. "I don't know what he does or doesn't know."

"Then we ask him tonight," I say, though it makes something in my chest ache. "Find out for certain."

"Kim." His voice is gentle, as if the way he says my name can translate into physical comfort. "If that's truly what you want to do, I won't stop you. But we can ask Peterson the same questions, and we already know she's part of this group."

"But if he's been lying to me—"

"Then he's been lying to you," he says. "But he wouldn't do it to hurt you. From what you've told me about Taka, he cares about you. I'm sure any secrets he kept were to protect you."

"You don't know that."

"And you don't know that he's been keeping this from you," Cross counters. "You're not going to gain anything by worrying about it right now. Whatever the answers to your questions are, they're going to be the same tonight whether you spend the next couple of hours thinking yourself sick or not. Now, c'mon," he says, reaching for the door handle, "we've got police work to do. Or do you not want to get this solved?"

I sigh. "Do you always have to be so logical about things?"

"Only on days that end in Y," he says with a grin. "You ready to work?"

"Yeah, yeah," I say as I step out of the car. I slam the door shut and meet his eyes across the top of the car. "Thank you."

"Of course," he says.

I walk around the back of the cruiser and meet him as we both head toward the front doors of HQ. Out of the corner of my eye, I glance at him and catch him smiling softly to himself, his eyes on the ground in front of him as he walks. There's a glint of satisfaction in his eyes, and I nudge him with my elbow. He stumbles a little and frowns at me.

"You don't have to look so smug about it," I joke.

"I'm not smug."

"You're a little smug."

He scoffs and pushes the front door open. "I don't have time to discuss this, Detective Phillips. Some of us have work to do."

I laugh and follow after him. "All right, Detective Cross. Let me know when you find some."

I head to my desk, while he heads to the kitchen. Throwing my jacket over the back of my chair, I pull up my notes from the Baker case and find Ruth Peterson's phone number neatly filed away. I stare at the digits for a long moment, then huff out a breath and dial. The phone rings a few times, and a young, male voice answers.

"Office of Mrs. Peterson. May I ask who's calling?"

"Detective Kim Phillips," I say as Cross sets a cup of coffee on my desk before sitting. I nod my thanks and continue talking to the receptionist. "I'm trying to reach Mrs. Peterson in regards to an active investigation."

"Oh, I see," the receptionist says, clearly caught off guard. "Mrs. Peterson is out of the office at the moment. Can I take a message?"

"She should have my number already," I say before rattling it off again. "Have her call me as soon as possible, please. This is about a homicide."

"Of course, Detective," he says. "I'll make sure she gets your message as soon as she's back."

"Thank you." I hang up and grab the cup of coffee, taking a careful sip before thanking Cross.

"Peterson wasn't available?" he asks.

"You'd think a Seer of her ability would know when to be in to take a phone call," I joke. "Did Abramo submit his report on our Doe yet?"

"Yeah, and you should take a look at it," Cross says. "He noticed something odd about her stab wounds."

I frown and pull up the report. It reads like a standard autopsy report until I get to the section describing the cause of death. The further I go, the more unsettled I become.

"Cross," I say slowly. "What am I reading here?"

"According to Abramo, she didn't die from the knife wounds. Internal bleeding, sure, but the knife wounds were superficial."

"It's like they just burst," I say, horrified. "How would that have happened?"

Cross meets my eyes across the desk. "Maybe we're not as done with Steve as we thought. He gave you his full name, right?"

I go for my keyboard and pull up the CPD's database. "Yeah, Stephen Christopher White. Let me see if he comes up."

I type in his name, then wait as the program churns through its data. After a moment, it tings cheerfully, one entry returned.

Stephen Christopher White, born September 2, 1980, and registered as a Shaker in early 1999.

"Shit," I say, shocked. "He was a fucking Medium."

CHAPTER TWENTY-FIVE

I spend the next hour or so reading whatever I can find on Steve. He left a paper trail of sorts. There's no record of him attending college, though I manage to track down a high school graduation announcement from a small newspaper in rural Iowa. There's nothing after that for a few years, and then he shows up again as part of a crew that picketed unfair working conditions on an oil derrick in south Texas. They made enough noise to have a small piece written about them in a local paper. He pops up again a year later in Oklahoma, though this time it's for petty theft. Another theft charge in southern Indiana, then minor assault in Gary. The last record I find for him is an arrest warrant for another assault, this time with a deadly weapon, issued a few weeks ago out of the Circuit Court of Cook County.

"He was clearly escalating," I tell Cross after showing him the rundown of Steve's movements and arrests.

"They were in a basement. Her internal injuries would've required significant force, and there was no sign of a blunt instrument down there," Cross says. "How do you think he did it?"

"He was a Shaker. I wouldn't be surprised if he used

his abilities while he was attacking her."

"That's fucked up."

"Yeah," I say, shivering. "He said that our Doe fought him, though. Maybe she was the first Medium he found himself up against."

"Maybe," Cross says. "We're going to have a hell of a time tracking his victims down if there are more. His MO could've been to make it look like accidents. This autopsy reads more like a car wreck than a murder."

"I'll get a call list together, start reaching out to the local police departments. You should probably go see Abramo, make sure we're reading his report right."

"You'll be all right on your own?"

"Yeah, I've got this," I say. "I'm going to be making phone calls for the rest of the day. There's no reason for you to sit here and watch."

"Okay." He stands and grabs his coat. "You'll send me Taka's address? I can meet you there later tonight."

"Shit," I say, quickly pulling my phone out. "I still need to let him know you're coming. I'll text you the address later?"

"Sounds good. See you tonight, partner."

"Later," I say, pulling Taka's number up on my speed dial. The phone rings a few times but clicks over to an answering machine.

"Hey Taka, it's Kim. I wanted to give you a heads-up that I'm bringing someone with me to dinner tonight. It's not anything serious, but I want you to meet the guy." I pause. "Not because of anything serious. He's Sighted, and

I was hoping you could help him find a Mentor. So, yeah. Medium stuff. Nothing important. But I wanted to give you a heads-up so you had time to cook for everyone. Though he might not stay for dinner. I don't know. That depends on if you can help him or not. Whatever, I'm rambling. I'll see you tonight. Bye."

Remind me how you're a detective again, Priya says, aghast. *That was awful.*

Shut up. It was fine.

We'll see what Taka has to say tonight, she says with a smug grin. *I bet you five bucks he thinks you're bringing a date.*

You don't use money.

Even better for you, then. If you lose, you won't have to pay up.

I roll my eyes and return my attention to the computer screen. *We've got more important things to deal with right now. There are at least three states we know Steve was in, with at least four different police departments we're going to have to work with. And if we find out there* are *other victims, we may have to bring in the Feds.* I groan and start searching for contact information for the police department in the Texas town where Steve first shows up. *There's going to be so much paperwork.*

I spend the next couple of hours looking up contact information, making phone calls, and faxing information to other police departments. While the guys in Texas struggle to remember Steve, the officer I speak to in Gary remembers him vividly.

"Real weird guy," he says when we speak. "I wasn't upset to see him leave town after his case was dropped."

"Dropped?" I ask.

"Yeah. It was the oddest thing, but we couldn't get anything to stick. No physical evidence, no witnesses, only the victim saying that White was the one who attacked her. He had an alibi, though."

"Who was it?"

"His boss," the officer says, clearly annoyed. "Said that White was at work the entire time. Had video to prove it, too. But the vic kept telling us that White was the one who'd attacked her. We weren't able to square the two and ended up having to drop the charges."

"Did you know he was a Medium?" I ask.

"That's part of why we were able to convince the grand jury to bring charges, but the prosecutor decided not to take it to trial. He didn't think it'd stand up in court."

"Great," I say with a heavy sigh. "Any chance you can look into cold cases in your area for me?"

"You think White's involved in something else?"

"I think he might have been, yes."

"You got him in holding? Is he talking?"

"He's dead. He's not talking to anyone."

The other officer grunts into the phone. "Well, you send me the MO, and I'll see what I can find. Might not get it to you for a couple of days, though. You know how it is."

Unfortunately, I do, but I send him the information anyway, along with my number. It's the same story with the other police department in Indiana. I consider following up with the Cook County Prosecutor's office but decide to leave it for tomorrow. It's getting close to five, the entire day spent researching and making phone calls, and if there's anything that Taka dislikes more than tardiness, it's tardiness with a bad excuse.

I'm pulling my things together, getting ready to leave, when my phone rings. I check the caller ID and frown when I see Banks's information on the screen.

"Detective Phillips," I say as I push back my chair, which lets out a low howl in protest. "What's up, Banks?"

"Are you busy right now?"

I look at the clock again and bite my lip. "I might be. Why?"

"That marker you told me about, the second one? I need to talk to you about it. Now."

"So, talk." I slide my arms into my jacket, my cell phone tucked between my ear and my shoulder. "I'm about to leave the office."

"I can't do it over the phone," she says. Something about her tone makes me pause, and a thread of disquiet eases its way into my chest. "You need to come here. Now."

"What's going on?" I ask. "Is everything okay?"

"More or less," she says, and her voice quavers a little bit. The crack in her usually confident demeanor sets alarm bells ringing. "I can't talk about it over the phone. How soon can you get here, Detective?"

I pick up my pace, nearly jogging as I hit the doors to the parking lot. "I'm going to be in my personal car, so no lights or siren, but if I push it, I can get there in fifteen."

"Okay," she says. "Please, I need you to hurry. I don't know wh—"

The phone hangs up, and I curse.

Is everything okay? Priya asks as I fumble for my car keys.

I'm not sure. The engine rumbles to life, and I back out of the lot quickly, hitting Sixty-Third Street and rushing toward the highway. *She sounded like she might be in trouble.*

We'd better hurry, then.

The road flies beneath my car as I zip my way north. Street lights flash to life as darkness falls. The sunset turns the clouds a deep, fire red, and as I pull up to the cemetery where the second marker is, I fight a shiver even though the heat is turned on full.

Banks's black coupe is parked near the front of the cemetery, and I pull up next to it before stepping out of my car, holster unbuttoned, hand resting on my gun.

You see anything suspicious, I tell Priya, *you let me know. I'm not sure what we're walking into here.*

Hopefully nothing, Priya says, but she doesn't sound convinced.

With evening falling, the cemetery feels abandoned and forgotten. There are no cars, no signs of caretakers or visitors leaving for the day. A backhoe, digging arm resting limply against the ground, sits in the distance, the last rays of sunlight glinting off the glass of its empty cab. I scan the graveyard and still when I see a solitary figure standing next to a familiar stone marker.

I approach Banks slowly. She's facing the marker, her back to me. Dry grass crackles under my boots, and she turns as I approach, her hands clasped together in front of her.

"Detective," she says shakily. She takes a quick step toward me, wrings her hands, then turns back to the marker. "I'm sorry to drag you out here, but you have to see this."

I slowly move my hand from my holster, but I leave the safety clasp undone. "What's this about, Banks?"

"It's the binding on this marker," she says. "I don't like what it's telling me."

"What's it telling you?" I ask, taking a cautious step closer.

"It's hard to explain," she says, crouching down to run her fingers over the marker's carved surface. "But this one isn't just for binding a ghost or controlling power. It's specifically forcing forgetfulness. This series of runes here"—she presses her palm against the front of the marker, then traces a cluster of symbols—"would make whoever was Bound to this marker forget who they were or why they were here."

"You mean whatever ghost was here before, the binding would have stolen their memories?"

"Something like that." She stands and wipes her hands off on her pants. I can't tell if she's trying to clean off dirt or sweat. "What was the ghost who was here like?"

"She wasn't all here," I say carefully. "Her mind seemed scattered, unfocused."

She kept singing, Priya Sends to the both of us. *It sounded like a nursery rhyme.*

Banks nods slowly. "That sounds like what this would do. Come here, though, I want you to see this."

I take a hesitant step closer. She wrings her hands together again, glancing over my shoulder, then back to my face. Her skin is pale and as I watch, a bead of sweat gathers at her temple and slides down the curve of her face. I still.

"Why couldn't you have told me that over the phone?" I ask, frowning.

"Just"—she lets out a heavy breath—"come over here, please. *Please.*"

I take another step so that we're only a few paces apart. Her eyes are wide, her breath coming fast. "What's going on? You sounded like you were in trouble."

"That's because she was," a masculine voice says from behind me.

I spin, hand reaching for my gun, when I feel a viselike grip around my entire body, locking me in place. I hear Banks curse quietly behind me.

"Why couldn't you *trust* me for once?" she asks quietly.

"None of that, now," he says. "Nice to finally meet you, Detective."

A man walks into view from around a large mausoleum. His long black hair is pulled back into a ponytail, and thick eyeglasses stop me from being able to tell his eye color. He's older than I am but not by much, maybe only five or ten years. Crow's feet peek out around the frames of his glasses, and they become more visible as he smiles, though there's no humor or kindness in his expression. Something about him is familiar, but I can't put my finger on it.

"I'm sorry," Banks says. She sounds defeated and panicked, and her breath comes hard and fast, though I can't turn around to see her. The grip on my body tightens, squeezing itself around my chest in a painful rush. I fight against the invisible hand, and it tightens hard enough that I can feel my ribs creak.

"Who the fuck are you?" I ask as I try to think of a way to break free.

"Is that important right now?" He smiles, and the vise tightens.

My breath is forced from my lungs, and I gasp for air. The man's smile grows.

"I thought you would put up more of a fight," he says. "He said you would be more of a challenge than our usual fare."

"You let me go, and I'll show you how much of a challenge I can be." I force the words through gritted teeth, and he laughs.

"Where's the fun in that?" he asks. Slowly, he walks toward me, stopping inches from me. He reaches up and runs a finger over my cheek, and I snap my teeth at him. Startled, he pulls his hand back quickly, eyes wide, and he grins again. "You *are* a fighter, aren't you?"

"Who the *fuck* are you?" I ask again.

"His name is White," Banks says from behind me, voice shaking but strong. "He told me before you got here."

"You shut your fucking mouth," White says with a snarl. Banks yells in pain behind me, and I struggle again, though it doesn't do me any good.

"White?" I ask, the puzzle pieces slotting into place as realization sweeps over me.

"My brother says hello," he says with a snarl, and my vision goes black.

CHAPTER TWENTY-SIX

W hen I come to, I'm leaning up against a stone wall, my hands tied tightly behind my back. It's cold, and my breath frosts the air in front of me. There's a weak beam of light coming in, probably from a streetlight or something nearby, and as I squint in the darkness, I make out dust, dead leaves, and a large stone casket in the center of the room. It seems to be part of the mausoleum itself—it and the floor having come from the same, massive block of stone, the casket painstakingly carved from the rock. If I stretch my legs out, I can probably kick it, but instead, I don't move, pretending to still be unconscious.

Priya, I Send with a tight, focused beam. *What's going on?*

She doesn't appear, but I can feel her nearby. *He's got you locked up in a mausoleum in the cemetery. Banks is on the other side of the coffin, but she's still out.* I can feel her anxiety singing down our bond. *He's outside, pacing and talking to himself.*

He's a Medium?

Maybe, she says. *I can't be sure. I don't see another ghost around him, so he may just have some of the Sight.*

And some of the Shaker abilities his brother had, I add, wincing as I shift to ease the ache in my ribs. The movement doesn't help and sends another pang of discomfort through my body.

I try to loosen the bindings on my hands, wiggling my wrists back and forth to loosen the rope. It starts to chafe against my skin, burning the longer I move. I hold back an impatient sigh.

Any chance you can get these off? I ask Priya, trying to ignore the stinging pain as the rope bites into my irritated skin.

Give me a second, she says. Her cool touch on my wrists soothes my abraded skin, and I wait as she pulls power from our bond, trying to gather enough energy to undo the knot. After a moment, the rope loosens, and when I move my arms this time, the rope comes away enough for me to slip one hand free.

Fuck yes, I say. *Thank you.*

Rubbing at my wrists, I quickly take stock of my surroundings. Checking for weapons first, I come up empty. My gun is gone, though my shoulder holster is still on, and my knife is missing from my boot. My cell phone is also missing, as is my badge. All that's left is a piece of chalk, tucked deep into the lining of one of my pockets.

Shit.

Carefully, I make my way around the casket, trying to be silent. Banks is lying on the ground, her hands also bound behind her. I sidle around her, eyeing the large, ornately decorated metal door that appears to be the only exit. Creeping back to her side, I touch my fingers to her neck, feeling for a pulse. Her heartbeat seems to rush to meet my touch, and as I feel the strong beat of her heart against my fingers, I let out a quiet, relieved sigh.

I'm going to try to get her up, I tell Priya. *Stand guard. Let me know if he starts coming toward the door.*

The rope around Banks's wrists comes away after a few moments of frantic tugging at the knot, my fingers numb from the cold. I lay Banks on her back and gently shake her.

"Hey," I whisper, praying that the thick stone of the mausoleum will stop my voice from carrying. "You need to wake up, you idiot. That cup of coffee was *not* worth this shit."

Banks groans, and I clamp my hand over her mouth, trying to stifle the sound. Her eyes fly open, wide and terrified, and I shush her, trying to calm her down while tightening my grip around her mouth.

"It's all right," I say. "It's me. Calm down and stay quiet. He's outside, and he's got my gun."

Her eyes widen again, and her breath is hot and fast against my palm.

"I'm going to take my hand away, but you have to be quiet," I say, trying to pitch my voice so that it's soothing, rather than intimidating. I'm not entirely sure I succeed, but Banks nods, and I slowly pull my hand away from her mouth.

She sits up, shivering, and looks around the darkened space. "Did that motherfucker put us inside a tomb?"

"Not important," I say. "We have to figure out how to get out of here. He's got my weapons, and he's got at least some Shaker abilities."

"Is he a full Medium?" she asks, voice trembling.

"I don't think so."

"Thank God for small miracles." Her typical carefully pulled-back hair is loose and hanging in tight curls around her face. She pushes a strand back. "So, how are we going to fuck this guy up?"

"I'm not sure. I've got chalk, that's it."

She grins, her teeth flashing white and feral in the darkness. "That's more than enough, then. Hand it here."

I fish the small piece out of my pocket and pass it to her. "What are you thinking?"

"Stay out of my way, and when it's time, I'm going to need you to power it."

I frown. "I don't have my knife."

She turns her face toward me, the thin light flashing off the pair of silver studs in her ears. "Sterling," she says, noticing my eyes following the low glint of metal. "And sharp as hell."

Banks reaches up and pulls one of the studs out before handing it to me. She moves to the left side of the door, near the hinges, and I crouch down to the right. One eye on the metal door, one eye on Banks, I watch as she starts furiously scribing runes and sigils across the solid stone floor. The chalk rasps quietly in the still silence of the tomb, and it sends a shiver up my spine, the fine hairs along the back of my neck standing up.

What's White doing? I ask Priya, watching Banks work.

He's got your gun out, but I don't think he's used to it. He's waving it around, and… Kim, I think he's talking to his brother, she says. *But I don't see any other ghosts. And you and Cross, you Burnt Steve, Right?*

I think so. What's he saying?

He's talking about… Jesus, he's talking about killing people, Kim. Women. It sounds like they were working together, and Steve went off on his own. The assaults in Indiana. He… She swallows. *This guy's been tracking his brother since then, trying to catch up.*

Shit. Does he seem sane?

No, Priya says firmly. *He seems… lost. Like Steve was the one in charge, and now he doesn't know what to do. I thought it was bad before, but this… You have to be careful. I don't think you're going to be able to predict what this guy will do.*

I can barely make out White's voice from the other side of the door. I move closer, pressing my ear up against the cold metal. I can only make out a few words, but it's clear that he's yelling at someone who isn't there.

Kim, Priya Sends, her voice a whisper only slightly louder than Banks's scribing, *he's coming toward the mausoleum.*

He still has my gun?

Yeah, she says.

"Banks," I whisper furiously as I move away from the door. "Whatever you're doing, you need to finish it. *Now.*"

"Prick your finger," she says, the chalk dancing across the floor as she continues to write, "and get ready to move."

I jab the stud into my thumb. At first, it just indents the surface. There are years of scars there, small, thin white lines gained after countless circles and bindings. It's tough and thick, and I wince as I press the earring harder into my skin. After a long, terrifying second, it pops through the surface and buries itself into my flesh. I gasp, then wrench the stud out. Blood seeps from the wound, and I hold my hand at the ready, waiting for either Banks's signal or for the door to open.

He's reaching for the door, Priya says. She's panicked, her voice high-pitched and tight in her throat. *Kim, get ready to jump him or something. Go for his legs once the door opens. He's got the gun up, so if you take him by surprise, he won't be able to shoot you. I don't know what Banks is trying to do, but it's not—*

"Now," Banks says on a harsh whisper. "Fucking *now*."

I slam my hand against the chalk lines spread out across the floor as the door opens. Muted light pours in from the doorway, but it's wiped away from the light of whatever thing Banks has scribed. For a moment, I see White's dark hair and the glow of sigils glinting off of his glasses, but then I have to turn away, eyes watering in pain. I throw my arm up, half to block the light and half to brace for an attack that doesn't come. Instead, a sound like screaming begins, a wind swirling around us from out of nothing. My hair whips around my face and eyes, and I reach for the stone casket. My hands bite into the roughhewn rock as blond strands sting my face. The wind grabs at my clothes, trying to pull me toward the bright, swirling light that continues to grow behind me. Stark shadows dance in jerking, grotesque movements on the far wall, and I look away, something about the sight making an instinctive part of me want to run and hide somewhere far, far away.

Jesus Christ, Priya breathes. *Holy fucking shit.*

There's a strangled scream from behind me, and I draw myself closer to the stone casket, fighting to keep a hold on the stone as the wind picks up and starts grabbing me, tearing my jacket open to flap in the wind.

"What the fuck did you do?" I shout to Banks, trying to find her in the chaos of light and wind and swirling debris.

"I broke open one of those tears," she yells from the other side of the casket. "Something got White. Oh God, it was…"

I finally look behind me, and what I see steals the breath from my lungs in a terrified rush. A pillar of light stands before the doorway, a semicircle of wards that holds a yawning darkness at bay. Something moves inside of it, a slithering serpentine motion that puts my fight-or-flight response straight to flight. A malformed hand presses against the light, and the darkness screams as it pulls away. There's a hint of gnashing teeth, and that screaming sound starts again, only this time I can see the dark throat that it comes from. Eyes flash in the dark, red as embers in a fire, and it lets out a twisted, multivoiced laugh.

"How the fuck do we close it?" I yell, my fingers digging deeper into the rough stone of the casket.

"I don't know," Banks says, and her voice sounds like she's sobbing.

"Well, *fuck*," I say, more to myself than to her.

Priya, I Send. *Thoughts.*

Shield, break the circle, then Bind it.

That sounds risky.

I don't know what else to do, she says. I catch a hint of strain in her voice.

You okay?

It's trying to pull me in, too, she says. Now that I'm looking for it, I can feel the strong, persistent tug on our bond.

Well, it can get fucked, I say. I force myself to stand and reach for Banks's hand where it's grasping the casket's carved lid, her fingers dug into a jagged channel that runs around the rim of the lid.

"Get over here," I yell, and she forces herself to her feet and drags herself around to the other side of the casket with me between her and the dark opening. With the heavy weight of stone between us and the tear, we have a modicum of protection against the growing wind. I face it, watching as whatever dark creature prowling the boundary screams again, its twisted voice like hundreds of people dying and crying out for help.

"Stay as close to me as you can," I tell her, and she immediately wraps her arms around my waist, tucking her head into the space between my shoulder blades. I try to ignore the way her nails bite into my skin, even through my jacket and shirt. "I'm going to shield us. Hold on."

I close my eyes, trying to block out the terrifying sight in front of me, and draw power. It tugs away from my hands, getting drawn into the darkness, and I pull harder, teeth gritted. Slowly, it comes back to me, filling my internal stores until there's a molten core of power roiling in my gut. I let out a breath and a shield springs to life around Banks and me.

The wind around us immediately dies, though leaves and debris are still tossed up and around the inside of the tomb. They slap harmlessly against the shield, and Banks whimpers into my back.

"Did you do it?" she asks.

"Not yet."

I feel her head rise from my back, and she curses.

"What the fuck were you thinking?" I ask, watching as another, smaller, predatory shape moves in the darkness, testing the light that separates it from us. It snaps at the other creature, which snarls with a chorus of voices, and the smaller creature retreats with a whimper.

"I was thinking," she says, "that there was a homicidal maniac with magic powers waiting to kill us."

"Did you even think of an exit strategy?"

"No," she says, angry and annoyed, "but I figured it would be better than being crushed or stabbed or shot to death."

"Well, you'd better figure out how we're going to close this damn thing," I say. My shield flickers and an errant gust of wind whips my hair into my eyes. "I'm not going to be able to hold this forever."

"I've still got the chalk," she says. "Can you get us any closer?"

"You want to go *toward* the giant, spinning death thing?"

"Fuck you," she says, "and yes."

"Fine," I say, and press my lips firmly together as I

shuffle toward the dark hole in the world. Something crashes into the light barrier, and I freeze as the whole thing flickers under the strain. Voices laugh from the other side of the boundary.

"Hurry the fuck up."

Banks crouches down and starts writing another series of runes. I don't even try to pay attention to what she's doing, instead funneling all of my focus and attention into keeping the shield up around us. Sweat gathers on my forehead, and an ache blooms between my shoulder blades, as if my body is bearing the weight of the shield. My knees shake, and the shield dims for a moment.

Banks writes faster.

After another moment, she lets out a soft sigh. "I need you to power this," she says. "You're going to have to put as much energy into it as you can. I don't know if it'll work otherwise."

"If I fail," I say, crouching down next to her, "you do whatever you can to get out of here, and you bring Ruth Peterson back."

She frowns. "The Seer?"

"Not important," I say. "Just do it."

"Okay." She nods. "Whenever you're ready."

I take a deep breath. *See you on the other side,* I Send to Priya. Panic zips through our bond, but before she can say anything, I press my still-bleeding thumb against the new lines of chalk.

Power sweeps out of me in a wave, followed quickly by ice cold. I grit my teeth to stop them from shivering and watch as the new line of runes and sigils slowly bursts to light. As if struggling through a fog, each symbol glows softly and gains in intensity. Blue, red, and green flames lick over each character, twisting and curling as they fight their way toward the already-burning light between us and the tear.

My vision goes black around the edges, color fading as the world turns gray around me. I fight against it, forcing more power from my body and into the runes. I don't hear the wind or the creature howling with its many voices, only a high-pitched ringing that gains in intensity as the world dims.

I fall to one knee, head spinning, and watch as the symbols finally meet the existing wards, then leap into bright, burning white light.

As the tear seals, it creates a vacuum, and air rushes in to fill the void. A deafening pull hurts my ears. My shield drops a heartbeat later, and I fall forward, gasping for breath as I struggle to stay conscious. Banks lets out a whoop, and my whole body shivers, muscles cramping as I curl around my knees, head pressed against the cold stone, fighting for warmth.

"Fuck, yes!" Banks shouts again. Her feet scrape across the stone ground and stop. "Oh, shit. Detective." She drops to the ground next to me and puts her hand on my back. "You're gonna be okay. Just keep breathing."

"Fuck you," I say, but the words come out a little slurred. "M'fine."

You're not fine, Priya says, her voice a mix of anxious worry and relief. *Can you Heal yourself?*

I mumble something and a creeping warmth moves its way from deep within my stomach to spread into my chest, arms, and legs. Banks's hand on my back stills, then pulls away.

"Why are you glowing?" she asks hesitantly.

"M'magic," I say, my words still slurred.

Priya sighs. *She'll be fine in a moment. Just let the Healing do its thing.*

When the warmth reaches my fingers, I relax into it. Smooth waves of heat pass through me, and I roll onto my back with a soft groan. Opening my eyes, I find Banks looming over me, brow furrowed. She's lit softly by gentle green light. I glance down as if from a distance, surprised to see the light coming from me. I wave at her, then close my eyes again, enjoying the way the Healing courses through my body to ease my bone-deep exhaustion.

"Well, shit," Banks says on a sigh. "You're full of surprises, aren't you?"

I exhale as the Healing finishes working its way through me. Eyes open, I look at my thumb to find it healed and the old scars faded to almost nothing. I push myself up, dry leaves falling from my back and hair.

"What the hell happened?"

CHAPTER TWENTY-SEVEN

"You want to, maybe, have this conversation somewhere else?" Banks asks, gesturing around the mausoleum.

"No," I say as I stand. "Here's just fine."

She sighs and wraps her arms around her waist with a shiver. "Can we go somewhere a little warmer at least?"

Still warm from the Healing, I watch her breath fog the air.

You should get somewhere warm before the adrenaline rush wears off, Priya says pragmatically. *You're going to crash.*

"Okay, fine," I say, relenting. "Let's go."

Banks hesitates for a moment, then turns around and walks out of the still-open doorway of the tomb. I look around the entryway, hoping to find my gun, but it's as gone as White is. I guess it was dragged into Death at the same time he was. I groan, realizing the paperwork nightmare that I'm going to have to wade through, and walk outside.

Night has fallen. There are a few lights spread along the unpaved roads of the cemetery. Other than those pools of illumination, the graveyard is covered in the thick, inky blackness of midwinter night. Banks is standing to the side, looking around us with a furrowed brow.

"Do you still have your keys?" she asks me, her gray eyes meeting mine as I walk toward her. "My pockets are empty."

"Shit," I say as I scan the cemetery. "We'd better hope he didn't have them on him whenever that thing took him. Let's see if we can find his car."

"Yeah," Banks says with a shiver.

It takes us a few minutes, and we end up finding the car more from sound than from sight. White had turned all of his lights off but left his Ford Explorer idling nearby. The driver's side door opens with a squeal of unoiled hinges, and I flip the headlights on. Light cuts through the darkness before us, creating shadows from the gravestones that look like fingers reaching from the darkness. Banks looks away and opens the back door, reaching inside and up to turn on the ceiling light.

My badge and knife are sitting haphazardly on the passenger seat, and I lean across the driver's seat to grab them. Banks rummages around on the floor for a moment and lets out a triumphant shout.

"Here we go," she says, shaking her keys, the metal jangling loudly in the empty cemetery.

I open the center console and find an unfamiliar wallet, along with some opened envelopes and food wrappers. Leaving it for later, I check the glove compartment. My keys fall out onto the passenger side floor, along with a pile of other wallets and keys. Mouth turning down, I grab my keys from the pile. There's no sign of our phones.

"What're those?" Banks asks, peering over the driver's seat to look at the pile on the floor.

"Trophies, probably." I exit the car. "I'm going to have to get your fingerprints so Forensics doesn't get confused when they process this thing."

She goes a little pale. "You think this car is a crime scene?"

"Either that or he and his brother used it to commit their crimes. C'mon, get out of there."

She exits the car carefully, and I turn it off before I go to shut the door. A faint buzzing stops me, though, and I follow the sound to where it originates under the driver's side seat. Tucked up under the bar to move the seat back are two cell phones. The one buzzing is mine, and I assume the other is Banks's. I weave my hand into the small space, grab both phones, and answer mine.

"Phillips," I say, holding the other phone out to Banks. She takes it and mouths a thank-you before moving away from White's car.

"Where are you?" Taka asks, his voice crisp with anger.

I flinch. "This is going to be really hard to explain over the phone."

"Then you had best get here soon. My patience is thin this evening, especially with the unexpected company."

"I left a voice mail?" I say, my voice rising at the end of the sentence and turning it from a statement to a question.

"One I did not receive," Taka says. "I will speak with you when you arrive."

He hangs up, and I take a deep breath, pulling the

phone away from my ear. Looking at the front screen, I see a series of missed calls from both Taka and Cross. I curse softly and turn back to Banks. I walk up to her, and together, we move away from the Explorer.

It takes us a moment to get oriented, but we eventually find our cars parked where we left them. I silently thank God for criminals too lazy to hide evidence. Banks hesitates outside of her vehicle and looks to me.

"We can talk in my car," I say, recognizing her unspoken fear, before opening the door and climbing in. The engine turns over and purrs to life. She opens the passenger side door, sits, and slams it loudly. It's quiet and awkward in the car, and exhaustion starts seeping in along the edges of my mind. I rub the bridge of my nose.

"So," I say, startling her a little. "What happened?"

"He followed me," she says quietly. "Or, rather, he followed *you*, and then he followed me. He didn't make much sense when he started talking. Said a lot of stuff about his brother, but I didn't know what he was talking about. I still don't, not really. But once he figured out that I knew you well enough to have your number, he made me call. You know what happened after that."

"Are you okay?" I ask, though I want to ask about what he said. "It's a lot for one night."

She laughs mirthlessly. "I guess. I've never been kidnapped. Held hostage? Whatever you want to call it, it's a first."

"There are victim's counselors with the CPD you can talk to," I say, but she cuts me off.

"Fuck that shit." She glares at me, and the tightness in

my shoulders eases at the familiar, predatory gleam in her eyes. "I'm shaken, yeah, and I'm going to be double-checking all of my doors and windows for a while, but I'll be okay."

She pauses and looks down at her hands, furrowing her brow at her fingers, which she's tangled together. "Honestly? I'm more frightened by whatever was beyond the tear. That was…"

"Yeah," I say as the silence in the car becomes pensive, thoughtful. I frown. "How did you even *do* that?"

She smiles, one side of her mouth quirking up into a softened facsimile of her usual bravado. "I undid whatever those markers have been doing."

"You undid them? How'd you figure that out?"

"I've been staring at those damn things for days now," she says, a hint of frustration coating her voice. "You spend that much time studying a binding like that, and it becomes a fairly straightforward process to reverse it."

"Well, shit," I say, shaking my head.

"You don't have to worry about me doing it again," she says. "I can't power the runes myself, and there's no way in *hell* I'd open one of those things again. Not after… Anyway, it'll be fine." She frowns at me. "Why did you want me to find Ruth Peterson?"

"She's involved," I say. "With the markers, I mean. She's apparently in charge of the organization that's putting them up around the city."

Banks's eyebrows go up, crowding into her hairline. "For real?"

"Yeah. An informant told us about it."

"The ghost at the Confederate Mound?"

"A *confidential* informant," I say. She rolls her eyes but lets it go.

"So, what do you do now?" she asks. "I mean, you aren't going to be able to charge that guy for what he did."

"I'll get it written up and pass the information on to Cold Case. They'll review outstanding cases, send his and his brother's information to other police bureaus, and hopefully, something'll shake out. We have his brother's DNA, and there's always a chance we'll find some of his on his car. Best case, it hits on an unsolved case, and some family somewhere gets answers."

Banks nods. "I can't say I regret what happened to him, but I'm glad you'll still be able to do something about that creep."

I glance at the dashboard clock and sigh. "Are you okay to drive? Do you need me to take you anywhere?"

Her eyebrow rises again. "You have somewhere to be?"

"Yes," I say. "Dinner with Taka."

Understanding washes over her face. "Are you late?" She takes in my expression and shakes her head. "Okay, yes. Definitely late. I should be okay. Just… If you can wait until I get in my car?"

"Yeah," I say as she gets out. "I'll wait."

She smiles her thanks. "I'll be in touch, Detective. I still have questions for you."

"And I want to talk to you about what he was saying when he took you, but for now? Just stay out of trouble, okay?"

"I'll do my best," she says before shutting the door.

I wait for her to get into her car, turn on my headlights, and hurry out of the cemetery. The road flies beneath me as I hurry to Taka's. I call Cross, but he doesn't answer. I leave a voice mail that's probably more confusing than my silence, but I figure the effort will count for something. I also call HQ, telling the officer on duty about White's Ford and its likely connection to our double. He promises to pass the information along the chain and have someone from Forensics come and get the car. With that worry off my plate for the time being, all that's left for me to focus on is the drive.

I'll admit, though, that I'm distracted as I draw closer to Taka's home. Part of my mind is focused on driving, but another part mulls over what happened in that mausoleum, about the hole that Banks tore in reality, and the darkness that moved beyond it.

Priya, I ask, breaking the silence, *do you think that all of the afterlife is like that?*

You mean dark and full of terrors?

Game of Thrones *reference aside, yes.*

I think, she says after a moment, *that parts of it must be. I was raised to believe that there are planes of existence that we inhabit before reincarnation. Some are good, some are not. What we saw tonight… Well, Banks opened a small hole in the barrier between us and Death. And same as there is evil and darkness in life, there must be evil and darkness beyond. We saw some of that. But there's also goodness and light here, and I think it must be on the other side as well. So, is all of the afterlife like that? No, I don't think so.*

I smile softly. *Very metaphysical of you.*

I've got a lot of time on my hands, she says with a grin. *And you don't have enough romance novels.*

It startles a laugh from me. *We need to talk to Ruth, figure out what this all means and what we can do to help.*

You think she'll let you? Frank made it seem like it was a tight-knit community, not one that you could easily walk into.

Well, I say, apprehensive as I approach Taka's home, *I've got three Affinities now. I figure that'll get my foot in the door.*

Priya frowns, serious. *Do you think you'll get any more?*

Honestly? I have no idea. I'll be happy if this is where it stops.

And Riley? she asks.

He needs a Mentor, I say, *and I need to stop drawing runes on him. It's a little ridiculous at this point.*

Priya laughs. *I can't argue with that, but I meant about what's going on between the two of you. Everything else seems to have calmed down, right? Are you going to talk it out?*

I pause, thinking. *Yes,* I finally say. *I promised him I would.*

And?

And we'll see how it goes, I guess. There are plenty of reasons why this is a bad idea.

Other than the whole working together thing, what's stopping you?

I eye her with more than a hint of disbelief. *You've seen me date. You know how I get.*

You'll be fine, she counters, brushing aside my concerns. *Riley won't let you get away with shit.*

I sigh. *We'll see.*

After another quiet moment, I slow to a stop before Taka's house. The lights are blazing, and Cross's car is in the driveway. After pulling up behind it, I take a deep breath before turning the key and climbing out of my car. There are still a few leaves clinging to my jacket, and I brush them away as I walk to the front door. I raise my hand to knock, and the door swings open, an aggrieved Taka standing at the entrance, glare already in place.

"*Tadaima?*"

CHAPTER TWENTY-EIGHT

"Kim," Taka says stiffly, "*okaeri.*"

He steps aside, and I walk in, shoulders hunched and feeling like a chastised child. Cross is sitting awkwardly at the low table in the living room. Our eyes meet, and I can read the implied *save me* in his gaze.

"I'm so sorry I'm late," I say, though part of me is annoyed that I'm going to have to explain myself—a full-grown woman—to Taka. "It's extremely complicated."

Taka gestures toward the table. "Sit, then talk."

I take my shoes off, then go to sit at the table next to Cross. He flashes me a quick, reassuring smile, and though it's a minor thing, it does help. Taka makes himself comfortable on the other side of the table, and I have to fight back the sudden sense of déjà vu. It's like I'm back in high school, coming home past curfew and getting ready to be chewed out.

"Would you like to explain why you're late?" Taka asks.

I consider giving him the unvarnished truth.

A serial killer kidnapped Banks and me and locked us in a mausoleum where we broke open the barrier between life and death to stop him from killing us.

As I open my mouth to explain, I look at Taka, examining him in a way I haven't in a long time. He has bags under his eyes, his skin a little sallow, sunken. He looks tired in a way he didn't on Sunday, and I wonder what the truth will do to him, how it will weigh him down more. So, I hedge instead, unwilling to burden him while he looks so worn out.

"It's complicated."

"So you said earlier," Taka says. "Would you care to elaborate?"

I look to Cross, who gives a helpless shrug. "It was work related," I say, unconvincingly. "A suspect kept me late."

Cross frowns, but I put a hand on his knee, silencing him with a tight squeeze on his leg.

Later, I think, hoping he gets the message from my fingers digging into his thigh. *I'll explain later.*

"If you want to keep secrets, that's your choice," Taka says tersely before standing. "You are an adult, and you do not owe me any explanations."

I fight back a wince. *Later,* I think. *I'll tell him later.*

He walks into the kitchen and comes out a moment later with a serving tray, stacked high with steaming dishes.

"However," he continues as he passes out bowls of udon, "for future reference, if you are going to be late, call beforehand. Now, introduce me to your… friend."

I turn to Cross, who's blushing like a child who's been reprimanded. "This is Detective Riley Cross," I say, taking one of the bowls. "He's my partner with the Chicago Police Department. He's developed the Sight."

Taka takes his own bowl from the tray, acting uninterested but clearly perking up at my words. "It's a pleasure to meet you, Detective Cross," he says. "Kim has not mentioned you to me before."

"She's only had good things to say about you," Cross says with a charming smile. "Thank you for inviting me into your home. It's beautiful."

I watch as the ice around Taka starts to melt, Cross's easy way with people thawing his ire where my own evasiveness has only made it worse.

"Thank you," Taka says and takes a sip of broth from his bowl. "That is very kind of you. Now, tell me about your Sight."

"Yes, sir," Cross responds. "It started a few months ago."

Taka glances at me and back to Cross. "When Kim Burnt that creature, Baker, yes?"

"Yes."

"What have you been able to do?"

"Kim's taught me how to use Second-Sight and how to Send, though I've only spoken with Priya."

"You're able to see Claire, my partner?"

Cross's eyes go distant, and he nods.

"Good. Can you speak with her?"

Cross's brow furrows, but after a moment, he nods again. "Yes, I can."

"Good, good," Taka says, rising slowly from the table.

"I will see if I can find you a Mentor. It will take some time, of course. Our community is small and dispersed. Do you have a number?"

Cross hands him a business card emblazoned with a CPD detective's badge.

"I will call you when I've found someone," Taka says, tucking the business card carefully into a small, metal case. "In the meantime, continue working with Kim. She may be terrible at keeping to a schedule"—he shoots me an icy glance—"but she is intelligent and a good teacher."

After that, the rest of dinner goes about as well as expected. Cross does an awful lot to smooth Taka's ruffled feathers, though he's still distant with me. After the night I've had, I do my best to stay out of the way. For the most part, I nod my head and make affirmative sounds in the back of my throat, hoping Taka won't ask any further questions. I figure I'll broach the subject of Ruth Peterson and her secret organization later. Considering his mood, it's safe to assume that any uncomfortable questions will go unanswered tonight.

After I clear the bowls away and we finish our tea, Taka turns to me. "I will see you—*just* you—next week?"

"Yes," I say, standing at the implied goodbye in his voice. "Of course."

"Good. We will talk more then. In the meantime, stay out of trouble. I will see you out."

We're hurried out of Taka's home, though it's entirely polite and mannered with no obvious sense of urgency or annoyance. I can tell, though, that he's fuming, and I ready myself to apologize as he ushers us out.

The front door closes behind us before I have a chance. Cross and I stand on the front porch, breath clouding the air.

"That was interesting," he says as he straightens his coat around his shoulders. "Any chance you could explain why you were over an hour late?"

"Yes," I say with a sigh. "I'm not sure you're going to like it, though."

"Try me."

I make my way to the car, gesturing that Cross should follow me. He tucks his massive frame into the passenger seat and pushes it back so his long legs are comfortable instead of crammed against the dash.

It's hard to explain what happened to him, but I try my best. His face is white, any and all color washed away as I describe the dark, predatory shapes that lingered on the other side of the barrier. By the end of the story, his color is slightly improved, though he doesn't look any less worried.

"And what about Banks?" he asks, shifting his body so he's leaning against the passenger side door. "What are you going to do about her?"

"She can't scribe anything on her own. I don't think she'll be a problem."

"No chances of her disarming these things or interfering with the process?"

"No," I say vehemently. "Even if I didn't trust her, she was as terrified of that tear as I am. She's on our side."

"Okay, good." Cross looks down, thinking. "And Steve

had a brother?"

"Yeah," I say with a sigh. "It'll complicate trying to pin down any other crimes they might have committed, but we've got his car. It's a place to start."

"Those wallets will go a long way toward finding their victims," Cross says. "What a shitshow. And we're no closer to finding out why he was in that basement in the first place."

"Maybe something will shake out after we talk to Peterson."

Cross gives me a skeptical look.

"Or not." I run a hand through my hair and find another leaf. I toss it to the floor of my car with a huff. "I guess we'll find out then."

"And Taka's going to find me a real Mentor, huh?" Cross asks, his mouth twisted in a soft smile.

"Whoever he finds will absolutely do a better job than I have."

"I didn't think you were doing a bad job," Cross says, and I laugh.

"You don't have to be nice to me," I say. "I promise you, you will not hurt my feelings."

"In that case," he says, trailing off as I laugh again. "You ready to call it a night?"

I look at him from across the car and suddenly realize that, no, I'm not. But it's also late, and we can't stay parked in Taka's driveway all night.

"Yeah," I say, straightening up from my half-slouched position against the driver's side door. "I should be getting home."

"I guess I'll see you in the morning then," he says as he reaches for the door handle. Stopping, he turns back to me. "Walk me to my car?"

I laugh. "It's right there." I gesture to his car parked directly in front of mine.

"Humor me." He flashes me his most charming, boyish grin. I roll my eyes, leave the car running, and step out. He walks around the front of my car, my headlights outlining him in clear, crisp light, and waits as I join him by the front bumper.

I follow him to his door, and as he jiggles his keys in his hand, he turns to me, a slight frown on his face.

"Phillips," he says quietly, looking down at me, "I'm going to try something, and I need you to trust me."

"What are you going to do?" I ask, struggling to read his expression.

He smiles. "Just trust me, okay? I'll stop if you ask me to, but I want you to follow my lead first. Okay?"

Hesitantly, I nod. "Okay. I trust you."

"Good."

He takes a step forward and reaches up to cup my face, his warm hands cradling the weight of my jaw. His thumb strokes over the planes of my cheek, dragging a slow line of fire across my skin before he shifts his hand to thread into the hair at the base of my head. My skin breaks out into goose bumps at his touch, ice and heat cascading down my neck until my whole body shivers with it.

"That's good," he says quietly, his eyes dropping to my

mouth as it falls open on a small gasp. "That's very good."

His head starts to dip, his eyes half-lidded and dark. I can barely breathe, barely think, but my mouth tilts up, my hands suddenly grasping at his arms as his lips come to rest, oh-so-softly, against mine.

Everything is washed away in the sudden overwhelming feel of his mouth on mine. His lips are full and soft, moving gently against mine, asking for more. I gasp again, and he shifts closer, changing the angle until our lips are pressed tightly against each other. He sips at my mouth with teasing brushes, and I'm helpless to resist. I don't know when my fingers find their way into his hair, but they tighten against the soft curls at the nape of his neck, pulling him closer to me to deepen the kiss.

I'm lost in him, my body pressed against his, my fingers tangled in his hair, my mouth and lips and tongue tangled with his. He moans against my mouth, and I swear my knees turn to water at the sound. He catches me, pressing me tighter to him, and I can feel the hardness of him against the softness of my stomach. Awareness rushes through me to pool in my gut, turning my blood to fire.

He pulls his mouth from mine, panting for breath, and touches our foreheads together. When I try to bring our mouths back together, to repeat the kiss, his grip in my hair tightens slightly, stopping me.

"I'm trying to go with it," I say, my voice deep and gravelly. "You should let me do that."

I feel his smile more than I see it. "I need to think," he says. The words send another shiver through me, and his hand tightens in my hair again before softening into a caress. "I can't think like this."

"Thinking is overrated," I say. He laughs and presses a quick, unsatisfying kiss to my lips.

"You're going to be the death of me," he says. His hand in my hair loosens, stroking its way down my back to rest at my waist. His other hand traces the line of my jaw, tilting my face up so that I meet his gaze. His green eyes, usually so bright, are dark with desire, the pupils blown wide as his eyes move slowly over my face.

"God, you're beautiful," he says, and I tilt my head, looking away from him as I shake my head.

"Don't say that."

"I'll say whatever I damn well please," he insists. "You are infuriating and exciting and so goddamned gorgeous, sometimes I can't breathe. And you'd better get used to hearing it because I'm not going to stop saying it now that I've started."

"You're one to talk," I say, taking a careful step back. His hand at my waist tightens, tries to pull me back in, but I keep him at a slight distance, my fingers on his neck rubbing soothing circles there. I give him a thorough once-over, dragging my eyes from his face to his broad chest, narrow waist, long, lean legs, and back up again. He grins at my obvious inspection before his mouth softens, his eyes falling to my lips again.

"What do you want to do about this?" He pulls me against him again. I fall into it, letting my body press up against his in a slow, careful move that has him groaning softly.

"I can think of a couple things," I say, burying my

fingers in his hair and pulling his mouth to mine. "None of which involve clothes."

He laughs, then kisses me again, the caress deep and drugging. I lose track of the minutes, surrendering to the growing ache that he coaxes out of me with every touch.

"I guess I'd better stop calling you Cross," I say when he pulls back to trail his lips down the line of my jaw. He laughs, nuzzling at the soft skin of my neck until I tilt my head to the side, granting him access to trail biting kisses down the column of my throat.

"I kind of like the way you say it," he says to my collarbone, lips tracing their way across the slope of bone and skin.

I laugh, and he catches it with his mouth against mine, both of our lips curved into smiles. He pulls away again, and I can't breathe for a moment, happiness choking the air from my lungs. He smiles down at me and brushes my hair from my face to tuck it behind my ear. He trails his fingers over the gentle slope of it, and I shiver again.

"We're going to actually talk about this," he says, his fingers lingering for a moment before he takes a step back. "But you were taking too long."

A pang of anxiety hits me, sharp and tight. "I'm not great with this stuff. The vulnerability thing," I say.

"Could've fooled me." He presses a warm, comforting kiss to my forehead. "Stop overthinking this."

"I promise to try," I say.

The lights on the front porch flash, and I'm immediately pulled back to high school and late nights necking in the driveway. Heat floods my face. Cross looks to the house, then waves, a wide smile across his face. Groaning and mortified, I bury my face in his coat, my embarrassed laughter lost in the warm wool.

"I think Taka wants us out of his driveway," Cross says, and I shake my head against his chest.

"You are the worst."

"You like it," he says. I lift my head from his chest, mouth open to respond, and he stops my words with his lips against mine. I sink into the kiss, then pull away. Shaking out his lapels, I keep my eyes trained on the hollow of his throat. Gently, he tips my face up till I meet his eyes.

"I'll see you tomorrow morning," he says, his thumb pressed against the jut of my chin.

"Yeah," I say, throat tight as he moves his thumb up to catch the pout of my lower lip. He trails the pad of his thumb over its gentle arch and pulls his hand away, leaving my heart pounding. I swallow, hard, and take a step back.

He gives me a slow once-over, sending a shiver through me before he gets into his car. Frozen to the spot, I stare at him while he starts his car and rolls his window down, elbow resting on the frame as he leans out.

"You have to move your car," he says, smiling with more than a hint of smugness. "You've got me blocked in."

I stammer something and hurry back to my Ford. After climbing into the driver's seat, I shift into reverse and pull onto the street, parking along the curb. Cross moves past me, winking at me before he turns and heads off down the street.

I put my head against the steering wheel with a groan.

Priya squeals in delight from the passenger seat. Tilting my head to the side so I can see her, I have to fight back a laugh when I catch her dancing.

You're the worst, I say, but there's nothing but warmth to the words.

At least something good happened today, she Sends before she breaks into singsong. *Kim's got a boyfriend, Kim's got a boyfriend.*

Are you twelve? I ask, laughing as I put my seatbelt on and shift the car into drive.

Tonight? Yes. Yes, I am. I am twelve years old, and you have a boyfriend.

He's not my boyfriend, I say. *We haven't talked about what we are.*

Well, you're something, *and that's good enough for me.* She whoops again and settles back into the seat. *For now.*

I roll my eyes again, but I can't fight back my grin. There are still plenty of things for me to worry about, but that was one hell of a kiss, and I suddenly find I can't care too much about the rest.

Epilogue

I t's dark. It's been dark. Unending, unyielding, the darkness that had first engulfed your soul now engulfs everything else. You cannot see, but your other senses are alive in this place. You can feel creatures moving around your legs, their fur like spider silk, their teeth the only flashes of light in this wretched place. They do not stalk you, only slink along after you, recognizing that you are the greater predator here, though you've not been here long. You hear their labored breaths, can smell the fetid stink of it as they exhale in warm, panting gasps. Though they make poor companions, it is better than being alone.

Together, you and the stream of creatures that trail after you walk. You're unable to tell how far you've gone or how much farther you can go, but you continue to put one foot in front of the other, reaching with your senses for any changes, any weaknesses that exist in the darkness.

The first sign is the almost imperceptible light that seeps through. A pinprick in the black, like a solitary star, twinkling in a never-ending sky. When you reach it, though it's small, it nearly blinds you. Your own teeth flashing, you grin and press your finger to the hole, blocking the light.

Then you dig the point of a claw into the hole and start tearing.

Soon, you think, watching as the hole slowly grows.

Soon.

GLOSSARY OF TERMS

Medium — A person possessing the ability to interact and communicate with the afterlife and spirits of deceased people. Mediums make up about 0.2 percent of the population, depending on the area. They Bond with ghosts who have yet to Turn as the final step of their training, which increases their power and stops the ghost from Turning.

Turning — When a ghost loses their sense of reality and becomes dangerous to living people. After Turning, ghosts may cause damage to property, as well as people.

Affinity — The specialized skill set a Medium possesses. The seven Affinities, from most common to least, are Burner, Reader, Healer, Speaker, Shaker, Seer, Passenger.

Burner — This is the most common type of Medium. They can speak with and exorcise ghosts and usually work in criminal justice or as independent contractors.

Reader — Gains memories and emotions from physical objects. Clarity of images and depth of information is dependent on their power and how long they're in contact with the item. The longer they spend trying to find out information from something, the better it is, but there is a limit to what they can discover. Most items will not trigger anything when a Reader is in contact with them, but some items that have a strong psychic aura will cause them to fall into a vision without warning. Second most common type of Medium.

Healer — Possesses healing abilities and can view internal structures. They are regarded with extreme respect and sought out regularly by hospitals and convalescent homes. They tend to be very caring individuals, who form significant emotional bonds with the people they trust and love. The strength of the Medium determines how severe of an injury or illness they can heal. Third most common type.

Speaker — Can communicate telepathically with other Mediums and people who have a predisposition for the supernatural. Work with Burners and Readers regularly. Also tend to work in special forces or the military due to their ability to Speak to people. The strength of the Medium determines how far and how many people they can Speak with at a time. Fourth most common type.

Shaker — Can move things and people without physically touching them. The weight of the item or person they can move is determined by the Medium's power. They tend to work in dangerous construction jobs, like underwater drilling and high-rise construction and repair. They are also commonly found working in disaster areas, especially earthquakes, as support teams. Fifth most common type

Seer — Can see into the future or past. The length of

time into the future or past and the clarity of what they See is based on their inherent power. Generally work in the financial, military, or political sector. Sixth most common type.

Passenger — Can possess people for brief moments. Very little is known about this Affinity as it is so uncommon. They have been steadily declining in numbers since the early 1800s. Almost no Mediums of this type are alive currently. Seventh most common type.

Second-Sight — The specialized vision that Mediums use to view and interact with elements of the afterlife. Said to appear as a brightly lit outline of the living world.

Sending — When a Medium or ghost shares a memory or thought with another Medium or ghost. Used as a form of communication for Mediums and their partner ghosts, as well as Speakers when communicating with other Mediums.

Circle — A circle written in chalk used by Mediums to do various things, such as Burning a ghost or Seeing something that happened previously in a location. The function is determined by the sigils and runes used to construct the circle. Powered by the blood of a Medium, otherwise inactive. Will completely disappear after being used.

Runes — Arcane marks that describe the nature of things. Used in circles to describe what the circle is supposed to effect.

Sigils — Arcane marks that link runes together and focus arcane energy in circles. Directs and channels energy in circles.

Wards — Sets of sigils and runes used outside of a circle to protect an area from entry or exit. Generally used on Mediums' homes to stop malevolent or unknown ghosts from entering. Can also be used to stop a ghost from leaving an area.

DRAMATIS PERSONAE

Detective Kim Phillips

Homicide detective with the Chicago Police Department. Also a Medium with Burner, Reader, and Healer Affinities.

Takahashi "Taka" Kikuchi

Medium with Burner Affinity. Mentor to Kim Phillips.

Andrea "Andi" Banks

Lifestyle reporter with the *Chicago Tribune*. Sighted, with an expertise in runes.

Priya Rachamalla

Kim Phillips's ghost partner. Was a Healer when alive.

Detective Riley Cross

Homicide detective with the Chicago Police Department and partnered with Kim. Newly Sighted with unknown abilities.

Lieutenant Leanne Walker

Kim Phillips and Riley Cross's superior officer with the Chicago Police Department.

Officer Taylor

Uniformed officer with the Chicago Police Department.

Officer Hernandez

Uniformed officer with the Chicago Police Department.

Gary

Forensics technician with the Chicago Police Department.

Stephen Christopher White

One of two murder victims found at Sixty-Fourth and Wolcott.

Doctor Frank Abramo

Medical Examiner with the Cook County Coroner's office.

Comfort Bell

Medium with Healer Affinity. One of the Binders of Joseph Baker. Deceased.

Joseph Baker

Medium with Passenger Affinity. Deceased.

Caroline Moore

Medium with Shaker Affinity. One of the Binders of Joseph Baker. Deceased.

Sadie Phillips

Medium with Burner Affinity. One of the Binders of Joseph Baker. Kim Phillips's grandmother. Deceased.

Elijah Abbot

Medium with Shaker Affinity. One of the Binders of Joseph Baker. Deceased.

Emmett Brennan

Medium with Reader Affinity. One of the Binders of Joseph Baker. Deceased.

Dave

Medium with Burner and one other unknown Affinity.

John

Comfort Bell's ghost partner.

Ruth Peterson

Medium with Seer Affinity.

White

Brother of Stephen Christopher White.

ACKNOWLEDGEMENTS

I started writing *Healer* in February of 2018. I'd found out at Christmas that I was expecting my second child, and I felt a huge sense of urgency to finish the manuscript well before he was born. As with most things that are on a rushed deadline, I found myself blocked entirely by mid-spring. I set down the draft for months, agonizing over where the story should go and what I should write. When my son was born in August, I was no closer to finishing than I had been in April.

Honestly, it was gutting. I'd never been blocked so badly on a manuscript before, and I knew that I was only getting further and further intro trouble as my editing deadline approached. I finally admitted to myself that the story I had originally planned just wasn't going to work, and I ended up ripping out almost thirty pages from the draft, leaving a skeleton of a story behind.

As painful as that process was, it ended up being for the best. I sat down in January of 2019, determined to have the novel finished by April. I wrote every day, no matter how my personal or professional life interfered, and with little concrete idea of where I was going. But by April, I had a finished manuscript that I was happy with. I shipped it off to my editor, and now, here we are.

There are so many people I need to thank for their help with *Healer*. Thank you to the members of the Indianapolis Police Department who answered my questions and took the time out of their busy schedules to talk to me about the plot line I ended up tossing out: Officers Nick Gallico, Frank Miller, and Michael O'Connor. Additional thanks to the medical specialists I spoke to, again about the plotline that got binned: Doctor Armor and Eric Skelnik. While I didn't use the information gathered from these amazing resources, I sincerely appreciate their time and expertise, and I hope to one day write that story.

My husband, again and as always, deserves huge credit here. It's hard enough writing a novel but juggling a newborn and a kindergartener makes it nearly impossible. He stepped up, though, and made sure to give me the time and space I needed to get *Healer* finished. Thank you isn't enough.

Michael, Jennifer, and Susan, my writing partners, were also indispensable. Their feedback and quick turnaround as I steamrolled through *Healer* helped keep me focused and on-pace. I couldn't have done this without them.

My editor, Nikki Busch, who's been in integral part of making the *Affinity Series* the wonderful story it is. Thank goodness the italics didn't get messed up this time!

And my dad, who taught me to find joy in storytelling and engaging my audience. That sense of satisfaction I get when I tell a story well is due entirely to his example.

And last, but absolutely not least, I want to thank my fans. When I was struggling the most with *Healer*, you were a constant reminder that there were people cheering me on around the globe. You kept me writing, even when I wanted to give up. Thank you for your support, and I sincerely hope you enjoyed *Healer*.

Speaker, the next book in the series, is scheduled for release next year. If you want to get updates on its progress or just see how I'm doing, feel free to follow me on Twitter (@p1013) or follow The Affinity Series on Facebook.

Thank you all, again, so much.

J. S.

About the Author

J. S. Lenore was born and raised in the suburbs of Chicago. She attended Elgin High School, graduating within the top ten of her class. She majored in Japanese Studies at Earlham College and graduated with honors before getting her Masters in Teaching, also from Earlham College. She started creative writing at a young age, mainly writing fanfiction, but did not find much success until after graduation. In 2013, writing under the handle p1013, J. S. Lenore posted her first fanfiction for MTV's *Teen Wolf*. This story, titled *The Full Moon Like Blood*, and others gained a moderate following. In the same year, she decided to branch out into original fiction, writing the rough draft of *Burner* during National Novel Writing Month. She is currently working on the fourth book in The Affinity Series, *Speaker*.

J. S. Lenore currently lives in Indianapolis with her husband, two children, two cats, and zero ghosts.